Playing the Hand She's Dealt

David Fingerman

Smilowitch and Blackwood
Minneapolis, Minnesota

Acknowledgements
I'd like to thank The Minneapolis Writers' Workshop and
The Southside Writers' Group for their constant
encouragement and critiques. A big thank you to Scott Jarnot
and Lt. Steve Burke for making themselves available for my
many questions and kindly offering their expertise. Thank
you to Isabel Gomez for your friendship, encouragement and
keen insight. And thank you to my editor, Cindy Davis, and
Linda Smith, Linda Houle, and all the Dreamspell staff.
Any mistakes, miscues, and inconsistencies regarding law
enforcement and financial investing are to be blamed on the
author. I either twisted the situations to advance the story or
failed to understand.

df

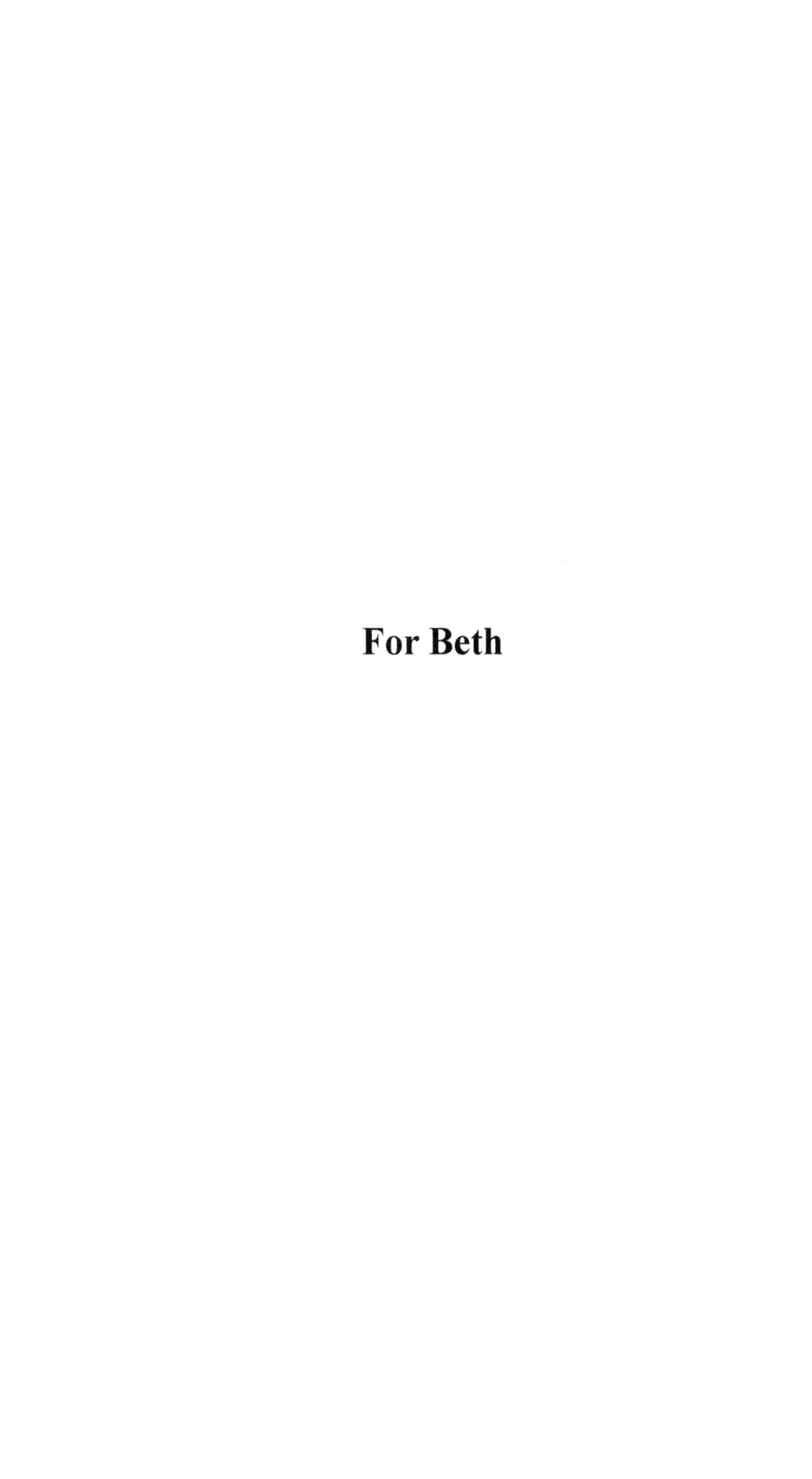

For Beth

Chapter 1

Sweat trickled down Walter Farkos' brow as a man clad in black walked straight to the hidden safe. Four paintings lined the wall. Odd, the stranger seemed to know exactly where to go. He removed the Degas and placed it on the floor, leaning it against the curio that held Walter's trophies and medals from all the way back in high school. The intruder pried the false panel off the wall and gingerly touched the safe's dial. Walter refused to struggle against the binds that held his wrists to the arms of the chair. The Victorian swivel chair just set him back seventy-five hundred dollars. He didn't want to risk damaging his new antique.

Shouting would be pointless. The walls were thick, the windows double paned. Even if they weren't, the velvet drapes would soak up the sound. His wife and kids would be of no help. Muriel was vacationing with 'the girls' in the Hamptons. Walter Jr. lived on the other side of Minneapolis, Elissa lived in Edina, and Jessica was out east attending Yale.

The silent man dressed like a ninja with sunglasses spun the dial back and forth. The safe didn't open. He tried the combination again. And again, nothing. Walter grinned behind the man's back. Two days ago the asshole would've emptied the safe.

Very few people knew where the safe was located. His wife and kids, of course, and he could think of two, maybe three friends who might. But the day before yesterday, on a whim, Walter changed the combination. Only he knew the new sequence of numbers.

The man walked toward him with a purposeful stride while reaching into his pocket. Walter cringed, not knowing what the canister might be that the thief now held. The stranger brought it up to his own throat and spoke. "What's the combination?"

Walter had heard the same metallic voice before, from an old friend suffering from throat cancer. The artificial voice box amazed and disgusted him at the same time. Two simultaneous thoughts made him shudder. One, his old friend dying of the dreaded disease, and two, this man in front of him hiding his voice for a reason. The ninja-burglar appeared to be in too good of shape for throat cancer. *Do I know him?* Walter studied the man's size and posture, the way he moved as he approached. Though nothing remarkable, it did seem familiar. He recalled the men from his office, then the men from his club. He gave up. It could be anyone. He never paid much attention.

A sharp rap sent a jackhammer of pain through Walter's head. The intruder hit the exact spot where a welt had risen above his left eye, the same spot that laid Walter out when he stepped into his study to investigate a noise. On hindsight, he should have called the police, but the alarm never went off. Now he knew that whomever this man might be, he was clever enough to bypass the system.

The stranger leaned over. "The combination." The fake voice rang in his ear.

"Fuck you!" Walter spit on the black mask.

The man stood up and reached into his pocket casually pulling out an Exacto Knife. The quality was top-notch. It must have set him back thirty or forty dollars. The handle fit perfectly in his hand. It even had little indentations for the fingers. Then the blade came out about a quarter of an inch.

The binds dug into Walter's wrists as he finally began to struggle, no longer thinking about the value of the chair. A quick slash across his belly opened a flawless slit in his shirt. Blood seeped out of the cut staining the white silk.

"I paid seventy-five dollars for this shirt."

"The combination," the robotic voice repeated.

"Do you think I'm going to tell you because you ruined my shirt? Hardly worth that."

"Is it worth your life?"

The voice had an eerie effect. The words came out clear enough, but with no emotion.

"If you kill me you'll never get into the safe."

The man set his voice box on the oak desk, then grabbed a handful of Walter's thick gray hair and jerked his head back. He sliced across Walter's neck, not deep enough to do any permanent damage, but enough to make a point.

Rivulets of blood oozed down Walter's throat,

soaking into the collar of his now worthless shirt. The blade slid back into its chamber and the man slipped it back in his pocket. He picked up the voice box.

"Think hard. This is your last chance. I have no desire to kill you, but if I have to leave empty-handed, your life means nothing to me. Is your life worth so little to you?"

Walter sneered at his captor. "How do I know you won't kill me after I give you the combination?"

"Faith," the tinny voice rang.

"Forget it. If I'm going to die anyway, I'm not letting the likes of you profit from my death."

The man slammed his gloved fist onto Walter's left hand. Walter screamed.

The fake ninja reached into his pocket and came out again with the Exacto. This time the blade extended to its full length.

"Three joints on each finger, ten fingers, you do the math. Then I move to your toes. After that I get creative."

He laid his voice box down and grabbed Walter's left hand, forcing it open, the palm pressing against the arm of the chair. Holding it securely, he used his other hand to place the blade just below Walter's cuticle on the pinky finger.

Sweat rolled down Walter's face mingling with the blood as it reached his throat. His eyes gaping. "If I tell you do you promise not to kill me?"

The blade disappeared inside the handle, leaving a small but harmless cut on Walter's finger.

Reluctantly, Walter spit out the numbers.

As the lunatic walked across the room and tried the new combination, Walter once again struggled with the binds. The arm of the chair loosened below his left wrist. He wriggled his arm more until a crack of wood shattered the silence.

The masked man, surprised at the noise, spun and charged. Walter struggled with the broken arm of the chair and wiggled it down until he had a good hold on the wood. Because of the restraints, he could only use the strength of his arm. He swung.

The attacker ducked to his right. Still, it knocked

him off balance enough that he tripped into the desk, his sunglasses falling to the floor. Leaning over he picked up the marble paperweight, some achievement award from 1997, and raised his arm.

The man stood like a statue. The two stared at each other. Walter's jaw dropped as he recognized those eyes. Then the arm came down and those eyes were the last vision Walter Farkos ever saw.

Chapter 2

She saw the steel-eyed glare behind his sunglasses. Unblinking, he sat frozen, but Louise noticed a flash of a spasm at the corner of his left eye. An involuntary muscle contraction might have given his hand away. Then again, it could've just been nerves. She hadn't been doing this long enough to feel confident about her interpretations.

Louise Miller held a seven and eight of clubs. It was an okay starter, but not a great one. The dealer laid out a seven of diamonds, king of clubs, and an eight of hearts. Her opponent opened with a small bet, not even matching the pot. Still, everyone but she had folded. She figured he had a pair of kings and thought about raising but decided to slow-play and only called his bet. The next card the dealer flipped up was the two of clubs. It didn't help him at all, but gave her a possible flush.

This time, the man across the table matched the pot. That gave Louise more confidence. If she went all in and he called, he'd still have chips left over but she'd be the chip leader at the table. Instead, she decided to call. She didn't want to scare him and have him fold.

The dealer flopped the eight of diamonds as the last card. Even better than a flush, Louise had a full house – eights over sevens. On the inside Louise screamed with joy. On the outside she prayed her face remained unreadable. The player across the table checked to her. *Did I give something away?* She thought maybe a small bet might keep him in. Then again, he'd have the top two pair with kings and eights. *He should be feeling confident. So why didn't he bet?*

"All in." Louise pushed the remainder of her chips to the middle of the table.

Without hesitation, the man called.

Usually, the person who places the bet is the first to show their cards. The guy with the sunglasses didn't wait. He slapped a pair of kings on the table, giving him a full house of kings over eights.

She dropped her cards face up on the table, letting people know that she'd had a good hand. Stunned, all she could do was rub her temples. "Nice hand," she mumbled as she pushed back her chair.

"Ouch." A sympathetic voice came from her left.

Another added, "I would've played it the same way."

Louise wished them all luck and walked away from the table. The board showed she came in four hundred and thirtieth place out of the six hundred and twelve that started the tournament. If she only could have outlasted another four hundred and four players she would have been in the money round. The five hundred dollar entry fee that was supposed to be her share of the mortgage, instead paid for two hours of torturous entertainment. That last hand was by far the best she'd been dealt, and it was still a loser.

"The story of my life." She walked out of the casino and into the bright sunlight.

Louise wondered if Karla would loan her the money, but quickly decided that required another explanation of where the money had gone. She'd made up too many lies in the past few weeks regarding money. Karla didn't have anything against gambling, at least not until it interfered with daily life. Louise felt pretty sure that, in Karla's eyes, losing mortgage money would be crossing the line.

Hell, this is all Karla's fault anyway. It had been she who introduced Louise to Texas Hold 'em. After Louise quit the police force, Karla told her this was a fun and safe way to get an adrenalin rush. An inexpensive evening, she said. They'd each have fifty dollars, and they would play for two hours or until the money ran out—whichever came first.

Louise thought it was stupid until she won one hundred and fifty dollars her first night. Karla won twenty-five. The next week Louise won seventy-five dollars and Karla came out fifty ahead.

"This is easier than collecting extortion money when I was on the force," Louise said.

"You'd better tell me you're joking."

"Well, duh."

Then, instead of job searching, Louise snuck out during the day when Karla was at work. The cheap tables soon bored her. She left two-dollar antes behind and graduated to the eight-dollar ante tables. Then came the point where she had to win back the money she lost. *If I can only* break even, I'll call it quits, she thought as she slid deeper and deeper in the hole.

Andrew would be good for a loan. She also wouldn't have to think up any new lies. The ones that worked with Karla would work fine on her brother. The Internet fraud one where someone drained her bank account sounded plausible for this situation. She figured a ten-minute lecture on computer security would certainly be worth five hundred dollars.

--

The unseasonably warm spring weather made sweat roll down the man's face. He sat behind the tinted windshield in the crowded parking lot, turned the key and listened to the engine's soft hum. Reaching over, he flipped on the AC. As much as he wanted to remove the blond wig and peel off the beard, just to be safe he left them on. He'd finished his work and now came the hard part – waiting.

It didn't take long. The ex-cop slipped on her sunglasses as she walked toward the parking lot. He had planned on waiting a lot longer to watch the fun, but she came out early. "You must really suck at poker."

He watched from two rows back as Louise, with her stupid red ponytail, got into her car. *Hell, it wouldn't take much. Lose about fifteen pounds, get your hair done, put on some makeup and you might actually be a looker.* He smiled as he observed, and waited. A chuckle escaped his lips as the bitch threw open her door and, with a disgusted face, stomped to the front of her car and popped the hood. With glee the man put his car in gear. He had places to be and things to do, and timing was important.

The hood blocked her vision so she couldn't see that the BMW, the fanciest car he ever stole, went out of its way to drive down her lane. And now that it did, she still didn't look up from her engine.

How easy it would be to run her fat ass down, or better yet, crush her between this car and hers. But either scenario meant a hell of a mess, and even more likely that he'd get caught because that was just the kind of thing witnesses remember. Besides, he wanted the bitch to suffer.

With the windows sealed tight, the cold blast from the air conditioner erased the sweat on his face. He gave her plenty of room as he drove past so she wouldn't be alarmed and take notice.

"Your life belongs to me, dyke," he growled as he passed.

--

Louise fumed as she fantasized putting her fist through the engine. *Now what the hell am I going to do?* She couldn't call Karla or Andrew. The few friendships she'd developed while on the force were now out of the question. She had pretty much severed all ties there as she told everyone in her resignation letter that they could kiss her lesbian ass and go straight to hell.

She glanced up for a moment as a Beemer passed by.

"Asshole. You could've stopped and asked if I needed help." She knew for certain that if her breasts were a little larger, the prick would've jumped out of his car to help, or more likely offered her a ride. She couldn't decide what pissed her off more – that, or why someone would steal her distributor cap.

Chapter 3

The living room smelled of fresh paint and tobacco. Karla stubbed out her cigarette, then moved the reclining chair from next to the sofa to the corner by the stereo. Now she could plug in the headphones and block out the rest of the world while sitting in the comfy chair. She loved the turntable Louise had gotten as a moving-in present even though the motives were partly selfish. Louise loved her old LPs. But what she hadn't known was that Karla had quite a collection herself.

Peanut lay sprawled on the couch. The rottweiler watched her every movement, never raising his chin off of the arm. He tracked her with his one and only eye as she crossed the room and carried one of the end tables next to the chair.

Karla was about the only person she knew who actually enjoyed moving. Packing wasn't so great, but she enjoyed the unpacking and deciding where and how furniture should be arranged. She also knew that no matter what she decided, Louise would go along. Louise told her she should've been an interior decorator.

Even though they'd spent most weekends together at one apartment or the other, Karla was wary of the idea of a fulltime roommate. Despite her misgivings, she took the plunge and agreed to combine their money and buy a house. They discussed Karla's need for alone time, and Louise respected that promising she'd land a new job sooner than soon, hopefully one that started and ended an hour later than Karla's. Until then, she would be out searching and giving as much alone time as Karla needed.

Selecting an old Al Di Meola album from her crate, Karla flipped on the turntable and did her interpretive dance to the jazz guitar. She hoped Louise wouldn't walk in during her performance in front of Peanut. Interpretive dance never failed to crack Louise up. Peanut swiveled his head without lifting to keep his eye on her moves.

For twenty minutes she jerked and gyrated to the music. The phone rang, making an unwelcome interruption. She stopped in mid-spin, staggered to the record player and lifted the arm off the vinyl. "Sorry, Peanut. The show will resume in a minute." The dog didn't seem to mind one way or the other.

With her balance more intact, she rushed to the phone. Louise's cell number shone on the caller ID. "Hi," she answered.

A long pause greeted Karla.

"Louise?" Karla's voice held a note of concern.

"How ya doin'? How's the unpacking going?"

"It's going fine," Karla answered cautiously. "I haven't touched your stuff. Do you want me to unpack it?"

There was no answer.

"Louise, what's wrong?"

"I screwed up. Screwed up big time."

Karla waited. Finally, "Are you going to tell me, or do I have to guess?"

"I lost my share of the mortgage," Louise blurted out.

Karla let out the breath she'd been holding. Not good, but it could've been a lot worse. "What happened?" She cradled the phone between her ear and shoulder and reached for the cigarettes, lighting one up while waiting for Louise to respond.

"I wanted to get you something special for moving in with me, but I didn't have enough money..."

Karla sucked the smoke deep in her lungs. She didn't like where this was heading.

"So instead of saying the hell with it I noticed there was a Texas Hold 'em tourney. Well, aren't you the one that keeps telling me to go for it?"

"You lost it gambling? Don't you dare try to put this on me!"

"That's not what I meant. I really thought I was good enough. Maybe not to win the whole thing, but at least to get far enough to win some money. I mean, I can figure out odds. I can read people."

"Oh Louise," Karla groaned. "Most people in those tournaments have been playing for years. How long have you been playing – two months? Three? What were you thinking?" She took another long drag from the smoke.

"I was thinking we could use the extra money."

Karla didn't want to deal with Louise's defensiveness. She mentally calculated her finances and figured she could carry her roommate for a couple of months, maybe more. Exhaling a long plume of smoke, she asked, "How's the job hunting coming along?"

"Still pounding the pavement."

What the hell does that mean? "Have you applied anywhere?" Karla kept her voice as neutral as possible.

"A couple of places. Have a few more in mind, but I want to check 'em out first."

"Anything interesting?" Karla shook another cigarette from the pack and lit it with the tip of her old one.

"Not really. Security. One I want to check out is for a night watchman. That sounds like it might be kind of fun."

Karla wanted to trust her partner, but wondered if this might be another lie. Too many times these past couple of weeks Louise told her things that were suspiciously inconsistent.

"Why don't you just come home? We'll talk."

"Well, that brings me to the reason I really called. Someone vandalized my car. Well, not vandalized exactly, but stole my distributor cap. I'm stuck in the casino parking lot. Can you come and pick me up?"

"Why would somebody steal your distributor cap?" Another comment that didn't make sense.

"I have no idea. Can you come get me?"

Karla checked her pack of cigarettes. Only two left. She had to stop at the store anyway. "It'll probably take a half-an-hour, forty-five minutes."

"Love you." The phone disconnected.

"You'd better," Karla said into the dead line. "Hey, Peanut, wanna go for a ride in the car?"

The dog bolted off the couch and dashed for the leash that hung next to the door. He got on his hind legs and stretched, able to get the clasp of the blue nylon cord off the hook. He sat attentively at the door, waiting, the leash dangling from his mouth.

Karla still marveled at the dog and how he seemed to understand so many words. "Can I pee first?"

The dog didn't move, his eye gazing at her, waiting.

When Karla got out of the bathroom, Peanut still sat in the same spot, in the exact same posture. Despite the weeks of training and unconditioning his past, she clicked the leash on his collar and wondered what he might do if she changed her mind and told him no ride. She shuddered at the thought. Karla had never seen him mad, but the stories she heard when she'd been locked in that dungeon still gave her nightmares.

--

Louise concluded the distributor cap would not reappear on its own. She slammed the hood on her Saturn and did another quick scan of the parking lot before calling the dealership. They made arrangements to tow it and Louise grimaced thinking about how much more money this would set her back. She let out a string of curses while walking back to the casino.

The kids who worked the valet parking glanced at her in an odd way, as did the security guard sitting at his desk inside the front doors.

"Can I help you?" he asked.

A big man with a marine haircut shifted uneasily in his chair. Maybe he thought she might be a sore loser coming back to get some sort of revenge. Maybe went to her car for a gun? Maybe she should put him at ease before he did something stupid.

"Car trouble. I'm sure it's just a prank, but someone stole my distributor cap."

"Why would somebody do that?" His nametag read Chuck.

Because you're too fat and lazy to get up off your ass and do your job. "Like I said, I'm sure it's just a prank, but I suppose I should fill out a report."

With a harrumph, the man pushed back his chair, opened the desk drawer and thumbed through a folder full of papers until he found the right form. "The casino is not responsible."

Your concern warms my heart. "I can appreciate

that. Hey, I don't suppose you'd let me see the surveillance tape of the parking lot?"

The security man made a face like he just swallowed something vile.

"C'mon, law enforcement officer to law enforcement officer."

His eyes widened. "You're a cop?"

"Was." Louise held up her right hand and showed him the gnarled joints and flaking skin. The doctors told her she'd probably never have full use of her hand again, and it would often feel stiff. She'd most likely join the club of those who could predict the rain by how their bones are feeling. "Broke twelve bones in this hand. The cast came off a week ago."

"How did that happen?" His voice held a new respect.

Every time Louise thought about her hand she wanted to kick herself. *How could I have been so stupid?* Before she realized she'd be classified as permanently disabled and get a monthly check for life, she'd gotten drunk and mailed that scathing letter of resignation. Her lawyer said they could try and blame it on the Vicodin, but it would be iffy at best and up to the judge to decide.

"In the line of duty," Louise said. Her voice took on a far away quality.

"But how?"

Damn, he was insistent. "In a fight. That's all I'm going to say." Louise shivered as Elias flashed back for just a moment.

"That must've been one hell of a punch. Hope his face got it as bad as your hand."

Louise buried the chill that crawled over her body. "How about showing me that tape?" She tried to erase the scene of that awful night from her memory.

"You'll have to ask the supervisor of surveillance," he said.

While he called, Louise admired the security cameras hovering above every table. God knew what all else they had hidden, but she was sure it would be impressive.

"Ever have any trouble in here?" Louise asked in a

making conversation sort of way.

"Oh yeah, almost every day."

"Really? With all the security, I'm rather surprised."

"Mostly people who had too much to drink. They get pissed off about something and forget they're being watched."

"Anyone ever try and rip this place off?"

Chuck shook and head and smirked, settling back in his chair. "Just an occasional idiot trying to sneak a few chips off of someone else's stack. There was one guy who..."

"Can I help you?"

The man stood six foot two and weighed maybe one hundred and forty pounds soaking wet, a lot of it in his blonde and gray walrus mustache. He wore thick bifocals making the bottom half of his blue eyes look enlarged.

Louise held out her hand and introduced herself.

"She says someone broke into her car. She wants to see the tapes," Chuck said.

"I'm sorry to hear that. I can't let you back but I'll certainly take a look. Approximately, when did this incident take place?"

"She used to be a cop."

Louise winked at Chuck. She didn't need his help, and didn't particularly want it, but it was nice to have someone to stick up for you every once in a while.

"Had to be sometime between nine and eleven," Louise answered.

The thin man raised his bushy eyebrows. "A cop, huh? What happened?"

"I resigned."

Louise could read the man's mind. The woman couldn't cut it as a cop. She wanted to punch him.

Four young men walked in the door laughing and rowdy. Louise smelled the alcohol on their breath as they passed and guessed they might've just turned twenty-one. They all had athletic builds, the smallest of the four stood about five-ten. She couldn't tell if the swagger came from confidence or alcohol, or maybe a combination of both.

"We're gonna bust the fucking bank in this dive," one man crowed to his friends. His voice was liquor-loud.

The security guard said something quietly into his walkie-talkie but never got up from his chair.

Surveillance guy shifted his attention from the four back to Louise. "I'll review the tape and get back to you. And I'll forward anything of interest to the Hiawatha Police Department. Once you complete the incident report we'll have all the information from you that we need." The dismissal was curt.

Louise cringed. Not only was she getting the brush-off, but it would be some hick town cops handling the case. Unfortunately, the city of Hiawatha stood outside Hennepin County. She wouldn't be able to enlist the help of Andrew and the HC Sheriff's Department.

Louise hung out in front of the security desk enjoying the unexpected show as the rowdy men got louder. They were politely asked to leave. Politeness faded from the security guards as the questioning tone left their voices. One of the boys spat out a "fuck you" and cold-cocked one of the authorities.

As soon as the sound of fist connecting with chin was heard, the kid who threw the punch tore away from the melee leaving his three friends to the pack of wolves in uniform. He sped past the seated guard who went as far as to push his chair back, but never rose from it.

Louise stuck out her foot and caught the kid's ankle. He flew a good three feet before landing spread-eagled on his stomach. Before he regained his bearings, Louise had her knee planted in the middle of his back, twisting his arm back and instinctively reaching for a nonexistent pair of cuffs. Instead, she kept him in a wristlock until one of the men getting paid to do this work took over.

The four were taken to a room somewhere out of sight very quickly and professionally. Only the people who sat at the tables on the outer rim of the casino room had noticed the fight. They gave security a polite applause then returned to their games.

"Impressive," said Chuck.

"Yeah, you too," Louise panted. "You talked into that mike like a real pro."

Before he could say a word, another guard appeared.

"I need a 187B."

Chuck opened the draw and handed a form to his co-worker. "Hey Larry, the lady thinks I'm a wuss."

"You are a wuss," Larry answered.

Chuck grinned. "But she thinks I'm a wuss because I didn't join in taking those boys down."

"Since when do you care what other people think?"

Chuck shrugged.

"So why don't you explain it to her?"

"Don't think she'll believe me."

Larry strolled over and stood next to Louise. He towered over her by over a foot and hitched his thumbs in his belt loop. "It's like this, ma'am." He all of a sudden sounded like John Wayne, a pretty good imitation, too.

Louise stifled a fake yawn. "It's none of my business and I don't really care."

"Chuck here is a real rough-rider," he continued. "If we turned him loose, those boys woulda been carried out in a box."

"Thanks, Larr." Chuck's face glowed beet red.

"My pleasure." Larry took the form and wandered off.

"I stand corrected," Louise said, sounding like a southern belle. She fanned her face with her hand.

"Actually, if I left my post without finding a replacement, I'd be looking for a new job. They're very strict on that point." His color slowly returned to normal.

"My apologies. I guess I shouldn't assume."

"No big deal."

Louise stood in uncomfortable silence while Chuck pretended to neaten his desk. A loud cheer came from the casino followed by a smattering of applause.

A valet who barely looked old enough to own a driver's license entered the lobby. "Somebody call a tow from Saturn?"

"That was fast." Louise exited to the parking lot.

She jumped in the front seat of the truck and guided the driver to her car explaining her situation.

"You're kidding. Did you tell that to the clerk?" He sounded amazed.

"Told 'em the whole story, why?"

"If that's all it is, I could've just brought a distributor cap with me. Could've saved you a tow."

Louise boiled on the inside. Spending money when needed was painful, but okay. Wasting money was not. She tried to suck it up. It wasn't this guy's fault.

"It's all right. My friend is already on her way to pick me up."

"Let me talk to my boss when I get back. I'm pretty sure he'll let me waive the charge."

She guessed him to be in his mid twenties. Greasy blond hair fell over his eyes. The sleeves of his shirt were rolled up exposing muscular forearms. Jutting from below one sleeve was a tattoo of a talon and a partial wing. She wished his sleeves were rolled up a little higher. *If I were straight, I'd blow you.* "Thank you. I think you just restored my faith in humanity."

He expertly hitched up her car and drove away. There was an extra spring in her step as she walked back to the casino.

"Hey, you guys have any job openings?" Louise sidled up next to Chuck's desk. "I could park my butt behind a desk. I bet I'd be good at it. I've already showed I can handle myself."

Chuck became a little more animated too – in a good way. He probably didn't get many people coming up to chat. "I don't think so. We're pretty well staffed, but go to the desk behind the cashier's cage and ask for an application. You're obviously qualified."

Not sure whether he was enthused that she might apply, or just maybe hitting on her, Louise went back and requested an application. An attractive blonde with a wide smile and dazzling white teeth handed her the form. "The only openings we have right now are for janitorial and food service." Her voice oozed with obnoxiousness.

"I was more interested in security."

"Nothing at the moment. We'll keep your application on file for six months. If something opens up we'll call you for an interview."

I wonder how your smile would look if you were

missing a few teeth. "Thank you."

The cell phone buzzed as Louise finished writing and signed her name. She winked at the girl, laid the application on the desk, and reached into her purse. "It's me," Louise answered.

"Get your sexy butt out here. Valet boys are laughing at my car."

"Sic Peanut on 'em." Louise had no doubt Karla had brought the dog. They had built quite a bond.

Louise stuffed the phone back in her purse and dashed toward the exit. She thanked Chuck, not really sure what for, and saw what the valets were laughing at. Peanut sat wedged next to her in the front seat of the Beetle, his tongue slobbering the back of Karla's head. Louise couldn't stop laughing herself.

Chapter 4

Peanut sat cramped in the back seat, his head out the window, and basking as the wind washed over his face. Louise wished she could join him but instead sat in uncomfortable silence. She had as much desire to offer another apology as she thought Karla had to hear one, but still she figured she owed it.

"I had a full house – eights over sevens! Wouldn't you go all in with a full house? Who would've ever thought he'd be holding a pair of kings? That's the only way he could've beat me," she said in lieu of an I'm sorry.

Karla kept her eyes focused on the road ahead, refusing to even glance at her partner. "Since when does a pair of kings beat a full house?"

Louise sighed in exasperation. "There was a king showing. He had a full house too, kings over. I thought I was the wolf stalking its prey. I had no idea that I was the one being stalked."

"Sounds like he played you like a sap." Karla eased the speedometer over eighty.

"Thanks for your compassion and understanding."

Karla placed her hand on Louise's thigh. Louise couldn't help but smile as she closed her eyes and tilted her head back. She shared the rush of warm spring air with Peanut as the VW bug cruised down the freeway.

"Watch the speed," Louise said with her eyes still closed. "They love to set up traps."

The car slowed to sixty-five as other cars sped by, not a cop in sight.

"How do I get to Saturn from here?" Karla asked.

Louise opened her eyes and sat upright. "Mind if we stop at home first? I left my checkbook on the dresser. I'd rather write a check than bury myself any deeper in my Visa card."

Karla glared a demand of *What else haven't you told me?*

Louise pointed where off in the distance flashing lights could be seen. "You might wanna slow down a tad."

"Why? He already has someone pulled over."

Karla had to slow anyway because of the gawkers. Louise had the sudden urge to spill her guts and tell Karla about the drained bank account and her gambling addiction. Instead, she stuck her head out the window and mimicked the dog.

"My two children," Karla said.

An invisible barrier stretched across the road where the cop stood off on the shoulder handing out a ticket to some poor speeder. Once past it, the traffic thinned and sped up. The VW maxed out at eighty-five as Karla held the pedal down as far as it would go.

"When will you start being honest with me?"

Despite the wind rushing in her face, Louise heard the question and ducked back into the car. She didn't dare look Karla in the eye.

"I've got a problem." Louise waited for a reaction and got none. Karla gazed at the road as if in a trance.

"Gambling," Louise added, trying to keep her voice emotionless.

"How much?" Karla asked, matching her tone.

"How much of a problem?"

"Don't you dare be glib! How much money?"

"All of it. Twenty-five thousand."

Louise waited for the onslaught. The how-could-she-after-she-quit-her-job-and-they-just-bought-a-house-together lecture? What the hell had she been thinking? Instead, she was met with worse – silence. Karla's knuckles were shades whiter than the rest of her as they grasped the steering wheel. Not a good sign.

"Guess I'm not going to make it as a professional card player, huh?"

"Not funny."

Please yell at me. Pull over and hit me. Keep driving and hit me. Do something!

Karla slowed more as they approached their exit. "What about your PERA?"

"Spent it." She choked back the lump in her throat, thinking back to the day she cashed out her retirement fund. That had been her first clue that she might have a problem. "It was like I was standing outside of my body, watching. I knew it was wrong, knew I shouldn't do it, but I couldn't stop myself." A tear rolled down Louise's cheek.

Karla sucked in a deep breath and took her eyes off of the road long enough to gawk at Louise. "I don't think I've never seen you cry before. You're supposed to be the strong one in this relationship." Her voice cracked.

"Sorry. It won't happen again." Louise regained her composure and wiped the tear using her sleeve. "Do you still respect me?"

"Don't know. Makes you almost human. Not sure if I like that. I kind of liked dating Super Woman."

Inside, the eruption ebbed just a little bit. Louise reached out the window and scratched Peanut around the eye patch. He reciprocated by licking her hand.

"All right. This is what we're going to do," Karla said, breaking the tender mood between woman and dog.

Louise swiveled in her seat, facing the love of her life. "Tell me." She knew better than to act flippant.

"After we pick up your car, we're heading back home and working out a budget. Then we're going through the want ads."

"Yes, Miss Spires."

"Knock off the attitude. And until something permanent comes along, you're getting a part-time job. I don't care if it's flipping burgers or mopping floors. You will start bringing home some money."

"Just a minute," Louise interrupted.

"Don't go there," Karla interrupted back. "I'm serious. This is serious. You screwed up big time and I don't make enough to support both of us."

Louise slumped in her seat. "You're right." *Since when did you become the bitch of this relationship?*

The remainder of the trip home lacked conversation. No words were spoken until Karla parked in the driveway.

"You want to wait in the car while I run in and get my wallet?" Louise asked.

"Got to pee. Think I drank an entire pot of coffee this morning" Karla switched off the ignition and opened the door.

Louise got out and pushed forward the back of her

seat. Peanut bounded out and raced ahead of Karla to the front door. When he reached the front step he skidded to a halt and growled as best he could for a dog with severed vocal chords. Karla cocked her head at the dog as she arrived at the door. Louise caught up, grabbed Karla's shoulder, and yanked her back.

"Goddammit," Louise whispered. She hadn't touched her gun since she left the force. The .45 was sitting snuggly behind the bath towels in the linen closet. At least she hoped it was still in the linen closet.

The doorknob turned, unlocked. Karla held Peanut by the collar.

"Did you lock the door?" Louise whispered.

"I'm positive." Karla nodded as she matched Louise's tone.

"Keep a tight rein on him." Louise turned back toward the door, inched it open and peeked in.

A man with gray hair sat on the couch. Louise could only see him from behind. She closed the door just far enough that it didn't click.

"Give me the dog," she whispered, "and you get out of sight. Call the cops."

Karla snapped the leash on Peanut and handed it to Louise, then walked behind the car while digging through her purse.

"Should we wait for the police?" Louise whispered to Peanut.

He waited at the door, muscles tense.

"I don't think so either."

She flung open the door. Peanut charged. The leash tore out of her hand. The dog leapt over the back of the couch and pounced. The man flew to the floor under one hundred-twenty five pounds of rottweiler.

Louise raced around the sofa ready to jump into the carnage. She stopped suddenly, almost falling over. Peanut stood over the man, sniffing his face as Louise grabbed the leash and dragged him back to the front door.

"Karla!"

Her partner appeared from the side of the house.

"Take the dog."

Karla took control of the leash. The dog didn't resist. "What happened?"

"There's a dead man in the house."

Karla gasped, bringing her hand to her mouth. "It wasn't Peanut?"

"No, no. The guy's been dead for a while. Somebody beat him up pretty good."

Karla shook, leaning on Peanut for support. "The police are on the way."

Louise took her in her arms. In a tight embrace, she wondered how the people of this quiet street would think of their new neighbors when the cops did door-to-door interviews. They moved in only three days ago to a neighborhood chosen mostly because of the low crime rate. *Irony?* A new thought clicked in her brain and she released Karla, gently holding her shoulders and pushing her arms-length away.

"I think I know that guy."

Chapter 5

A Hennepin County Sheriff's vehicle stood out as it parked in a mass of Minneapolis Police cruisers. Relief spread through Louise's body as her brother stepped out and adjusted his wide brim hat. A ridiculous part of the uniform, she thought, but it seemed to fit well on Andrew.

"Over here, Deputy Dawg." Louise waved.

The officer taking her statement stopped writing as her brother approached. Both the cop and deputy stood at five-eleven. While Andrew was well toned, the police officer had to have been bulked up with steroids. Still, Louise thought that her brother could take him. Then she wondered why she thought that in the first place.

"Andrew, this is Officer…" She checked the nameplate under his badge. "Perkins." Not living in her former precinct, she didn't know this cop. "Officer Perkins, my brother, Deputy Andrew Miller." Her voice held a note of pride.

The two shook hands as Andrew took in the scene. Louise followed her brother's eyes. It seemed like the entire neighborhood stood anxiously on the other side of the street, waiting expectantly for something exciting to happen.

"Where's Wing Nut?"

Louise kind of liked that nickname her brother thought up but would never admit it, especially to him. "*Peanut* is in the back yard."

He nodded seeing Karla being interviewed on the other side of the lawn. "How's she doing?"

"She's a trooper," Louise answered.

"You're kidding." Perkins' jaw dropped.

Both brother and sister chuckled.

"Figure of speech," Louise said.

A detective walked out of the house with the coroner. Following, two uniforms carried out a sofa, and behind them, two orderlies pushed out a gurney carrying Walter Farkos in a body bag. Chatter from across the street stopped in unison, a noticeable silence.

"Detective Grant is going to want to talk to you," Perkins said.

As if on cue, the detective ambled in their direction. Louise nodded. Detective Gordon Grant was not her favorite cop. But then, she didn't think he was anybody's favorite cop. A driven man, he gave everything to solve a case. He despised himself and those around him when a case went cold.

Back when she was in uniform, she passed Grant in the hall a number of times. He never said hello, even on those few occasions when their eyes met. At first she thought he was just another homophobe ass wipe, but later discovered he was just an ass wipe. He treated all uniforms that way. The only time he talked to anyone below detective was when he needed something, and then it sounded like an order. Still, the man was competent at solving cases.

Grant patted the coroner on the back and headed over. He nodded a greeting and a bead of sweat dropped from his graying sideburn. He wore black slacks, a white cotton shirt, sleeves rolled halfway up his forearm, and a thin black tie. He could've just as easily stepped out from an episode of 'Dragnet.' Even his crew cut would have made him fit in with the sixties cop show.

"Good to see you again, Miller. How's the hand?"

How did he know who she was, let alone know about her injury? "You too," was all she could muster.

"Hell of a heat wave. Feels like the mid-eighties. Must be a record for April."

"Yes, sir," Perkins answered. "I'm sure it is a record."

Grant shot the officer his infamous unamused stare. "I'll take over here. Why don't you see if you can help out with crowd control?" The question never sounded less like a question.

"Yes, sir." Dejection registered in Perkins' voice.

The officer plodded across the street with slumped shoulders. When he mingled with other cops, Grant eyed Andrew.

"My brother, Andrew Miller," Louise said as an introduction.

Andrew stuck out his hand, and to her surprise, Grant took it. "Good work on the Boughton case."

Andrew's eyebrows arched. "Thanks."

"I was there too," Louise piped in.

Grant let go of Andrew's hand and gave Louise something between a sarcastic grin and a sneer, using only half of his mouth. His steel-blue eyes drilled into her.

"Tell me how you know Walter Farkos."

When he spoke, Louise thought that if the Schwarzenegger character in 'The Terminator' had blue eyes instead of red, that was them. She felt every one of the eighty-plus degrees as she tried to return his stare.

"Busted him for a DUI last year. That's the last I saw of him 'til I walked in my house this afternoon."

"You remember all your DUI busts? Impressive."

"I remember all of 'em where I had to draw my gun. This guy was a major league asshole."

"Sounds like we have a motive," Grant said.

"Fuck you!" Louise spat, then glanced over at Andrew. "What the hell are you smirking at?"

Andrew raised his hands in surrender. "I'm staying out of this." He searched for an excuse. "I think I'll go over and see how Karla is doing?"

"You do that." She actually appreciated Andrew for bailing over to her partner. If anybody could calm her down and set things right, it was her brother.

Louise regained most of her composure. "So, am I going to need a lawyer? If so, this interview ends right now."

"Nah, I'm ninety-nine percent certain it wasn't you. But just for shits and giggles, why don't we make it one hundred percent and you tell me where you were yesterday between three and seven p.m."

Louise didn't know if the cool breeze or the feeling of relief slowed her pounding heart. "At the casino, getting ready for this morning's tourney. I'm sure the cameras will have my smiling face."

Grant reached into his pocket for a notepad and started scribbling. When he finished he again gave that penetrating gaze into Louise. "So now the million dollar question – why would someone go through the trouble of sneaking a body into your home?"

Officially off the hook, this time Louise was not

intimidated by the stare. "I think the million dollar question is who?"

Grant broke the gaze. "Would that be who, or whom?"

"What?"

"No, really. I always get those two mixed up."

A uniform, another cop that Louise failed to recognize, approached, walking next to a woman with henna-dyed hair. She wore fashion blue jeans and a maroon button-down silk blouse.

"Excuse me, sir. This is Emily Harper. She lives in that stucco house." He pointed across the street.

Grant's personality changed to that of a caring human being. He showed a genial smile and held out his arm. "How do you do Ms. Harper? How can I be of assistance?"

Louise did a slight double take at the sudden transformation. The woman was smitten as she let him take her hand.

"I'm sure it's nothing, but the officer insisted I talk to you."

"You never know," Grant said. "Sometimes it's those minor details that will solve a case. Why don't you tell me what you saw?"

Now the detective's eyes had changed to a Paul Newman blue.

"I saw a van enter this driveway."

Louise wanted to jump in. *What kind of van? Did you get the color, the license plate?* But the detective obviously made it a point not to interrupt.

"This guy gets out and pulls out a rolled up carpet. I didn't think anything of it. We've got a Persian carpet in our rec room that was a lot like that when they were carrying it into our house. Although, it took two men to bring in ours."

Louise wanted to toss her in a chair and bitch-slap her. *What did the guy look like? Was there a bulge in the carpet? Like maybe a man wrapped up?*

Grant remained stoic.

"But there was something weird. Then I figured it out. The carpet was rolled with the carpet facing out, not the underside. Very unprofessional. It gets dirty that way. Anyway, when he was leaving, from what little I could see, the pattern looked pretty much the same. I figured they just liked that style."

"Where were you when you saw all this?" Grant asked.

"In my kitchen. I was unloading the dishwasher from our dinner party last night."

"What did the van look like?"

Thank you! Louise fidgeted, wishing the woman would talk a little faster.

"Hmm. Well, it was yellow, maybe white. No, it could've been a light green, or a light blue. I'm not really sure."

"Did it have any writing on the side? Any windows?"

Despite her own impatience, Louise was impressed at how well the detective kept a straight face. *He'd be a good poker player.*

"I don't think so. Wait – it didn't have any windows on the side, but I think there were windows on the back door."

"And did you get a look at the driver?" Grant continued patiently.

"Blond hair in a ponytail. I remember that part for sure. And kind of skinny, I think. Maybe not skinny, but not fat."

Louise wanted to lash out at the bitch.

"Do you think that you could recognize him again, maybe if you saw a picture?"

"I'm not sure. I don't usually pay close attention to those people."

"Those people?"

A chink opened in Grant's empathetic armor. Louise found something to finally smile about. *Keep it up, lady.*

"Oh, you know. The hired help."

Where the hell do you think you live, North Oaks? Louise was really beginning to like this interaction as Grant raised his eyebrows.

"You mean people that work for a living?" the

detective asked.

"No. That's not what I mean at all." Ms. Harper sounded flustered. "Some of my best friends are nonprofessionals."

Open your mouth a little wider, lady, and you can fit in both feet. If they hadn't just carried a body out of her living room, Louise would've been enjoying herself.

"Do you think you could come down to the station and look at some photographs?"

"Oh no, there's no way I could possibly find the time. Between PTA, Kristine starting soccer, and Christopher with his tennis, it's all I can do to get dinner on the table when my husband gets home. I'm sorry. In fact, I'm already late. I still need to get to the supermarket."

Grant eyed her up and down while Louise watched with avid attention. The detective raised his hand and rubbed it through his short hair. The hand came away sweaty.

"How old are your children?" Grant asked.

"Kristine is twelve, Christopher is nine."

Grant whistled long and low, shaking his head. He focused on the notepad and wrote as he spoke. Any friendliness had disappeared from his voice.

"Do you mean to tell me that with two small children, it doesn't bother you that there's a murderer running loose in your neighborhood?" Whatever he'd been scribbling, Grant made an emphasis dotting that final period before snapping the book shut. "We'll be in touch." It sounded like a threat. He turned his back to her.

Squirm out of this one, bitch. Louise had a new respect and a new admiration for Gordon Grant.

"I'd give my life for those kids!" Emily choked on the words. "Of course I'll do anything I can to help."

The mischievous grin disappeared from the detective's face before he turned back to the repentant mom. His voice became that of a consoling friend. "I know it's a pain in the rear, but we really do need your help. You seem to be the only one who might have seen his face. Maybe after you get the kids off to school tomorrow morning you can stop in. Would that work?" Grant put his arm around her shoulder and guided her in the direction of her house, meaning he was done with her.

"I think I can do that," she said.

Walking with her as far as the boulevard, Grant handed her his card and whispered something in her ear. Louise couldn't make out what he said.

The mob surrounded Emily Harper as she stepped up to the curb on the other side of the street.

"Instant celebrity status," Louise said as the detective approached.

"I'd bet a paycheck that when we catch the guy, she'll be telling anyone who will listen that we wouldn't have been able to do it without her help."

"No bet. What did you whisper to her?"

Grant shook his head. "The typical PR bullshit; doing the community a great service. Make her feel important."

"I don't think that will be a problem," Louise said.

"Speaking of paychecks, Miller, any itches to rejoin the force?"

For the second time that afternoon, Grant amazed her. How much did he know?

"None at all. Besides, even if I did, I think I pretty much burned any bridges I might've had."

"I saw the letter. It was amusing more than anything else. Brass got a pretty good laugh out of it."

Anger and embarrassment welled inside her. Louise couldn't remember writing anything funny, and certainly hadn't meant to. "Let's just say I have authority issues. Besides…" she held up her damaged hand.

Grant waved away her hand issue. "Bones heal. It's your attitude that made you such a good cop. It's those ass-lickers like Perkins over there who'll be getting the promotions, but it's the cops like you that actually get things done."

Louise now thought of Grant like a friend instead of a superior. "Are you listening to yourself? Hell of an incentive. Take orders from idiots for half the pay?"

"Oh hell, Miller. You want to sit behind a desk all day and play politics? Besides, the perk is that you get to drive your captain nuts and you both know there's not a damn thing he or she can do about it because if they get rid of you, their crime statistics go up, and the mayor comes down."

"They have their ways too." Anger grew in Louise's voice.

"What? So you didn't get to go to your friend's funeral. Well boo-fuckin'-hoo. Guess what? He didn't give a shit. He was dead."

His words punched her in the gut. Louise wanted Andrew and Karla's support but they were no longer there. She frantically searched for the tan uniform of the deputy that should have stood out amongst all the black police ones.

"Andrew? Karla?" she called out.

"I saw them walking around the house, toward the back."

With a little air back in her lungs and her head not reeling as much, Louise leered at Grant. "Is there anything you don't know about me?"

"Yeah." An intensity etched into Grant's face. "I don't know why you quit. They were just about ready to pull out the sergeant's chair for you."

"I think you mean out from *under* me."

The detective shook his head. "You could've been an exception to the rule, a smart-ass who might've climbed up the ladder. I could see you as a detective within five years. You and me are a lot alike, Miller."

"You're a lesbian, too?"

"Trapped in a man's body," he said without missing a beat.

Too bad she'd never gotten to really know this guy. He certainly seemed to know a lot about her, and that was irritating. Although, he might make a good mentor. For the first time since she quit, Louise thought about maybe asking for reinstatement. Grant had a little clout; maybe he could call in a favor or two.

"What's up?" Andrew called.

He and Karla hurried toward her, worry etched on their faces.

"Just wondering where you guys went."

"Everything okay?" Andrew asked.

"We went to check on Peanut," Karla said.

"Everything's fine," Louise said.

The scene died down. A few neighbors grew bored with Emily's eyewitness account. A red tow truck with 'Doug's Towing' emblazoned on the side, drove into the Harper driveway. Emily broke away from her remaining friends and ran into the tow truck driver's arms before he fully got out of the truck.

Their voices easily carried across the street.

"Oh Dougie, you will not believe the day I had."

"Somebody said they saw on the news there was a murder right by our house and they hadn't caught the guy yet. I came home as fast as I could."

"I'll be goddamned," Grant whispered only loud enough for the other three to hear. "Her husband is one of 'those people.' I think that's the worst case of denial I've ever seen." He closed his eyes and shuddered as if shaking away cobwebs. "Maybe it doesn't count if you own the business."

Louise slowly shook her head as the couple walked into their house. "Edina white collar tastes with a Minneapolis blue collar budget."

Andrew and Karla shrugged in unison.

Four men carrying bags of evidence and equipment walked out the front door of Louise and Karla's home.

"Hey, Vince, you guys done already? That was quick," Grant called.

"The guy was tidy. Looks like a beeline to the couch and out. Didn't wander around. Got samples from the carpet, but that's about it."

Grant turned back to Louise. "Well, I guess the good news is you don't have to stay at a hotel tonight."

"You going to be okay going back in there?" Louise asked Karla,

Karla stared at the front door for a good fifteen seconds before answering. "I'm not going to be scared out of my own home."

"I'll be in touch, then. If anything comes to mind, give me a call." Grant nodded his goodbyes.

The detective got into his Ford Taurus and drove off.

The last of the police cruisers followed him down the street, and the last of the onlookers went back into their homes.

"And then there was one." Louise grinned and punched her brother in the arm.

"I suppose I should get back on the street, huh?"

"Damn straight. My taxes are paying your salary. Get your lazy ass back to work."

Andrew took off his hat and gave his sister a peck on the cheek. "You've been waiting to use that line since you've been off the force, haven't you?"

Louise grinned but didn't deny it.

After giving Karla a hug, Andrew walked back to his squad and called, "I'll stop by after my shift and take you two out for dinner."

That brought smiles from the two women.

After he drove away the smiles vanished.

Karla wrapped Louise's hand in hers. "And then there were none."

Chapter 6

The doorbell chimed and Walter Jr. observed his half-sister from across the dining room table. She dabbed her eyes with a cotton handkerchief then stuffed it into her purse.

"We don't have to answer that," he said. "They'll go away eventually."

The doorbell rang again. "Go ahead," she finally said.

Walter dragged himself past the living room to the front door. Through the peephole George Jeffers slid a comb through his gelled hair, then shoved it into his pocket.

"Oh Christ," Walter whispered. He debated with himself whether to turn around, but decided to get it over with. Opening the door, Walter mumbled out a "Hey George," deliberately showing a lack of respect to his elder and his father's business partner.

Jeffers didn't notice, or ignored the slight, as he let himself in and grabbed the young Farkos in a bear hug. "I'm so sorry for your loss. Your father was a great man, and my best friend."

Walter thought about telling him what his father had really thought of this 'best friend,' but figured there might be a more opportune time – like maybe at the funeral in front of a lot of people.

"Thank you," he said, pushing away.

"Hello." Elissa entered the living room, her handkerchief clutched in her hand.

"Muriel, it's been far too long." George stepped around Walter like a piece of furniture.

"That's my sister, Elissa Jarvis." Walter raised his hand to cover the grin. "This is George Jeffers – uh, Dad's best friend."

Crimson spread across George's face but he didn't miss a beat. "I'm so sorry. Not wearing my glasses." As he reached her he stopped and squinted. "Of course, now that I'm closer I can tell you're much younger."

"My stepmother is three years older than me," she answered curtly.

"Again, I apologize."

This time, George Jeffers reached inside his sport coat and pulled out a pair of glasses. They were wire rims with round tinted lenses, the kind John Lennon wore in the sixties except George's pair had that bifocal line cutting across the middle.

He slipped them on. "I can see."

His attempt at humor made Elissa leave the room without a good-bye or even a pleased to meet you. Walter wished he had the guts to follow his sister's lead.

"What can I do for you, George?"

Jeffers took an uninvited seat on the couch, a blue floral print that dated back to the days of Walter Sr.'s first wife. Walter Jr. scanned the room for other artifacts that predated his mother. In the corner stood a grandfather clock. Next to that, a curio cabinet holding a menagerie of glass birds. He especially liked the red cardinal and the blue jay on the top shelf. When the time seemed right, he'd ask his mom if he could have them. Hell, he'd ask for the entire cabinet. Hopefully, before she threw out or sold everything having to do with the original Mrs. Farkos. Maybe he could take them now. Would she even notice?

George slipped off his glasses and put them back inside his coat. "I just stopped by on the chance you or your mom might be here, to let you know you have my deepest condolences."

"Thank you." Walter fidgeted, wanting to know what his sister was up to. "I'm kind of busy, George." He glanced at the clock. "Thanks for the condolences. Is there anything else?"

Taken aback, he responded, "Well, yes. I'd also like to be a pallbearer."

"I'll discuss it with the family. Now if you'll excuse me, I have a lot to do before Muriel gets home."

Jeffers had little choice but to get up as Walter walked away. "You refer to your mother by her first name?"

"I really don't see how I refer to my mother is any of your business…George."

"In my day we had more respect for our parents and our elders." Sympathy had left his voice.

"That was a long time ago, George. Now people

actually have to earn respect before being treated to it." He compared the time on his watch to the grandfather clock. One of them was three minutes off. "I also have to pick up my sister at the airport."

Jeffers walked to the door, and stopped. "I know that you're grieving, so I'll overlook your manners. I also came because I have some business to talk over, but I can see this isn't the time. Again, I'm sorry for your loss."

Walter's dad's best friend slammed the door behind him.

Elissa walked back into the room. "Good job, step-bro. I'm impressed."

"What a fucktard."

Elissa placed a hand on his shoulder. "I'm going to make some tea. Want a cup?" The grandfather clock chimed at the half-hour. Walter shook his head.

"Drew loves that clock. I want it before your mother sells it on eBay."

Walter nodded, feeling a little disappointment. He liked the clock, especially above the face where a dial rotated, telling the different phases of the moon.

"How is your hubby? Still whale hugging and sending positive vibes to plug the hole in the ozone?"

"He's doing fine."

Walter liked the cute way she smiled, especially when it was at her husband's expense.

As long as they were talking possessions, he thought now would be a good time to ask. "Um, do you mind if I take the bird cabinet?" He realized she had more of a right to it than he, but if she said no, he'd still take the cardinal and blue jay.

"That's fine, except for the hummingbird."

Walter studied the delicately blown piece of glass with the tiny stained green wings, and long yellow beak inside a purple flower. Beautiful artwork, but it would probably look a little faggy inside his apartment.

"Deal," he said.

"That's the last present I ever got her." Elissa dabbed her eyes with a hanky as she headed toward the kitchen. Walter didn't know if she was crying for her mother or her father. Then it hit him that his big sister was now an orphan. He caught up with her and hugged her tight. She buried her face in his shoulder, muffling the sobs and hugging him tight.

Walter quickly twisted his position so that she wouldn't feel the stirring beneath his waist.

--

The plane landed fifty-five minutes late. Jessica Farkos waited impatiently for the passengers in front of her to get the hell moving. Finally able to get her bag out of overhead, she slowly made her way down the narrow aisle while behind her a suitcase nudged into her calves, prodding her along.

"Knock it off!" She whipped around and glared at the kid who was all of seventeen. "I can only move as fast as the guy in front of me."

The kid became momentarily stunned. Jessica felt bad about snapping, but it had built up from the cab being late, security singling her out for a bag search, an hour delay, and finally, a flight turbulent enough to make her reach twice for the barf bag. *Oh yeah, and my dad was just murdered.*

Once inside the terminal, Jessica searched for her twin brother. They had made no arrangements for him to pick her up, but she did tell him the flight number and time. It was more of a surprise that he hadn't shown up. Maybe he was in the bar – a natural thing to do with the plane being so late.

A smattering of business people sat in the lounge watching a basketball game on the TV, while a family of four occupied one of the eight tables. There was no sign of Walter. Jessica walked up to the bartender and ordered a gin and tonic.

"Got some I.D.?" The black man had a square jaw and a nose that had been broken probably more than once. He had a natural streak of gray hair over his left ear that shined in a sea of thick black.

"Oh c'mon, I've been told I could pass for thirty." Even while she talked, Jessica reached into her purse for her driver's license.

"All the more reason," he said.

She slid the license across the bar, wondering the tactful way to properly flirt with this guy. The bartender picked it up with thick calloused fingers and studied the age.

Jessica saw him do the subtraction in his head. "I'm guessing you used to be a boxer."

He ignored the question until he figured out she was twenty-two, then smiled and slid the license back. "It's the nose, ain't it?"

Instead of waiting for an answer, he started mixing her drink. Within seconds it sat on a napkin in front of her. Jessica slid a ten across the bar and was mildly annoyed at how little change she got back.

"You haven't seen a guy with brown hair, brown eyes, who looks like he could be my twin brother, have you?"

The bartender concentrated hard on her face before shaking his head. "Been pretty slow. Not many people today and nobody even close as good looking as you—male or female. Sorry."

Jessica beamed as she downed half her drink and did another quick scan. "Any other pubs around here?"

A clean-cut man in a tailored suit tapped his glass on the bar. The bartender acknowledged him with a wave.

"When you get to the end of the terminal, turn left. It's right by the Sunglass Hut, across from Harley Davidson. Ike's is the main bar."

"Thanks. I'm sure that's where he's at." She polished off the rest of her drink, leaving the remainder of the ten on the bar.

"Was he supposed to pick you up?" the bartender asked.

A stupid question, Jessica thought, but she sweetly answered yes.

"Then he ain't going to be there, either."

"Besides being a boxer and a bartender, let me guess, you're also a psychic?" She meant it to sound flirty, but it came out condescending.

The bartender took no offense. "Unless he bought

his self a ticket, he ain't getting past security."

Embarrassed, Jessica slapped her palm against her forehead. "How could I be so stupid?"

There were a number of things the bartender could've done or said to deepen her embarrassment.

"Happens to the best of us," he said with a smile, showing off a gold-capped front tooth. "He's probably down at baggage claim."

Jessica took out another five, and her card, and placed them both next to the remaining change on the bar. She winked and used her sexiest walk as she strutted away. As slyly as she could, Jessica took a compact mirror from her purse to see if he might be watching. The man was shaking his head, but still smiling as he left the money on the bar but swept her card into his shirt pocket and went to tend his other customer.

Wandering past the stores, Jessica wondered when the airports around the country started doubling as indoor malls. She couldn't figure why people would pay top prices for the same souvenir you could get in L.A., Minneapolis, or Boston. And Harleys? In an airport? *No, don't put it in a bag; I'll drive it out.*

Down at baggage claim a number of people from her flight stood around the carousel waiting with newly arrived friends and family. No Walter. Jessica concluded that her brother was not going to meet her. She hitched the strap of her bag higher up on her shoulder then began the trek to the taxi stand. No more than five steps taken she felt a tap on her back.

"Hey, lady, got any spare change?"

Jessica spun around to the raspy voice. A grin spread across her face as she hugged her brother. "I knew you wouldn't strand me."

Walter held her at arm's distance. "Let me look at you." His eyes never left hers "You a lawyer yet?"

"By next year at this time I'll be studying for the bar." Her face became somber. "How you holding up, baby brother?"

She started calling him baby brother when they were eighteen. When exchanging birthday cards he gave her one saying she would always be older than him, even though it was only by a couple of minutes.

Walter released her arms and took a deep breath. "Actually, I'm doing okay. It's not like we were all that close. Hell, we hardly ever saw each other. The hard part is that he was murdered. It's so sudden, ya know? And then taken to a stranger's house? What kind of sick joke is that? That's just weird."

"Any clues at all as to who might've done it?" Jessica asked.

Walter slid the bag off of his sister's arm and slung it over his own shoulder. "No clue. But you know cops, they don't tell you anything until they got someone in custody. And you know how private Dad was. Who knows how many enemies he might've had?"

Jessica nodded. It occurred to her that she hadn't really known her father at all. That hurt.

"Oh, by the way, when you get settled, some detective wants you to call him. He said he just wanted to ask you a few routine questions."

Jessica nodded.

"Is Muriel there?" Her mother's name tasted sour on Jessica's tongue.

"Not yet." Walter checked the time on one of the many airport clocks hanging from the ceiling, reminding passengers how long their flights were delayed. "As a matter of fact, her plane is supposed to arrive in about an hour-and-a-half."

"Shit," Jessica sighed. "I suppose I wouldn't mind waiting." She perked up. "Hey, we can take the train to the Mall of America. I'll buy ya a drink or two."

"I hate the mall. Plus, I bet dad's liquor cabinet is just as stocked as the bars there and a hell of a lot cheaper."

"But it would be silly to make a second trip to the airport," Jessica said.

"Who said anything about two trips? My quota is one trip to the airport per day."

"Then why are we standing around here?"

Luggage slid down the carousel chute. "Is this everything?" Walter nodded at the bag on his shoulder.

They headed toward the car. "Careful. My whole life is in that bag."

Chapter 7

Louise plopped down on some pillows where the sofa used to be. *Evidence my ass!* But with bloodstains on the cushions, she really didn't mind all that much that the police had carted it out. On the other side of the room, Peanut was curled up, his chin resting on Karla's foot. Karla, sitting on the comfy chair, shuddered as she glanced up from her needlepoint. The TV set was on but the dog was the only one showing any interest in the documentary about wolves in northern Minnesota.

"I forgot to ask," Karla said. "How much did your car set you back?"

Louise grimaced, wondering if she'd now have to account for every penny. "They were great. Only charged me for the distributor cap. Didn't even charge for the tow."

Karla nodded and resumed her hobby.

Seconds before the doorbell rang, Peanut sprang to his feet and made a dash for the door. Louise hoisted herself up and followed.

"Have you decided where you want to go for dinner?" Louise asked. "You know how wishy-washy Andrew is."

To her surprise, it wasn't Andrew standing on the other side of the door.

"Hope I didn't come at a bad time." Detective Grant held out his hand for Peanut to take in his scent. In his other hand he held a manila folder.

"Not at all." Louise said. "We're just waiting for my brother. Thought you were him, actually." She stepped aside and waved him in.

Karla put down her needlepoint and clicked off the TV as Louise followed Grant into the living room. "Good evening, Detective. This is an unexpected visit."

"Gordon," he corrected her. "I'm off duty."

"Since when are you ever off duty?" Louise asked.

"Well, I hope you came with good news. Can I get you something to drink? Coffee?" Karla asked.

Grant studied the Miro print hanging above the fireplace and gave it an admiring nod. "Nothing, thanks, and afraid not. Just stopped by as a professional courtesy." He handed Louise the folder. "Your arrest report on Walter Farkos. I'd appreciate if you'd go over it and let me know if anything jumps out at you."

Louise glanced through the papers and nodded. Karla took a seat back in her chair while Peanut sank to the floor. Grant remained standing.

"Prelim shows multiple blunt traumas to the head are what did him in. Carpet fibers on his skin, in his clothes and hair are being analyzed. Someone spent a good deal of time cleaning him up before rolling him in that rug." He focused on Karla. "You're positive your door was locked when you left?"

Karla didn't hesitate. "Absolutely."

"The guy is good. No sign of forced entry. I'm looking forward to asking your neighbor a few more questions tomorrow morning, like if she saw him put down the carpet and open the door, or if someone answered."

"No one answered the door," Louise said flatly.

"Not you two. But didn't it ever occur to you that there might've been more than one? Maybe someone snuck in the back, answered the door to make it look natural."

Louise's jaw dropped. It had never occurred to her.

"I'm not saying there was more than one. Just covering the bases."

"Oh my God. Two," Karla whispered. She got up from her chair and headed toward the kitchen. "I need some coffee. Anyone want anything?"

As if it was his job, Peanut got up and followed.

"No thanks," Louise and Grant said in unison.

Louise cocked her head at Peanut. "Guess whose dog he is?"

At that moment, thoughts of becoming a detective like Grant dashed out of Louise's mind. There could've been two people! It was an obvious deduction.

"What's driving me nuts is, why you? It's got to be someone who knows you pretty damned well, and someone who's really got it out for you."

Ice traveled through her veins as Louise hugged herself trying to get rid of the goose bumps that rose on her arms. "You mean like maybe another cop?"

Grant spoke softly, but every syllable succinct, "Watch where you're treading here, Miller. Think very carefully before you answer this next question. Do you know of any police officer that would want to try and frame you for a murder, or just put you through hell?"

Louise didn't hesitate. "Maybe two or three dozen, off the top of my head."

"I'm serious. This isn't a game."

Louise snapped. "You don't have any idea how hard it is to be a woman trying to be an equal with a bunch of good ol' boys. Add being gay and you might as well paint a giant target on my back. Hell, it would be a lot easier to ask who didn't hate me enough to pull this shit."

Karla followed Peanut back into the living room. She shot Louise a flash of sympathy, and then focused on the detective, waiting for his retort. When none came she took her seat and sipped coffee.

"Okay Miller, you got me. I guess I'm going to need you to make a list."

Peanut got to his feet and trotted to the front door.

"Is he trying to tell me something?" Grant asked.

The doorbell sounded and the door swung open. Andrew sauntered in. The nub that was Peanut's tail quivered, making his entire rear end vibrate. Andrew's knees cracked as he squatted and tapped his chest. The rottweiler jumped on his hind legs, resting his front paws on Andrew's shoulders while slobbering his face.

"I think his promise of taking us out to dinner is just an excuse to come over and play with the dog," Louise told the detective.

"Nonsense," Andrew said. "This is just an added perk. How ya doin' Wing Nut?"

"Good evening, Deputy."

"Detective."

"You can call him Gordon. He's off the clock," Louise chimed in.

Andrew stood up and eyed Grant. The detective nodded.

"So, did you catch the guy?" Andrew pressed his

hand on Peanut's head, scratching the dog's ears, and at the same time making sure he wouldn't jump.

Grant shook his head. "Was in the neighborhood and thought of a couple more questions I wanted to ask your sister before I went home."

"Care to join us for dinner, detective?" Andrew asked. "If you girls don't mind. There's an Asian place on Lake and Hennepin that I hear is pretty good."

Karla showed as much surprise as Louise.

"I'll take a rain check. Got some stuff I need to catch up on."

Louise hoped her relief didn't show.

"Walk me to my car, Deputy?"

Andrew raised his eyebrows. "Certainly."

"I'd like to see that list tomorrow," Grant said. He faced Karla. "Nice seeing you again." He let Andrew lead him to the door, careful not to let out the dog.

Louise waited until the door had closed completely and the men were well down the sidewalk. "What the hell!"

"Yeah," Karla said. "What do you think he wants to talk to Andrew about?"

"Huh? I'm wondering who the hell Andrew thinks he is inviting Grant to dinner? He never cleared it with us first."

Louise went over, opened the door a crack and watched from the entry while the men talked. The detective and her brother stood in the street by the driver's door of Grant's car and spoke soft enough that she couldn't hear. The fading daylight made it impossible for her to even try and read their lips.

The temperature had dropped at least twenty degrees from that afternoon and a cool breeze whipped its way into the partially open door. Karla shivered and went back into the living room. Louise stayed, basking in the chill. Soon spring would turn to summer, and that meant four months of sweltering temperatures and constant sweat. She was already looking forward to fall. The only plus to the heat, besides not having to shovel snow, was that her hand didn't feel as stiff.

The conversation ended as the detective got in his car and Andrew walked back up the path to the front door.

Louise waited impatiently for her brother.

"So, what was that?" She closed the door behind him.

"He thinks you should be a cop again. He has some kind of misguided impression that you might listen to me."

She punched him hard in the arm. "That's not what I'm talking about. I'm talking about him joining us for dinner."

Andrew rubbed his arm. "What's wrong with that? He seems like a nice guy."

"Where the hell did you get that? Nice guy, my ass."

Louise walked into the living room, looking to Karla for support. Karla concentrated on her needlepoint, purposely ignoring them.

"That's it," Louise pouted. "I want to go to an all you can eat place."

Andrew cringed, as did Karla.

"You know, it wouldn't hurt to have a friend or two still on the force," Andrew said.

A sly grin spread across Louise's face. "You clever bastard. Now that I'm off the force, you want a connection. You're devious, Andrew. I didn't think you had it in you."

Andrew shrugged. "Fine, think what you want. Can we go to that Asian place now? I'm getting hungry."

"I gotta get my purse." Louise sauntered down the hall.

From the bedroom, Louise overheard Andrew speak to Karla.

"Grant is right, she should ask for reinstatement. She'd make a good detective. Would you talk to her? Maybe she'll listen to you."

"She's got some other issues that need to be taken care of first." Karla's voice had a mixture of anger and sadness.

Louise snatched her purse and strode back with a purposeful gait. "Let's go," she said before Karla had a chance to narc her out.

--

The blond wig rested on a Styrofoam head in front of a mirror hanging in his bathroom. He ran a brush through the fake hair. "It was a good plan." He jerked the brush through a snag and brushed harder until hair started falling out. "Then what the hell went wrong?" he shouted. According to the news there were no suspects. *The body was in her living room for Christ's sake! How could she not be a suspect?* "They never even brought the dyke bitch in for questioning!"

He tore the wig off its mount and flung it to the floor. Ready to stomp on it, he caught his reflection in the mirror and didn't like what he saw. Burying his rage deep inside once again, he carefully picked up the blond tresses, set it back on the Styrofoam and calmly brushed one hundred strokes. What was supposed to be a major turmoil in her life turned out to be a minor inconvenience. It was time to carry out plan B.

Chapter 8

Andrew ordered the Szechuan Vegetable Delight;
Louise, the Kung Po Pork; and Karla, the Chicken Chow
Mein. All three admiringly eyed the waitress as she walked
from their table. Her silky black hair flowed down the
middle of her back while the slit in her red satin dress
showed a pleasing amount of slim thigh.

"Can we take her home with us?" Louise asked. "No
offense sweetheart, but there's something about Asian
chicks."

"Oh yeah," Karla answered without hesitation.

"Don't make me sorry I brought you two here,"
Andrew muttered.

A paper lantern showing a gold dragon hung above
the table with a low watt light bulb inside. In the middle of
the table sat a lit candle in a dark red ornamental holder.
Even in the dim light, Louise could see the blush on
Andrew's face.

"I don't believe for a second you weren't ogling at
her too."

"At least I have the decency to keep my mouth
shut."

"Whoa." Louise and Karla shared a conspiratorial
smile.

Karla shook her head. "Men. Can't live with 'em…"

When no response came after that, Andrew said, "I
heard it different."

The women cracked up. Louise pushed her chair
back and stood up. "I gotta hit the can. Don't speak too ill of
me while I'm gone." She gave her brother an evil smirk.
"Karla will tell me everything."

Louise wove her way around the tables and pushed
open the door to the ladies room. Relatively clean, a chart
hung on the wall that made known it had last been cleaned at
seven o'clock. Locking the door, Louise took a seat and
willed the weight of the world to fall off her shoulders. They
weren't even totally unpacked yet and the simple laidback
life she and Karla had planned was already falling in the
dumpster.

The body on her couch she had no control of, as bizarre as that was. "But a pair of kings?" *How could I have not seen that?*

Louise pressed the handle and willed her troubles to flush away. At the sink she splashed water on her face. In the mirror dark bags hung under her tired hazel eyes. *Is that a gray hair?*

"Screw it! A new day starting now." She practiced smiling before returning to the table.

Her new attitude faded when she saw Karla's face. She didn't know what Andrew said to her, but whatever it was, upset her a lot.

"What's going on?" Louise pulled her chair from the table and sat.

"You're a horse," Andrew said.

"Oh yeah? Well you're a pig."

"No, I'm a dog. Loyal and honest and I work well with others." If I was born a year later I'd be a pig."

"I'm a snake," added Karla, using her artificially cheery voice that Louise knew so well. "It says I'm wise and intense. Ooh, and beautiful. That's me." That last part didn't sound as artificial.

"And you're a horse" Andrew pointed at the zodiac chart on her placemat. "Wow, the Chinese might have something with this. Often ostentatious and impatient. These are pretty accurate."

Karla bowed her head and played with her napkin. The realization crashed in on Louise. Andrew hadn't said anything to her.

"She told you, didn't she?" Louise glared at her brother, forcing him to look her in the eye.

Louise didn't feel mad at Karla, and that surprised her somewhat. What also surprised her was the anger she held toward Andrew. She couldn't understand why, unless it was that pitiful expression on his face.

"Why didn't you say anything?" Andrew asked.

"I think it has to do with people maybe finding out?" Sarcasm dripped from her voice.

"Did you honestly think no one would? You really thought you'd win the money back?"

Louise hoped for some support from Karla but knew none would be coming. Words formed in her brain, but on the way to her mouth they collapsed in a bunch of mangled syllables. "Look," she finally said. "I don't want to talk about it now." She went from defensive to offensive and grabbed the Farkos report from her purse and slapped it on the table. "Let's talk about something interesting, like who would break into my house and dump a stiff."

"*Our* house," Karla said.

Her plan had worked. It got them, at least Karla, off the gambling subject. "Our house," she corrected herself.

Andrew took the report from Louise. "The gambling conversation isn't over."

Paging through the report, Andrew stopped. She knew he was at the part where she'd drawn her gun. She waited for a reaction but he only concentrated on the report. When he finished, Andrew slid the papers back. Louise picked them up, tapped the sheets back into alignment and slid it across to Karla.

"You want to read it?"

After a long pause Karla began reading. "If you were still on the force there's no way I'd read it, but now that you're off and I don't have to worry about you, what the hell."

Louise waited for a response from her brother.

"Other than you going crazy with your gun, it doesn't seem like all that an unusual arrest. How many people do you think know about it?"

The waitress came back balancing a tray on one hand and another glass of Du Kang for Karla in the other.

"How many is that?" Louise whispered to her brother. Below the table he showed her three fingers.

The tray held six plates and a large bowl of rice for the three to share. Expertly, the girl put an empty plate in front of each person, and the plates full of food next to them. She placed the bowl of rice in easy reaching distance of them all.

The aroma wafted around the table. Louise inhaled the smell of spices and pepper coming off of the Kung Po. In front of Andrew sat a rainbow of vegetables. Light brown patches barely seared their skins as steam rose up. Even Karla's chow mein smelled appetizing. The celery was fresh and not drowning in sauce.

"Is there anything else?" the waitress asked.

"Everything looks great," Andrew answered.

The waitress beamed and walked away with an extra wiggle in her step.

Always the gentleman, Andrew passed Karla the rice and then offered the bowl to Louise, who declined, before serving himself.

Carefully chewing and swallowing before speaking, he asked again, "Who-all knows about your run-in with Farkos?"

Politeness didn't enter into Louise's demeanor. She spoke with a mouthful of pork. "Well, just about any officer in the precinct, you, Karla, and whoever Farkos told."

"That's disgusting," Andrew said at her lack of manners. "I can ask Grant if he found out if Farkos had any enemies, but for the time being, let's assume it's somebody who has a grudge against you, and how that might tie into Farkos."

Louise stopped chewing and pondered his statement. "The only one that put us together was Paul Handley. He assisted on the arrest."

"Any bad blood between you two?"

Louise shook her head as she shoveled another forkful of food into her mouth. "Quite the contrary." She suddenly started gagging. The gagging contorted into a painful cough.

Andrew chuckled. "Serves you right."

When the coughing fit ended, Louise picked up her napkin, wiped her mouth and dabbed at her eyes. "Choked on a pepper, and thanks for your concern. Anyway, Paul was about the only cop on the force who didn't seem to have a bug up his ass about me."

"Sounds like that would make him a prime suspect," Andrew said.

"Very funny, pig."

"Horse," Andrew interrupted.

"Horse's ass," Louise answered back.

That brought a giggle from Karla, who licked her index finger and made an imaginary check in the air. "One for Louise."

Louise leaned over to her brother. "Only three?"

Hey, have you talked to Paul lately?" Karla pushed the report back to Louise.

"Moved up north after he retired. He and his wife bought some touristy gift shop. Haven't heard from him since he left." Louise sounded forlorn.

"You should call him," Karla said.

The waitress came over and asked how everything tasted. With her mouth full, Karla circled her thumb and index finger. Louise gave the thumbs up. Andrew said, "Excellent."

"Let me know if there's anything else I can bring you." She had no trace of an Asian accent and her smile radiated seduction.

Louise fantasized for a moment then Karla's knee brushed hers and she quickly erased the thought.

"Thank you," Andrew said.

When she walked away, the waitress brushed the tip of her finger across Andrew's shoulder.

"Ooh, looks like somebody has the hots for my brother." Louise watched the waitress' sexy walk.

Three times Andrew tried to pick up a chunk of pepper with his chopsticks. Each time it plopped back into his plate. "She just does that to get a bigger tip," he mumbled.

"I bet it's going to work, too," Louise said.

Andrew gave up, and like a mighty hunter, skewered the pepper with one chopstick. "Do you think Handley might've mentioned it to anybody?" He took a bite of the stabbed veggie.

Louise half-shrugged. "He might've, but I can't imagine why."

"You might want to ask him," Andrew said.

"We can invite him and his wife for dinner," Karla added. "You've talked about him enough. I'd like to meet the great Paul Handley."

Louise finished a mouthful this time before

speaking. "One, I don't think he'll want to drive to the city just for dinner. Two, I have no idea how to get hold of him."

"Okay, let's table that for now. Do you know anything about Walter Farkos' family?"

Louise shook her head and motioned for the waitress. The girl stood at a nearby table taking an order, but signaled she'd be right over.

"Nothing," Louise said. "The case never went to trial so I never had anything more to do with it. I assume he pled guilty and that was the end of it. When I talk to Grant, I'll ask to see the probation report."

"What can I get for you?" the waitress asked.

Louise twisted in her chair and looked up at the perfect teeth smile. "I'd like a box—"

"Make that two," Karla chimed in.

"And my brother would like your phone number."

"Louise!" Andrew turned toward the equally embarrassed girl. "I apologize for my sister."

The red started in the girl's cheeks and spread across her face, hiding the smooth alabaster white skin. "I be right back." She walked to the kitchen as fast as her high heels would let her.

Waiting for her to be safely out of earshot, Andrew spoke. "How could you? That was past rude!"

"You embarrassed the poor girl so much, she lost her American accent." Karla shook trying to hold in her laughter.

"Oh pooh. If she can't take it, she shouldn't dish it out. You saw the way she was flirting with you before."

Andrew squirmed in his chair. "I don't know if I can ever come back here."

"Don't be such a wuss. You're panties are showing."

All three clamped their mouths as the waitress approached. Karla focused on her plate, in fear of cracking up. Whatever embarrassment she showed when she left, the woman had made a remarkable recovery. She placed two Styrofoam boxes on the table next to Louise and a small plate with three fortune cookies sitting on top of the check by Andrew.

"Again, I apologize for my sister," Andrew said.

"It did catch me off guard," Her voice betrayed no

hint of being offended. "You can pay the cashier." She sounded American again.

Andrew passed a cookie to Karla, and with his index finger flicked another one to Louise. It ricocheted off the box and toward Karla as she dumped in the remainder of her food.

"Gimme." Louise reached across the table and snatched her fortune.

With a snap, Andrew opened his cookie. "Many surprises await you. Well, that narrows it down." He lifted up the check and underneath sat a scrap of paper. Written in red ink was the name, Ahn Kim, and a phone number. Andrew shoved the paper into his pocket, but not fast enough. Both Louise and Karla saw it.

"Well that's certainly a surprise," Louise said.

"Your fortune is already coming true. Gonna call her?" Karla opened her cookie, read the message and frowned. "'Relationships will prove to be a challenge. Patience and understanding will be needed to make it through.' Well that sucks." She nibbled the cookie and crumpled the message, dropping it in the remaining chow mein sauce.

Louise cracked open her fortune and read it to herself. Shivers prickled at her spine as she got up from the table. "Let's go."

"What did it say?" Concern crept in Karla's voice.

"It's just bullshit." Louise tore the slip of paper in half and dropped it onto the table. Pushing her chair back and getting ready to stand, she was too slow to stop Andrew whose arm shot out and snatched the scraps of paper. He held up the two pieces together, curled his lip and then handed it to Karla.

'A perilous journey lies ahead. Be wary of the path you choose.'

Chapter 9

Three men and one woman sat somberly at the round table in the meeting room. George Jeffers took a seat at the head of the table – the head of the table meaning where Walter Farkos used to sit.

"We have to move fast," Jeffers said.

Joel Spender and Leo Carp eyed him while Beverly Wimpole nervously stared out the forty-second story window of the IDS Center planted in the middle of downtown Minneapolis. Jeffers followed her gaze.

When the company moved to their new office almost twenty-five years ago, George liked to sit and watch the Mississippi River cutting its way between Minneapolis and St. Paul. With his telescope he could see past the city and into the suburbs, some of which back then were still farmland. Along came the expansion craze and smaller downtown buildings were demolished and replaced with bigger and taller skyscrapers. Now glass paneling from the office building across the street reflected the day's light. At night when he worked late, George often turned off the lights and watched the cleaning crew vacuuming carpets and emptying wastebaskets. On rare occasion he'd see someone hunched over their desk staring into a computer screen.

"He's not even in the ground yet," Spender said.

George returned his attention to the three and glided his hand through his salt and pepper hair.

"First order of business, I think we should close the office the day of Walter's funeral."

"I second that," Spender said.

"This is an informal meeting, Joel," George said.

Joel shrugged. "I still think it's a good idea."

"I think it should be a paid day off for the staff," Leo added.

George rubbed his chin while scheming. "How about this? We tell them they have to use vacation or sick time, but those who show up at the funeral, we'll give them a bonus of a day's pay. We can find out who's loyal to the company, and who's not."

"I don't like it." Leo spoke immediately. "I think it's

an underhanded way of doing business. All it will do is cause resentment.”

On the outside, George Jeffers remained calm and impassive. Inside his blood boiled as his anger rose. *That kike has been a thorn in my side since Walter made him a partner.* One day he’d have to do something about Mr. Goodie Jew-shoes, but that would take careful thought and consideration. He put it on his mental ‘things-to-do’ list.

“I respectfully disagree,” George said. “What do you think, Joel?” He knew Joel Spender as an ally and ‘yes’ man. He wouldn’t dare defy.

“I don’t know,” Spender said. “How about we give them a day off with pay, but encourage them to go to the funeral?”

“I wholeheartedly agree,” Leo said, cutting off Jeffers before he could speak.

George hid his chagrin at Spender’s sudden emergence of balls. “And what about you, Ms. Wimpole?”

The woman with mousy brown hair and green eyes twitched as she rubbed her hands together. “I don’t even know why I’m here.”

The tension broke and the men laughed, George Jeffers laughing the longest and loudest. “Well, Bev. Can I call you Bev?”

She nodded.

“Well Ms. Wimpole, as it so happens, out of all the junior execs, you, by far, have earned the most money for the company. The unfortunate demise of Walter Farkos leaves a seat open for a new partner. We’d like to offer that position to you.”

Beverly gasped as she pushed the chair away from the table, her shaking hands on the arms of the chair. “I don’t know what to say.”

“Say yes.” George flashed his bright toothy smile.

The other two men nodded their confirmation.

“Y-y-yes.”

“Congratulations,” George said. “Not only are you the first woman to be made partner, but at thirty-seven, you’re also the youngest.”

“Oh George, you shouldn’t be advertising a

woman's age," Joel said.

George rolled his eyes. "It's not like it's a secret to anyone in this room. We've all seen her personnel file."

"It's quite all right," Beverly said.

Joel and Leo shook her hand while George leaned back in his chair.

"Welcome aboard, Ms. Wimpole. Talk to the lawyers after the meeting and have them draw up all the legalities and get that out of the way. Now, as your first executive decision, what do you think about paying only the employees who attend Walter's funeral?"

Again she stammered. The redness in her face deepened. "Um, I think that it would seem political if we paid some and not others. I think we should treat everyone equally and just encourage them all to go to the funeral."

"So be it," George said. Underneath the desk his hands clenched into fists. *Maybe it wasn't such a good idea promoting a woman.*

"Next order of business, and I know that this will be hard, but I suggest we change the name of the company from 'Farkos, Jeffers, Spender and Carp' to 'Jeffers Spender, Carp and Wimpole.'

Beverly gasped again. Both Joel and Leo's jaw dropped.

"It's a fast paced world out there." George focused primarily on Spender. Even when Walter Farkos was alive, Spender had been George's closest ally. "Our investors are going to wonder why we're not keeping up with the times."

"I disagree," Leo said.

Of course you do. George wanted to wring his scrawny neck. It would be so nice to get rid of him, but Leo Carp made more money for the firm than anyone else, including George. The only way to get rid of him would be for some kind of accident to fall upon him. It was something to put on the back-burner – at least for now.

"FJS&C means financial investing confidence. Our investors have confidence in us. People admired and trusted Walter. If we dropped his name now, they'd think of us as just another heartless, soulless corporation. No offense to you, Ms. Wimpole, but I don't think we should make any rash changes and add your name to the marquee just yet."

"None taken," Beverly said, smiling at Leo.

Joel Spender was a lackey, but as was just proven moments ago, not always a pushover. "What about you, Joel?"

He cleared his throat. "Well, we've been talking about getting a new ad campaign going. I think now would be the most opportune time to do that *and* change the name."

George eased his fists and rested his hands on top of the table.

Joel continued. "I think our old clients will stick with us no matter what we call ourselves. And with a new campaign we can go after the young ones who've never heard of Farkos, Jeffers, Spender and Carp."

"And what about you, Ms. Wimpole? What do you think about the new name?" George asked.

Her face still glowed pink, but Beverly seemed to be relaxing into the situation. "I can appreciate what Mr. Carp says, but I have to agree with you and Mr. Spender."

"Excellent." George slapped his palms on the table in a quick drum roll. "I'll leave it to you and Joel to clear things with the lawyers and head up the new campaign." "Any problem with that, Leo?" His voice was smug.

Carp dejectedly shook his head. "No problem."

Jeffers stood up from the table feeling superior to his three junior partners. "Last order of business, Walter's clients. As senior partner I'll take it upon myself to divvy up his clients between the four of us."

"Wait a minute!" Leo Carp sprang to his feet.

At six-foot-one, George stood two inches taller than Carp. Carp was spindly. George outweighed him by a good fifty pounds. He'd love it if the Jew wanted to tango.

"Why don't we go round-robin, each picking clients? You're senior, George, you have first choice, then Joel, then me, then Beverly? We keep going around until there are no more clients."

Jeffers rolled his eyes at Spender and Wimpole like they shouldn't believe what Carp was saying, either. "If this were a democracy, Leo, you would probably get your way. But this investment firm is no democracy. Not on a decision this big."

Walter Farkos had seen to that. He had built the company from nothing and always remained in control with fifty-one percent of the stock. Always agreeable to listen to opposing views, and often willing to leave it to a vote, he made it clear that if there were a tie, his view would win. And on those rare occasions when a matter was not open to debate, he'd left no doubt as to who ran things.

"It's how Walter would've done it," George said. "As senior partner, and at least for now the major shareholder, it's my right and obligation to do it this way. I know most of Walter's clients and their personalities. I know who will be best suited for whom."

"You mean like who gets the biggest portfolios," Carp said.

Jeffers let out a conciliatory sigh. "Listen, Leo. I know we don't always see eye-to-eye on things, but I promise I will be fair."

Leo slumped back in his chair. Joel and Beverly both seemed indifferent.

"I think this meeting is over."

The three junior partners walked out of the conference room. Jeffers stayed behind, facing the window as they left. Outside, a few wispy clouds lazed above the horizon. Bicycles traveled the path along the river. George pondered what was in Walter Farkos' will. He knew Walter's probate attorney and thought about breaking into his office. But why? The will was in custody of the probate court. One implausible idea after another, he tried to come up with a scheme to see that damn document before anyone else.

As the sun sank deeper, George's ghostly reflection in the window became fuller, more regal. He saw the reflection of a leader who runs a billion dollar company – tall with a commanding presence and a hint of a smile to show compassion and humanity.

With a click, the florescent lights flickered out leaving the office bright enough to see, but in shadows. George Jeffers walked into the empty hall, listening to the faint hum of the fans from the computer room. What felt like minutes had stretched to almost two hours that he'd been staring out that window. It hadn't helped. He still had no idea how to be first to get hold of that will.

Casually walking down the hall, he passed offices and all of the personalized screen savers. When he walked past his own, his computer showed nothing but a blank screen. He'd disabled the screensaver because he found it distracting. Continuing to the end of the hall, he stopped at the suite Walter had once called his home away from home. Tomorrow he would start packing Walter's things. By the end of the week George Jeffers would be reveling in his new corner office.

Chapter 10

Without a cloud in the sky and despite a perfect spring temperature, he kept the windows in the car rolled up. The previous night he had a dream that his wig, along with his clothes, blew away in a windstorm, leaving him exposed to a crowded parking lot. In the dream he couldn't be sure if they were laughing at him because of the wig or the nudity. It didn't really matter, they were still laughing. He'd never read much into dreams before, but this one he interpreted that he'd better be very careful.

Parked at the end of the block, he waited as the garage door went up and the Saturn backed out. The blonde had already left for work in her VW. He assumed correctly that Miller wouldn't stay boxed up in the house all day. If she had, he'd have been back tomorrow, or the next day, or the next. Patience was his virtue.

After the Saturn disappeared from sight, he pulled into the driveway and pressed the button on the handmade remote. The third frequency he tried turned out to be the charm. The door whirred its way up. He drove his car in while glancing around for witnesses, noticing none. But then, in the middle of the week the entire neighborhood carried an eerie and deserted feel at one in the afternoon. Most of the families were double income, and with kids still in school most of the houses were ripe for a break-in. Security systems were a mere inconvenience he learned to work around.

But he was no burglar. His mission had purpose. His purpose? To destroy the life of Louise Miller; to slowly pick it apart until death would come like a relief.

He slid on a pair of rubber gloves and then stepped from his car. Like a summer Santa, he grabbed a lawn bag and flung it over his shoulder. He circled to the back of the house, closing the garage door. Instead of turning into the back yard, he detoured to the neighbors.

The Internet was a miracle sent by the gods. It saved a fortune in private investigator fees and witnesses. Any moron could Google anything, like an address or a phone number – in most cases for free – find out a person's name and where they worked. Hell, with a little patience and ingenuity, their whole meaningless life's story. Take for instance Miller's next-door neighbors, Ken and Marci Burlington. A childless couple, he a CPA and she an executive assistant, their house stood dormant Monday through Friday from seven-thirty in the a.m. until almost six in the evening.

He unlatched the wooden gate in the six-foot high fence. *Ahh, the need for privacy.* From inside the house, the Burlingtons' cock-a-poo raced to the sliding porch door and began its persistent barking.

Fortunately, the house was well insulated and the glass doors double paned. The racket could've been worse. Still, it confirmed his suspicions. If the Burlingtons even bothered to turn the alarm on, they would have the motion detector off. Prying open the doors would set off the alarm, but breaking through the glass most likely wouldn't.

He walked past the deck, crouched and peeked in the basement window into the laundry room. Common sense told him that window would be wired and even breaking the glass might cause enough of a disturbance to activate the alarm. Standing upright he spied the kitchen. That window might be wired too, but not as likely.

Do I really need to break in at all? Eyeing the vinyl siding he figured he probably did.

The dog yapped from the kitchen. The intruder reached into his bag and retrieved a two-gallon can of gasoline. With one sharp blow, the bottom of the can shattered the window. Shards of glass were strewn across the kitchen floor. The dog scurried back, avoiding the slivers, but never stopped the barking, no longer muffled by the closed house.

The thick smell of gasoline burned the man's eyes and nose as he unscrewed the cap. Because of the incessant noise, his head began to throb. Carefully clearing glass away from the frame, he leaned in with the can and splashed the wooden cabinets, taking an occasional shot at the dog. But the dog kept his distance, standing at the entryway that led into the living room. It didn't matter. If the flames didn't kill him, the smoke would.

To finish up, the red and white checkered curtains that hung loosely open by the sides of the window got a good dousing. Satisfied, he walked across the back yard, swinging the can as he went, sending splashes of gasoline across the lawn. The cock-a-poo raced back to the sliding door, alerting anyone who would listen about the intruder in his territory.

Once outside the gate, he sauntered into Miller's back yard. There was no fence to contend with. A long thin cable with a transparent red plastic coating was attached to the wall next to the back door. Haphazardly coiled, a leash-snap at the end of the cable rested on the top step at the bottom of the door. He picked it up and flung it across the yard. *She might as well have to walk across the yard next time she lets little poochy outside.* It occurred to him that all she'd have to do was pull the cable back from where it was attached to the house. *Unless there's nothing there.*

He reached into his pocket and drew out a Swiss army knife. Unfolding the Phillips head, be loosened the screws when an even better idea popped into his brain. *Why take it? She'd just get a new one.* Instead, he loosened them enough so one good yank would free the dog. *Maybe their little bundle of joy will get tangled up and choke itself to death, or maybe get hit by a car.* The thought of the dog writhing with cable digging in its neck, struggling to get free, made his throbbing head ease. "With luck you'll be joining your pal next door real soon."

Prank completed, he picked up the gas can and headed back toward the garage. Something in his peripheral vision moved. Something inside the house. A chill overtook his body as he swung around and the little pooch he imagined exploded into reality. A pair of eyes were staring at him. No, not a pair, one eye bore into him.

Fog misted over a small splotch of window from the dog's breath. A black patch covered one of its eyes, but the gaze from the other penetrated deep enough for two. He thought the beast might be growling, but no noise could hear from the other side of the window. Drool hung from its chin as it pressed its nose against the glass.

The man quickly recovered. "You are the biggest

and ugliest son of a bitch that I've ever seen." He didn't know if the mutt heard him, but he shuddered again when the dog appeared to be smiling.

Unnerved, he hastened to the front of the garage, pressed the button on his remote, and opened the door. Tomato cages stacked in the corner leaned on a sack of lawn fertilizer. He put the gas can behind the bag, partially hidden. Hidden enough that the women might not notice but the police would.

He threw the now empty plastic bag in the back seat of his car, trying to erase the picture of that dog leering at him. The fear of strangers laughing at his nudity would now take a back seat to the new nightmare his mind was now plotting – that damn dog drooling against the window. But in his new nightmare there'd be no glass separating the two.

Shaking his head vigorously, trying to get rid of the hellish images, he started the car and threw it in reverse. Halfway out of the garage he slammed on the brakes.

"Shit!"

With the car back into the garage, the man marveled at his own stupidity. That dog had done a number on him, played on his mind so he'd forget the most important detail. He made a beeline to the back of the Burlington house. When he rounded the corner, the yipping started again.

That won't last long.

He walked to the broken window. The scent of gasoline still permeated the air. He struck a match and touched it to the curtain.

As much as he wanted to stay and watch the flames spread, stay until the dog's barks became squeals, he knew he'd been too careless already. He jogged back to the car.

From the front of the house, everything seemed normal. Smoke would be spotted within a couple minutes, flames not long after. With luck he'd be half way home by the time a fire was reported.

After throwing the gloves in the back seat and the remote in the glove compartment, calmly and as naturally as he could, the man backed down the driveway as the garage door closed.

A bright flash from a house across the street caught

his attention in the rearview mirror. As he turned into the street it happened again. He slowly drove by, straining to see into the window, but the sun and shadows made seeing inside impossible. A third snap of light made his heart leap. He knew what that busybody was doing and he had to take a deep breath to avoid panic.

Spinning the tires, he screeched around the corner and then slowed, taking another right. He parked his car at the curb.

"Can things get any worse?"

With the plan becoming undone, he had to take more drastic chances. He cut across the block through someone's yard into the back lawn of the photographer. Tearing off the wig, he shoved it in his pocket. Hopefully the person with the camera never got a good look at his face.

He walked to the front of the house and up to the door. Wearing a façade of calm, he pressed the bell and waited. The wait lasted only a couple of seconds before a woman's voice through the intercom asked who was there.

"I'm a Minneapolis police detective. I'd like to ask you a few questions if I could."

"How did you get here so fast? I just called you. It couldn't have been over a minute ago."

A new wave of panic crept into his bones. He had to think and work fast. "I was already on my way here to talk to Ms. Miller across the street when the call came in to talk to you." He marveled at his deception. It sounded plausible.

"I'll be right there."

He spun around, not wanting her to see his face when she came to the door. A plume of smoke wafted above the house across the street. If the pukey little mutt was barking, he couldn't hear. *Maybe the stupid shit already got himself barbecued.*

The sound of a deadbolt slid and the door opened.

"Oh my," she said.

He turned back and saw her attention was focused at the rising cloud of smoke. She had a pink cashmere sweater draped over her shoulders, the long sleeves tied loosely in front of a yellow cotton blouse. Before she put her eyes to him, he shoved her into the house, away from the door. She flew backward into the wall. He jumped in after her, slamming the door behind him.

In shock, her hazel eyes grew double their size. He pounced on top of her, pressing his knees onto her shoulders, keeping her pinned. The crack of a backhanded slap across her face shattered the remaining silence. A trickle of blood broke from her lip.

"Lady, I don't have time to dick around. Give me what I want and I'm outta here. Where's the pictures?"

Recognition made her eyes grow even larger. She took a deep breath preparing to scream but he slapped her again. A red bruise already appeared on her cheek as tears rolled from her eyes.

"You think I can't kill you before the cops get here?"

"I've got children," she squeaked.

"I bet they'd like to see their mother again. Where's the camera?"

Something registered in her face. He hoped it was the gravity of her situation. "They didn't turn out. It was too dark in the kitchen and the flash made it so you couldn't even see out the window."

He glared into her, trying to find a sign of deception. "Show me, anyway."

"I put it away. Let me up and I'll get it."

Satisfied, he got off her and grabbed a handful of her red hair, yanking her to her feet.

"You're hurting me." Her head twisted so her cheek pressed into his shoulder.

He pulled harder, lifting her off the ground. "Get the camera," he whispered in her ear. He eased his grip.

Wincing, she led him across the entryway into the living room. A flat screen TV hung above a mantel on a white wall. On either side of the television were tastefully hung pictures of children from infant to preteen. On the left were photos of a boy, and on the right, a girl. Some were posed, others were candid action shots of the kids at the playground.

Centered above the TV hung a wedding photo of a smiling couple. The man wore the typical rented tuxedo and the woman a white wedding gown way too busy with frills and layers. Her hair was a darker red then, longer and straighter than what he now held in his fist, but overall she had aged well. He guessed she had gained no more than ten pounds from when that picture was taken. After two kids he was impressed.

"Nice family," he said.

She tensed and he knew she was waiting for the threat. He didn't disappoint. "When the cops get here, you're going to tell them it was all a mistake."

She nodded.

"You're going to tell them it was just someone delivering a package."

She nodded again.

"You know what's going to happen if you lie, don't you?"

She froze.

He spoke just above a whisper. "I'm going to come back and make you watch while I kill your kids, then your husband. After that I'll kill you."

Her knees buckled and the only thing keeping her up was her hair clenched in his fist. He shoved her to the carpet.

She crawled to the end table by the sofa and opened the drawer while trying to cover up the soft sobs. Among receipts and other scraps of paper, the woman grabbed a silver hand-sized digital camera. He snatched it out her grip and flipped it on.

"Please," she said. "You got what you want. You can just leave. I won't tell the police anything."

He opened the memory and found it empty.

"See. They didn't turn out."

He saw the pleading in her eyes. Blood had crusted around her lip and a welt had already blossomed on her cheek. He dropped the camera and reached out, offering his arm.

"You remember our conversation, right?"

Relief shone over her face and she took his hand. He hoisted her up, spun her around, and pressed her firmly against his body. She tried to take a step forward but he reached around her, grabbing the dangling sleeves of her sweater. He yanked and the sweater tightened around her throat.

The first couple seconds were easy. She was too stunned to move. He banded the sleeves around his fist, making a shorter, more powerful weapon. The struggle intensified when she realized what he had done. She clutched, trying to loosen the cloth digging into her neck. By the time she started bucking and kicking, a lot of fight had already drained. Still, she got a good back-kick on his shin.

"You stupid bitch. You've seen my face. You think I can let you live?"

In an instant of rage, he kicked one leg out from her and she toppled face first onto the carpet. He fell to his knees, all his weight landing on her spine. He jerked her head back and used the leverage to pull even tighter. She didn't resist, didn't even move. Still, he kept applying pressure. When he broke out of his trance, sweat poured down his face and he knew that she had long ago stopped struggling. The smell of fear permeated the air. The distant sound of sirens brought him back to the present.

He let go of the sweater and her face plopped down. He checked her pulse. None. He rolled off the body. The woman's eyes were wide open and staring at nothing, her lips purple. Next to her laid his wig. During the struggle she somehow tore his pocket. In near panic he shoved the hair into his pants and carefully scoured the area for anything else he might've dropped.

"Bitch! That was a good pair of slacks." He got to his feet and kicked at the sprawled body, calming himself. "Death by cashmere."

He walked into the kitchen and admired his work. Flames shot out of the roof in the house across the street as the sirens became uncomfortably loud. With luck maybe the fire would leap over and ignite Miller's house. He hadn't planned on that, but it would be an added perk. The sirens weren't from cops, but that didn't mean the police wouldn't be right on their tails, especially the ones that were already supposed to be on the way here.

"Don't panic. You've still got time."

He had just walked into the kitchen for the first time so none of his fingerprints were there. A cell phone sat next to a stack of mail on the kitchen table. He couldn't resist the temptation and picked up the phone and pressed 911.

An operator answered immediately.

Disguising his voice to sound feminine, he spoke. "There's a house across the street that's on fire." He recited the address.

"That's already been reported ma'am. The fire department is already on the way."

He was sure that the operator could hear the sirens in the background.

"The woman who lives next door, I think her name is Miller. I saw her carrying a gas can out of her garage and go into the back yard. I thought it looked suspicious."

"What's your name and address ma'am?"

The letters gave him the answer. "I'm Mrs. Emily Harper." He told her the address, figuring they already had it on their computer screen. "I think she saw me. I'm afraid for my life." Now flames could be seen in the house's front window.

"The police are on the way. I'll make sure they talk to you. I want you to stay on the line until they get there, okay?"

Shit! "I can't. I've got to go." He disconnected the line.

He was now nearing panic. That phone call had cost precious seconds, but still, the scenario formed in his mind that Miller might not only be arrested for arson, a murder charge would be the cherry on top of that lesbian sundae.

All right, what did I touch?" He focused on his own surroundings and slipped the woman's phone into his pocket.

Walking back into the living room he picked up the camera and put it into the same pocket as the phone. Confident they wouldn't be able to lift prints from the sweater, he nevertheless untangled it from around the woman's neck. If it hadn't stretched too much he might be able to re-gift it.

Two fire trucks pull up and men scrambled. More sirens were on the way, including the police. A few neighbors were gathering on the sidewalk.

"Don't you people have jobs?"

He jogged to the back of the house, and using the sweater to cover his hand, opened the door. Looking for prying eyes and finding none, he cut through the yards and back to the safety of his car.

Chapter 11

Fire trucks and police cruisers blocked the way when Louise tried to turn the corner on her block. The smell of smoke littered the air like smog. A police officer approached. Louise remembered his face, but not his name, from the other day when they took the body of Walter Farkos out of her house. She rolled down the window and read his tag.

"Officer Perkins, we're going to have to stop meeting like this. The neighbors are going to talk."

"Oh, they're talking all right." The man's face held no humor.

He nodded to another officer sitting in the squad barring entrance to the street. The car backed up, allowing Louise a narrow access.

"Detective Grant wants to see you, pronto. He's at the Harper house."

A pit grew to the size of a boulder in Louise's stomach as it dawned on her that somehow all this mess involved her. "I don't know who the Harpers are."

"Your neighbors from across the street."

Louise drove slowly down the block. A gauntlet of news vans and people crowded the road. She choked back a yelp when she got to Burlington house. Wisps of smoke wafted up from the roof. Their rose garden had been trampled, and the front door kicked in. Inside were blackened remains of furniture and charred beams. Outside in the front yard, Marci and Ken were talking with police and firefighters. Wrapped in a blanket in Marci's arms shivered their cock-a-poo.

Thank God for that. In just the few days there, she saw how Marci treated that dog better than a child.

She parked the car in her driveway, not bothering to open the garage. Another officer approached. "Are you Louise Miller?"

Louise opened the car door and thought about being flippant as she stepped out, but the seriousness on his face kept her from saying a word. She nodded.

"Come with me, please."

She followed, her nerves more jittery with every

step. The flurry of police activity made her heart pound as she approached Harper's house. *The fire's across the street. What the hell is going on here?* A tow truck sat abandoned in the driveway, the driver's door still open. She wanted to ask the officer what had happened, but from experience she knew he'd just tell her to talk to the detective.

When they reached the front door the policeman didn't cross the threshold, but leaned his head in and called for Detective Grant.

"She's here." With that he went back to the street, leaving her alone.

Louise thought about walking in, but she hadn't been invited. The click and whir of cameras were prevalent in the background when Grant came to the door. He looked a couple of years older than when she'd seen him earlier in the week. His accusatory presence made Louise feel like a Jehovah's Witness trying to convert an atheist. She thought it best to let him speak first.

Silence and glare made for an effective tool. Louise used it herself on many perps. She was ready to break when Grant finally spoke. "You have anything you want to get off your chest?"

"What the hell is going on?" Louise shook as she spoke.

After staring a little longer, Grant motioned for her to come in.

The air inside hung heavy with anguish. Doug Harper sat at the kitchen table, his head buried in his hands. All around him the professionals worked in respectful silence, only talking when they had something relevant to say, and saying it in subdued tones. The lighthearted banter used to relieve stress was conspicuously absent when a victim's family was within earshot.

Grant led Louise to the living room where the body of Emily Harper lay still.

Oh my god!

One of the techs snipped off a bit of carpet that had been stained with a fleck of blood. She put it in a plastic bag and marked it as evidence.

"The grandparents are picking up the kids from

school," Grant said.

Louise's eyes traveled from the body to the wall of photos, to the detective. She didn't like the way he studied her.

"Why are you showing this to me? I'm not a cop anymore."

After a long pause, Grant shook his head. "Miller, either you're one of the best actresses I've ever seen in my life, or someone's got it bad to destroy you."

Anger rose in her blood. A hot flash that had nothing to do with age made her forehead perspire. "What do you think?"

"Why don't you tell me where you were the last couple of hours? And while you're at it, it might be to your benefit to throw in the names of a couple of witnesses to corroborate it."

Louise stood dumbfounded. The intellectual part of her knew to keep her mouth shut until she talked to an attorney. The stupidest thing innocent people do is shoot off their mouths, implying suspicion. Like most stupid innocents, she knew she had nothing to hide so what would be the harm in talking? But unlike most, she had an alibi and plenty of witnesses.

"I was working," she said.

Grant pulled a small notepad from his breast pocket and flipped it open.

Louise waited until he was poised, ready to write. "I got a job through a temp agency. I'm a part-time floor-walker at Burke's Department store in Nordeast. And yeah, there's plenty of people that will vouch for me. Today's my first day. You gonna fuck it up for me?"

Grant ignored the barb. "Supervisor's name and the agency that sent you," he ordered.

Louise told him, while at the same time reading his face. *Can he really think I had anything to do with this?*

"What time did you leave the house? What time did you arrive at Burke's? What time did you leave?"

To Louise's relief, no one else seemed to be paying her any attention. "I left here about quarter to one. It's only a ten-minute drive. I'm supposed to work until five, but it was an extremely slow day so they sent me home at three." She decided that would be the last question she'd answer without a lawyer.

Grant motioned for a uniform and tore out a slip of paper from his pad. "Check this out for me, will ya?"

The officer took the information and walked away.

"Now!" Grant rubbed his eyes with his thumb and index finger. "What the hell have you got yourself into, Miller?"

Louise decided to forego the attorney. "You tell me. You're the detective."

Grant strode over so he could see into the kitchen. Doug Harper hadn't moved. He still sat with his face covered by his hands. The detective jerked his head and Louise followed him out the back door.

Even the smoke that drifted from across the street couldn't mar the smell of spring. The unseasonably warm April air made the trees bud prematurely. Lawns were already turning green after their winter's sleep. A flow of clouds lazily wisped past against a darkening blue sky. Louise let the cooling late afternoon breeze caress her skin. She needed to feel something pleasant with all the negativity that tightened its grip around her.

Grant broke the spell. "I didn't want Mr. Harper to have to hear this again." He held a mini-cassette recorder and pressed the button.

The 911 call wasn't the best quality, but Louise heard it clearly enough. A chill started at the base of her spine and raced up her back at the sound of her name. Goosebumps coated her arms.

"I swear to God…"

"Don't sweat it, Miller. Harper already told us that's not his wife's voice. I'm guessing it's the murderer. We're getting the voice analyzed, and I'd be willing to bet that they'll find it's a man."

Anger welled up in Louise, and she felt blood rush to her head. "Then what the hell you grilling me for, asshole? You know I didn't do it."

That finally got a rise out him. "Because it's my job, asshole. Deal with it."

The door opened and a policeman handed Grant back his slip of paper. "It checks out, sir."

"Thank you, Officer Meyer." Grant shoved the paper back in his breast pocket. "Good luck on the sergeant's exam."

The man like he got zapped with a Taser. He seemed unable to form words and finally nodded, disappearing back into the house.

The door swung shut, leaving the two alone once again.

"You totally made his day, if not his whole month," Louise said.

"He'll ace it, too," Grant said.

"I bet that when he handed that info back, he would've sworn you didn't even know his name."

"I keep an eye on the really good ones." He switched his focus to the back yard. "Unfortunately, it's a small list."

Louise crinkled her brow. She stepped off of the cement stairs onto the lawn. Grant stayed still. "What are you doing?"

About fifteen feet out, Louise stopped. "Do these folks have a dog?"

"Doesn't everybody in this neighborhood? You're the neighbor, you tell me."

Louise shot him a *get serious* look.

Grant straightened up. Louise could almost see the gears turning in his head.

"I don't think so. No sign of one. No bowls on the floor; no toys that I recollect." He stepped into the yard, approaching Louise.

"Watch where you step. Somebody left a little present."

Grant checked the soles of his shoes and the surrounding ground. He stepped back to the safety of the stairs.

"This going somewhere, Miller? God forbid, people have been known to break the law and not chain up their animals."

Louise took a couple of paces farther up the yard, then a couple more.

"Someone made a halfway decent shoe print in a pile of pooh. Looks like he left a little trail, too. And from the length of the paces, I'd say he was jogging, if not running."

Grant opened the back door and stuck in his head. "Sam, get your ass out here and bring your team."

Louise was in the adjoining neighbor's yard before Grant called out.

"You, get your ass back here and let the experts do their job. You're ruining a crime scene."

By the time Louise made it back to the steps, Grant had explained the situation and forensics started their work. They photographed and then meticulously carved out and bagged the dog shit. With their special lights and cameras, they began taking pictures of the lawn.

Caught off guard, Louise shuddered when Grant rested his hand on her shoulder. "So you'd rather be making minimum wage nabbing shoplifters than sucking it up and asking for reinstatement, huh?"

"Don't forget I now get an employee discount," Louise said.

Grant removed his hand and shook his head as he opened up the back door. Louise followed him in. As they passed the kitchen, Doug Harper raised his head. Louise had never spoken to the man before and only met his wife for the first time the other day in her yard. Still, she wanted to pay him her condolences.

"I'm terribly sorry for your loss."

Harper gazed at her silently for a moment, and then his eyes filled with rage. He sprang from the kitchen chair and charged. The chair flew into the wall behind him.

"You did this!" he screamed.

Officer Meyer stood in the kitchen and instinctively grabbed the man before he made it halfway to Louise. Grant had stepped in front of her ready to take him on in case he got past Meyer. But Meyer held tight and Harper fell to his knees before collapsing on the floor and curling up into the fetal position. He bawled like a newborn.

Grant whispered into Louise's ear, "I think we've done enough damage here." He gently took her arm and led her out the front door.

Louise held it together until they made it outside. The shivers overtook her body as they walked down the driveway. Someone had closed the tow truck door. She shut her eyes to will away the imaginary spiders crawling on her skin.

"Louise Miller?"

A woman with dark brown hair, short but stylish, walked up the driveway with purpose. About forty, she wore a gray three-piece pantsuit with a red scarf tucked under the jacket. "I'm Detective Kate Hanson, Arson Squad." She held out her left hand five strides before reaching them.

The first thing Louise noticed was the wedding ring. The diamond must've weighed over a karat. Louise took her hand.

"We've met," Louise said.

After three firm shakes, Kate withdrew her arm. "Have we?" Her voice filled with suspicion. "I don't remember."

Louise liked her instantly. No bullshit, strictly business. "I was a rookie and you were a lieutenant speaking at a symposium of women police officers. Congrats on the promotion."

The woman grinned, letting her human side show through. "Wow, that was ages ago. Good memory. By the way, I was sorry to hear you quit."

What the hell? Another one? Louise had always assumed the only ones that had heard of her were her fellow officers, her sergeant, and her captain.

"I'm trying to get her to ask for reinstatement," Grant said. "Maybe you can start working on her too."

Hanson nodded. "Just for the record, let me say that I don't think you have anything to do with your next door neighbor's fire."

"Her alibi checks out," Grant added.

"I'm sure it does. Still, I'd like permission to poke around your place. Being an ex-cop, I'm sure you know your rights, and I understand if you want us to get a warrant first."

It sounded to Louise like she went from colleague to suspect in one breath.

"Hey we're all friends here. Search away."

They made their way across the street and up to Louise's car. She opened the driver's door and pressed the button on the garage door opener attached to the visor. The door went up and the arson team went in. It took about three seconds for one of them to find the gas can.

"Is that yours?" Hanson asked.

"Never saw it before." Louise answered as if someone had punched the air from her lungs.

As they tagged and bagged the evidence, Grant took Louise by the shoulders and faced her. Louise didn't resist.

"This guy can get into your garage and maybe your house with no problem. I'd like to take a couple of officers inside and make sure he's not waiting for you."

The remark glance off Louise. Not quite comprehending, her mind swimming, she nodded, not sure what she had just agreed to.

Grant called to two officers and tried the door to the house from the garage. It was unlocked. The door opened a crack and the rottweiler tried to wedge in his head to pry it all the way open.

"Peanut!" The dog bounded to his human. Louise grasped his collar tight. She needed to hold onto something real.

"You don't look so good."

Louise blinked. Grant's face had been replaced by Hanson's.

"I'm a good person. Why is someone doing this to me?"

"You know that there's no real answer to that," Hanson let the dog sniff her hand and then patted his head. "There's a lot of crazies out there and you have to cope. For me, I go home and hug my kids each night. I read the Bible for solace."

Louise came around and snorted a chuckle. "I'm zero for two on that front, Detective."

"Well, we all have our own coping mechanisms. And you can call me Kate."

At least the woman wasn't one of those bent on converting the nonbelievers.

They stood in awkward silence waiting for Grant to give the okay. Actually, Louise hoped she'd hear gunshots and Grant would come out and say they got the son-of-a-bitch. Waiting for one or the other scenario, Louise looked across at the Burlingtons. Their next-door neighbors from the other side were consoling the couple, along with other neighbors Louise had never seen before. She'd join them as soon the Grant and Hanson were done with her.

"Figured as much with the dog being fine, but just for the record, it's clear. Best to be safe."

Grant and the cops stepped out the door into her garage. She slapped Peanut playful on the ass. He bounded inside and she closed the door, trapping him in the house. "I'll be in, in a minute." Grant stood next to her while the uniforms split up and went to their squads. "The dog would never let a stranger inside."

Grant nodded. "Like I said, better to be safe. I'm going to finish up across the street, then get going."

"I'm pretty much through here, myself," Hanson said.

The detectives shook hands and Grant walked away. Hanson turned to Louise. "He thinks you can have quite a future with MPD. So do I."

"It sounds like a conspiracy." Louise didn't like people talking about her behind her back.

Hanson smiled. "Maybe it is. Either way, let's do lunch when this whole mess is cleared up. Maybe I can convince you to rejoin the fold."

Louise rolled her eyes and Hanson laughed as she made way to her car. Alone at last, Louise figured it was time to say something to her neighbors. She had taken a couple of steps in their direction when Ken Burlington caught her eye. She put on her best sympathetic face.

"You!" His voice sounded like venom. "This has to do with you, doesn't it? You're responsible for this."

Louise froze. Shock replaced the sympathy. Ken took a step forward and she took a step back. "I'm sorry," she said, like she was the actual one to blame.

New tears rolled down Marci's face. "This was a nice peaceful neighborhood until you moved in!"

"Why don't you just leave?"

Louise didn't even recognize the person standing next to Marci who shouted that. Others around them glared while nodding their heads. A hand from behind grabbed her shoulder. Terrified, Louise was forcefully spun around. Officer Perkins glared.

"Why don't you go inside before a lynching breaks out?" He half guided, half pushed her toward her garage.

Louise stumbled to the door, fumbling with the knob before safely locking herself inside. She couldn't stop shaking. Using the wall for balance, she made her way into the bedroom and sprawled out onto the bed. Peanut jumped up and lay down beside her. She wrapped one arm around the dog, and reaching over to the nightstand with the other, she picked up the phone. It took a couple of attempts and heavy concentration to call Karla.

"Hello?" Karla's voice sounded like a dream as Louise pressed the phone to her ear.

"I need you," was all she could bring herself to say. She hung up and buried her face in Peanut's side to muffle the sobs.

Chapter 12

The unseasonably warm spring air did an about-face and plummeted past the normal mid-forties to the upper teens. Nimbostratus clouds had blocked any semblance of blue sky. Thick and dark gray, they threatened to drop snow on the few mourners who decided to go to the cemetery from the church. A cold wind snapped at the canopy over the gravesite and it felt to Walter Jr. like a late fall day. All he wanted to do was to go home. But no. After the graveside prayers he'd have to head over to – well, now it was Muriel's house – for the final good-bye party. At least that's how he thought of it – saying good-bye to Dad's old friends and hopefully never having to set sight on any of them again.

Uncomfortable in a folding chair, Walter shoved his hands deeper in the pockets of his overcoat. Sitting next to him, Jessica put her right arm around his left and hugged it to her body. He squeezed back and she rested her head on his shoulder. When the minister asked everyone to bow their heads, Walter craned his neck to see who all behind him had braved the elements.

George Jeffers was there, of course. *What an ass wipe.* Walter did have a brief moment of enjoyment when he told Jeffers he had forgotten the man's request and already had enough pallbearers. There were no apologies, just, "Nope, you can't."

He recognized Carp and Spender. In between them sat some mousy woman, cute in a librarianish sort of way. There were others from his father's company, Some faces he recognized, others he just assumed because they all sat in the same group. As for outside the company friends, there weren't many. Walter couldn't really blame people for not coming after church. Most who didn't show were older than Walter Sr. Hell, they were probably already at the house diving into the food and liquor.

"Amen," the minister said.

Walter whipped back around as everyone raised their head.

"Amen," came the response.

"I guess it's unanimous, the amens have it," Walter

whispered to his sister.

Jessica unsuccessfully hid a smile as she elbowed him in the ribs.

With the service finally over, the family members got up from their chairs. Muriel, sitting on the other side of Jessica, gave her daughter a giant hug.

Walter strode toward the minister, handing him an unmarked sealed envelope containing five hundred dollars in cash. "Great job, padre. You knocked 'em dead." He left before the man could respond.

"I'm going to miss him," he heard his mother whisper to Jess, still holding her tight.

Bullshit. You'll miss his money if he screws you in the will, and I'll bet his fortune that he will. Walter hadn't talked much to his father in a lot of years, but he'd been around him enough to know that good old dad thought of his wife as a whore. *Screws her in the will.* He wondered when was the last time his parents had sex, at least with each other. It had to have been a long time ago. He knew for a fact that his dad had kept a number of mistresses over the years – a double standard, but that was his dad. And with all the vacations Muriel had taken 'alone,' he couldn't believe she didn't have a lover or two, or three, or a few dozen hidden away. When the parents were together, they barely spoke to each other, let alone touched. Muriel even had her own bedroom.

"What are you smirking about?" Elissa asked.

Standing behind her, with his hands on her shoulders like he was steering her, stood Drew. Even in April the man had a tan that would make a surfer jealous. At least given the solemnity of the occasion, he had tied back his blond locks into a ponytail. Though the guy was a bleeding heart, had the face and hair that could go on the cover of a romance novel, and he was nailing the half-sister Walter was secretly attracted to, Walter had to admit that he kind of liked the guy. Well, at least didn't really dislike him.

"Glad you could unchain yourself from a tree long enough to show up," Walter said.

"Don't start," Elissa warned.

Drew held out his hand. "Good to see you, too. Still

creating garbage landfills wherever you go?”

"That goes for you too, buster,” Elissa chided her husband.

Walter smiled and shook hands. “Coming back to the house for the big gala?”

"Wouldn’t miss it,” Drew said.

"Hell, you’re family. Why don’t you ride back with us in the limo? There’s plenty of room.”

Drew shook his head. “Then who would drive the Prius?”

"Then who would drive the Prius?” Walter mocked him with a childish tone. He had hoped Drew would tell Elissa to go with the family in the limo while he drove the car, but he didn’t. “Hell, Drew, if the car was that environmental, they would’ve made it with recycled cans.”

"Don’t!” Elissa held up her index finger first to Walter, then to her husband.

"Truce?” Walter asked.

"Truce,” Drew answered.

--

More people had filled the house than were at the church. Walter took off his overcoat and sport coat, leaving them both draped over the nearest chair. People had formed their own little cliques creating pockets of space throughout the room. Fortunately, one of those pockets was by the bar. He loosened his tie while squeezing his way past the well wishers to the liquor cabinet. He poured himself a scotch. Downing it in one gulp, he poured another while sympathizers offered condolences. Jessica strode over.

"Was that the fun part?”

Walter took a shot glass for his twin and filled it to the rim. Like a pro, she emptied it with one swig, hardly making a face as it went down. She held out her glass for a refill. Walter raised an eyebrow but poured another.

"Don’t look at me like that. Christ, I’m sick of being gracious. People come up to me and tell me what a great man my father was. I just smile and nod. What do I tell them? That I really have no idea, I didn’t know the guy?”

Walter emptied the remainder of the bottle into a tumbler, dropped in an ice cube and took a sip. "Consider yourself fortunate. Not that I knew him a whole lot better, but from what I did know, he was an asshole." He plucked the ice out of the glass and stuck it in his mouth.

Jessica eyed him quizzically. "I talked to 'Lissa a few months ago and she said you and the old man seemed to be getting along pretty good."

Walter spit the ice back into the glass. "One day he said he wanted to start acting like a father. Felt real for a while." From across the room, his mother shot him a tipsy grin and started shoving her way over.

"Muriel alert," he said.

"Shit," Jessica whispered. She downed her second shot and turned to leave.

"Oh no you don't." Walter grabbed her shoulder. "You're not leaving me alone with her."

People parted as Muriel Farkos made a path for herself. She ignored the condolences and pushed away the attempted hugs while concentrating on not spilling her wine. Stumbling into her children, she gathered them into a hug. A splash from her glass stuck Walter's shirt to his back.

"How are my two favorite people in the world?" Muriel's voice carried a little too loud.

Walter broke away and in a jovial voice he spoke even louder. "We're just great, Mom. How the hell are you?" He took the glass out of her hand and placed it on the bar. Of course it had to be red wine, now his shirt was ruined.

Jessica also squirmed out of Muriel's grip. "We're still the same as we were during the ride home from the cemetery," she said quietly.

"Wasn't it a beautiful funeral? The flowers were so pretty," Muriel said.

"Oh look, there's Elissa." Jessica dodged Walter's attempt to grab her. Behind Muriel's back, she stuck out her tongue at her brother before disappearing behind a wall of people.

Muriel became suddenly somber. "I'm going to miss him."

George Jeffers ambled up and clapped Walter, Jr. on

the shoulder. "How ya holding up, champ?"

Walter wanted to smack him. "I'm twenty-two, George, not six."

"Hi George." Muriel's voice took on a seductive quality. "Wasn't it a beautiful funeral?"

She acted downright giddy.

"It was at that." George took her hand and held it while looking into her watery bloodshot eyes, then drifting down to her cleavage.

Walter took the opportunity. "Well, I can see you two have things to talk about." He stepped away, but Jeffers reached out with his free arm.

"Actually, it was you I came over to talk to." George released Muriel's hand. "Would you be so kind as to excuse us for a couple minutes? I've got a couple of business things I'd like to talk to your son about."

Muriel pouted. She was about to speak, but Jeffers put a finger to her lips. "I promise it will only be for a couple of minutes, then we'll sit and catch up. Promise."

Muriel perked up and snatched her wine glass off of the bar. "I'll be right over there." She pointed to the corner of the room.

George nodded, watching her strut, his eyes glued to her ass. "A lovely woman, your mother."

"Ever sleep with her?" Walter downed the rest of his drink, complete with ice cube.

Jeffers glared at the young man. "I'm very happily married."

"Well, that has everything to do with nothing."

Walter refilled his glass.

Finally, Jeffers spoke. "Not that it's any of your business, but no, I've never slept with your mother."

"What? You're saying my mother's not good enough for you?"

Walter was ready to fight. He wanted to fight. Jeffers was heavier and a couple inches taller, but he was also about thirty-five years older. The old fart would go down.

A flame ignited in Jeffers eye, but just as quick it died. A condescending smile crept across his face. "Look, I don't know why you don't like me, but I can assure you it's totally unwarranted."

"Is that right?" Walter spit the ice back in the glass. He ignored the scotch splashing on his hand.

"Yes, that's right." George scanned the room before turning his attention back to Walter. He lowered his voice. "I wanted to talk to you about your father's will. Have you seen it? Walter used to speak very highly of you, you know."

"No, I haven't, and no, I didn't know." Walter Jr. sensed a little pride along with the surprise.

"In fact," George continued. "I believe he's going to leave you the majority of his stock in our company."

"Is that right? And seeing as how no one has seen the will, just how would you know that, George?" He waited for the lie.

"He used to confide in me, told me what he was planning to do. He said you had a pretty good talent for investing. He wanted to bring you into the company. He was talking about retiring, and wanted me to take you under my wing."

Walter poured another drink. He'd heard enough of his father's rantings to know his old man would never confide anything to George Jeffers.

"And why would I want to do that?"

Jeffers chuckled and put his hand on Walter's shoulder. "I told him I'd be shocked if you agreed. I must say, your old man was a little naïve and delusional when it came to your relationship."

"Get your hand off my shoulder, George, or I'll fucking break your fingers."

Jeffers' voice took on the air of authority. "Like I said before, I know you don't like me. And you know what? I don't like you either."

Walter dropped another ice cube in the glass. "George, I think that's the first honest thing you've ever said to me." He held up the glass in salute, and took a sip.

"I think you're a spoiled brat who should've gotten a few belts to his backside." Jeffers' voice returned to that of a friend. "But I'm willing to overlook my personal feelings." Again, he scrutinized the room conspiratorially. "I'd like to buy you out. You'll have enough money that you'll never have to work another day in your life.”

Walter toyed with his glass. “And you’ll have enough shares that you’ll have total control of my father's company.”

Jeffers reacted like he’d been slapped.

“Oh relax, George.” Then he mocked Jeffers’ earlier actions and did his own scan around the room as if looking for spies. He motioned for George to come closer, and when the man bent down, Walter whispered, “Just between the two of us, George, did you kill my dad?”

Jeffers bolted upright, his face crimson. “I loved your father like a brother.” Spittle flew from his lips.

Now people did take notice.

“Kind of like how Cain loved Abel?” Walter asked.

Hate kindled in Jeffers’ eyes. Even as he noticed the outsiders’ stares, the loathing could not be doused.

“I refuse to stand here and be treated like a criminal!”

Walter propped his elbow upon the bar and leaned back. “You didn’t say no, George.” He secretly hoped that the man would charge, wanting to punch that self-righteous face.

“No! I did not kill your father, you little prick.” His voice carried, and then there was silence as if he’d flipped a switch and all of the words in the room had been shut off.

Jeffers motioned to his co-workers. Like everyone else they stared in utter amazement.

“We’re leaving!”

The Farkos Jeffers Spender and Carp contingent followed him to the door. All except Carp. Walter had only met him on a few previous occasions, but this was the first time he’d ever seen the man smile. Carp raised his glass toward Walter, and Walter nodded back.

“What the hell was that all about?” Jessica appeared at Walter’s side.

“When are they reading dad’s will?”

Muriel glared in his direction. Thankfully, she made no motion to get up and join them.

“I think Muriel made an appointment with the lawyer for tomorrow. Why?”

The alcohol took hold as the adrenalin rush wore off. Walter wanted to lie down. "I just assumed I was going to be cut out, but according to Jeffers, I might be able to take over the old man's company."

"Did he say anything about me?"

Hurt and suspicion resonated in Jessica's voice.

"Just that all of us kids would be well taken care of," he lied. He had no desire to create a rift between himself and his twin.

"What did you do?" Elissa now joined the duo. Her husband had not accompanied her.

"I think I might've figured out who killed our illustrious father."

Chapter 13

Andrew walked in after knocking, not waiting for an answer. Peanut stood at the alert already by the door. He scratched the dog behind the ears. Karla sat in a beanbag chair where the sofa used to be. Louise was stretched out on the floor, her head in Karla's lap, Karla twirling Louise's hair around her finger. They both faced the TV. A stand-up comic on the screen made the studio audience laugh hysterically. Neither Louise nor Karla showed any emotion. The phone rang and when no one made a move to answer, Andrew picked up.

"Hello?" After a couple of seconds of silence he checked the caller ID and hung up. "Unavailable."

"It's been like that all day," Karla said without turning around.

"Why don't you just unplug it?"

"We did that for a few hours, then I called you. Didn't bother after that," Karla said.

Louise stretched and twisted into a sitting position. Peanut strolled over and snuggled between her and Karla. Louise scratched his rear. He rolled over onto his back, his hind leg twitching as both she and Karla rubbed his stomach.

Andrew chuckled and took a seat by the stereo. "Wing Nut is one mean junkyard dog."

Karla hoisted herself up from the beanbag chair. "Can I get anybody anything? Coffee? Beer?"

"A beer would be great," Andrew said.

"Make that two," Louise chimed in.

Peanut's eyes followed Karla out of the room, but he made no effort to follow.

"The whole damn neighborhood is blaming me," Louise said.

Andrew reached for the remote and flicked off the TV. "That's what Karla told me. You know it's all bullshit, right?"

The phone rang again. Andrew glanced at the caller ID and answered. "You wouldn't believe the technology the police department has for tracing phone calls these days. We can have a unit there in minutes."

The line disconnected.

"It's not bullshit, Andrew." There was pleading in Louise's eyes. "It is my fault."

"You've got to be kidding me!"

"Seriously. If I never moved here that Harper woman across the street would still be alive, and my neighbor's house wouldn't have been torched."

Karla walked in carrying three beers. She handed one to Andrew and then sat back on the beanbag chair. She took over petting Peanut's stomach where Louise had stopped. The dog grunted his approval.

"Well, let's see," Andrew said. "If you hadn't moved here, Walter Farkos would still be dead, and who knows— maybe the crazy would've burned down your entire apartment building and a lot more people would be homeless, or dead. Don't you dare say the work of some sick freak is your fault." He twisted off the cap and chugged half the bottle.

"Yeah." Karla handed both bottles to Louise. "Can you open mine for me? My hand seems to be otherwise occupied."

The dog looked at Louise as if confirming the statement. Louise twisted the cap and handed the bottle back to her partner. She got to her feet and set hers, unopened, on the table.

"I gotta pee," she said.

Andrew waited until she was out of the room and spoke softly. "I think she'll be okay."

Karla sipped her beer and then rested the bottle between her legs while continuing to pet the dog. "Actually, she's gotten a lot better since I called you. She was almost comatose when I came home."

"She's tough." Andrew took another pull from the bottle.

The phone rang again. They ignored it. After four rings the machine kicked in and the caller hung up. Karla didn't say anything as she lifted the receiver, pressed the On button, and placed it next to the cradle. Louise walked into the room looking haggard. She'd changed into a Minnesota Wild sweatshirt that hung loosely off her shoulders. Andrew knew that she liked wearing the extra large, but still she might've lost a little weight. *Diet through depression. It would make a good book.*

"I think I need to be alone for a while," Louise said.

Andrew held up his hands in surrender. "I can take a hint."

Louise shook her head. "You stay. I'm going for a drive, maybe stop at the store on the way back and pick up some comfort food. You folks want anything?"

Karla perked up. "Cherry Garcia!"

"Anything for you, bro?"

Andrew thought for a moment and shook his head. "See ya in a while."

--

The cold wind slapped her face. It felt good. Outside the driver's side window Orion hung low in the sky. The constellation was set so far down on the horizon that the hunter seemed to be standing on the earth. Soon he would disappear for the summer, to be replaced by the Big Dipper. Louise felt a pang of regret. She always considered herself to be a kindred spirit with Orion but never figured out as to why. Maybe, because like the Big Dipper, it was about the only other constellation that she could easily pick out. Or maybe because as a little girl, she often gaze into the winter sky and saw him as her protector.

Nah, it probably had to do with the next few miserable months of heat.

She drove into the sparsely filled parking lot and got a spot not too far from the entrance. Her watch read just after nine o'clock. Smiling, she nodded to the security guard and walked up to the cashier, handing him fifty dollars. He carefully counted out the chips, two stacks of twenty and one of ten, slid them across the counter and wished her good luck.

One thing Louise liked about playing on a weeknight was she never had to wait for a seat. Across the vast expanse in the open room there were over sixty tables and less than half of them were in use. She wished she could play higher stakes, but with fifty dollars she could only afford the two/four table.

There were two open seats out of the nine-chairs. One stood directly opposite the dealer, the other, three seats left. She sat down at the latter. The dealer, bald on top and a gray ponytail in back, nodded a greeting and asked if she wanted to post now or wait. His nametag read Jake.

If she threw in her ante now, she'd have to do it again in three more hands when the deal rotated toward her. Instead, she'd use the time to study her opponents.

"Thanks Jake, but I'll wait."

Jake dealt out the cards, passing by Louise. The first person to bet tossed in two dollars worth of chips. Three people called, the rest folded. The dealer flipped up three cards. The middle-aged man sitting across from her had the most chips. He acted drunk but it could've been just that, an act. A guy sitting next to him had a small black widow spider tattooed on his upper cheek. His chip stack showed he was doing almost as well. The rest at the table were college-aged kids with chips ranging from about ten dollars to one hundred. Louise was the only woman.

The person who opened the betting checked. So did the kid next to him. The drunk threw in two bucks, the guy with the spider tattoo raised. The two young 'uns folded and the drunk called. The dealer flipped up the next card. The drunk tossed in four dollars and tattoo raised it to eight. The drunk gave tattoo an evil stare and called.

The final card came up. Again, the drunk put in four dollars worth of chips and, again, tattoo raised it to eight. Louise thought that the guy might be putting on an act when he called the raise.

"Let's see 'em," the dealer said.

The guy with the spider on his face flipped his cards and showed a straight. The drunk guy had been dealt a pair of threes down, and that's all he had. Still, he tipped the dealer a buck.

Holy shit, he really is wasted.

Tattoo guy racked his chips, over two hundred and fifty dollars, got up from the table and bid everyone goodnight and good luck.

"Opening on table twenty-seven," Jake called to the front. He dealt the next hand, again passing by Louise.

The opening guy checked. The kid sitting next to him bet two of his ten remaining dollars. The next two dropped, the third called, and the drunk raised it to four. The kid with only eight dollars left threw in two more. Everyone else folded.

Jake flipped up three cards. The kid now with only six dollars left cursed under his breadth and checked. The drunk flipped in two dollars. The kid slammed down his cards in disgust. Jake slid the pot to the drinker, who in turn gave him a two dollar tip.

Another round omitting Louise, and everyone except the sot checked. When he bet two dollars, they all folded.

You've got to be fucking kidding me.

The deal came around and she threw in her ante.

--

Louise had no idea how much time had passed. It had been time enough for her fifty-dollar stack to grow to over two hundred and fifty at one point, and it now hovered around two hundred. She had cleaned out the drunk. She would've won more of his money had he not kept tipping the dealer every hand whether he won or lost. Only one of the originals that she started with was still there. He tossed in the last of his chips. The replacements were decent card players. It took Louise a while to stop taking things for granted and start concentrating on her game again.

The cards landed in front of her and Louise peeked. A pair of black aces stared back. The check came to her and she bet two dollars, wishing she had moved to a higher stakes table. Three people called.

The dealer flipped up an eight, three, and ace—all diamonds. Louise checked. The player next to her bet. The other two called and so did Louise. The next card flipped up was the ace of hearts. Knowing that no hand could beat her now, Louise slow-played it and checked again. The man seated next to her checked, and the next in line bet four dollars. The one next to him raised it to eight. Louise called, and her neighbor folded. The final card was the queen of diamonds. Louise hoped that the other two both had high diamonds for the flush and she opened the betting with four dollars. The next in line called, and then the last guy raised it to eight. Louise raised it to twelve.

"I've got the ten of diamonds, but I'm guessing one of you has the king," the man said as he folded his cards.

The only remaining person raised the bet to sixteen dollars.

"I don't have the king," Louise said, but I bet you don't either." She raised it to twenty.

She instantly regretted opening her mouth. The man only called her raise. He flipped over his cards showing the king of diamonds.

Louise shook her head. I've only got two pair." She showed hers. "Red aces and black aces."

Appreciative sighs mixed with conciliatory groans circled the table as Louise raked in her chips. From nowhere a freezing chill stabbed at her back. She twisted in her chair. Karla and Andrew stood behind her. The euphoria of winning nosedived to despair when she saw the expression on Karla's face.

Unable to speak, Louise could only stare as Karla asked Andrew, "Can me and Peanut bunk at your place tonight?"

Andrew nodded and they both ignored Louise as they headed for the door. Louise got up from her chair and followed, leaving her chips in a pile on the table.

"It was only fifty dollars. That's all I would've used, just like when you first brought me here." Louise omitted the part that that was all she had. "I just needed to empty my mind of things. C'mon."

Karla stopped and spun around like she wanted to lash out but she struggled to remain calm.

"We'll talk about it tomorrow. Right now I can't even look at you."

Louise's heart broke as the two most important people of her life walked away. If she thought that if it would do any good, she would've gone after them. Instead, she plodded her way back to the table and slunk in her seat. She missed one hand and when she peeked at her cards, she held a seven and two, off suit – the worst hand one could be dealt in Texas Hold 'em. The bet came to her and she folded. The dealer flipped up seven, seven, two.

"If that's not a sign from God, I don't know what is. Good luck, gentlemen."

Louise gathered her chips and cashed them in. She should've been elated, but emptiness consumed her. This was bad. Karla had been mad before, but never enough to leave. At least Louise knew that she'd be safe with Andrew.

The dashboard clock read 2:45 when Louise started the engine. No wonder they'd come looking for her. Louise pictured them driving out to the casino, praying that they'd be wrong.

"I'm just a goddamned open book, aren't I?"

Speeding all the way back to Minneapolis, Louise stopped at the store and picked up a gallon of Rocky Road for herself and a few pints of Cherry Garcia, just in case.

The house was dark when she pulled into her garage. Louise felt as empty as her home, hoping Karla had changed her mind.

Opening the door from the garage, Louise reached around the corner for the light switch. There was a click but no light came on. Stepping inside and cursing under her breath, Louise heard a scuffling sound. Blinding light flashed inside her head as something hard smashed into the back of her skull. She hadn't time to feel the pain before she dropped into unconsciousness.

Chapter 14

Corwin meowed before Andrew got his key in the door.

"He knows Wing Nut is here," Andrew said.

Karla held Peanut's leash tight as Andrew opened the door. The dog wasn't the problem. Andrew's gray cat raced out the door totally ignoring the humans, instead purring while doing figure eights around the rottweiler's front legs. Peanut lowered his head and slobbered the cat, his tongue washing Corwin's face. Corwin's purr motor shifted into high gear.

With a little maneuvering they made their way inside. Karla unclasped the leash and sank into Andrew's sofa.

"Got a beer?" she asked.

Without a word, Andrew went to the kitchen. A moment later he came out with a can in each hand. He sat at the other end of the couch and watched as Peanut placed a paw on Corwin's back, holding him down while giving him a tongue bath. Andrew popped open the can and leaned over, handing it to Karla.

"You okay?" he asked.

Karla took a swig and closed her eyes. "I don't know what to do." She opened her purse and reached for her pack of cigarettes. "Do you mind?" she asked, pulling one out.

"Uh, yeah. Actually I do."

Karla shoved the cigarette back into the pack.

"You can smoke outside."

Karla shook her head. "That's okay. I'm just so frustrated, ya know?"

"I wish I knew what to tell you."

"Shit," Karla whispered before taking another gulp. "If we didn't just buy a house together, I think I might leave her." She looked pleadingly at Andrew. "I know she's your sister and all, but goddammit."

"I wouldn't blame you if you did." Andrew opened his own can and downed a couple swallows.

They both sat in silence watching the interaction between dog and cat. Each time Peanut took a break, Corwin playfully nipped at the dog's cheek until the face-licking resumed. The dog didn't seem to mind being ordered around by a cat.

"She's self destructing and there's not a damn thing I can do about it." Karla dabbed at her eyes before the tears came.

Andrew never took his eyes off the pets. "That dog could snap Corwin's head off with one quick bite."

Karla finished her beer. "You don't think she'd do something stupid, do you?"

"Oh yeah," he said, his voice distracted. *He could be chomping on Corwin's head before I got off the couch.*

"How stupid?" There was alarm in Karla's voice.

Andrew perked up. "What?"

"What do you think she might do?"

"About what?"

Karla cocked her head like Andrew might've lost his mind. "Have you heard a word I said?"

Andrew blushed and took another mouthful of beer. "Actually, I was wondering what I'd do if your dog decapitated my cat."

Beer sprayed out of Karla's mouth as she laughed and choked at the same time. "What a beautiful image."

Chuckling, Andrew got up and went back to the kitchen. Returning with a towel, he dabbed at the beer shower on his couch and carpet. Karla grew contemplative as he worked. When he finished, Andrew went back into the kitchen.

"Want another beer?" he called.

"No." Karla leaned down to pet Peanut.

When Andrew came back into the room, in his arms were a pillow and blanket.

"You can have the bedroom, I'll take the couch."

Guilt overtook Karla as she took another sip of beer. "Do you think she'll be okay?"

--

Louise lay on her stomach with her head jerked up, and arms stretched behind. Her legs bent painfully back at the knees. She could almost grip the toes of her shoes with her hands. The concussion-like headache, the strangling, the cramp in her leg, the shoulders feeling like they were going to explode, the rope binding her wrists too tight – all of these sensations forced Louise to open her eyes. A fuzzy, large black dot wavered in front of her while she tried to focus. As she twisted, the rope tightened around her neck making her gag. Instinctively she tried to bring her hands to her throat, but they didn't budge from behind her back. Hogtied, Louise was helpless. Fear now overrode all the physical pain.

"Welcome back to the land of the living."

The mechanical voice lacked any hint of emotion and that made goose bumps rise on Louise's arms.

"Don't worry, you won't be in the land of the living for long."

Louise blinked to clear her vision. The lamp was on and the blinds were down. The fuzzy black dot focused into a man all in black. He was dressed like a ninja wearing sunglasses.

"Who are you?" The words strained as rope bit into her neck.

The ninja held a device up to his mouth. "That's my dilemma," the mechanical voice echoed. "Do I tell you before I kill you, or have you die never knowing?"

Do I know this guy? Think, Louise! She struggled to remember all the cops she hated, and more importantly, those that hated her. Too many had similar builds. *This guy could be at least a dozen of 'em.*

"Each scenario has its advantages."

He took a step nearer. Louise struggled. The gagging became choking. She had to stop and concentrate on her breathing.

"But there's no need to rush the decision. We've got all night."

The emotionlessness of the tin voice reverberated in her every nerve.

"Why?" Louise asked.

He crouched so his face stood inches above hers. Louise imagined an evil sneer behind the mask. He held the voice box to his mouth, shook his head, and stood back up, walking behind her. Louise knew better than to twist her head around.

A tug at the rope where her wrists were bound to her ankles made Louise gasp for breath. The son-of-a-bitch was toying with her.

"My brother's a cop. He's bringing home my roommate right now. He will kill you." She hoped that the threat came off sounding authoritative and not as lame as it felt.

He plucked at the rope and then stepped back in front of her.

"Your brother is a deputy sheriff and he and your roommate," he had to pause so he could use his gloved fingers to motion quotation marks after the word roommate, "are probably back at his apartment talking about you, if they're not asleep yet. After all, she did ask if she could bunk out at his place."

Oh my God! This bastard knows me. He was at the casino.

"That's the reason I chose tonight to end your life. I knew we wouldn't be interrupted."

Louise strained to think back to the card game. This guy hadn't been seated at her table that she knew. She was also relatively certain he wasn't a cop. She would've recognized him. Maybe she didn't know him. Maybe this was his technique to freak out his victims. If that was his purpose, he was a master. If so, he had certainly done his homework on her.

Louise frantically tried to put her police training to work and recollect all the faces she'd seen at the casino. Other than the people at her table, no images came. She'd been so wrapped up in winning, then getting caught by Karla and Andrew, that faces of other people never entered her mind.

Letting the rope dig into her neck, Louise focused her vision to clearly make out her captor's build. If he did sit at her table, he would've been there at the end. It might be one of the college guys that sat next to the dealer. Then her mind wandered to her five years of arrests. Way too many to count; way too many to remember. A few stood out, but they should still be in prison. Maybe he just got released.

She had to rein in her thoughts. They were going in too many directions. *Focus, Louise.*

"Why?" Louise asked again.

Again, the ninja shook his head.

"Will murdering me fix whatever it is I did to you?"

He brought the voice box up to his mouth. "It won't change anything except make me feel better."

That brought a new set of chills coursing through her body. She took a chance. "Did it make you feel better when you killed Walter Farkos?"

The ninja stiffened. "You don't know anything about that. Don't think that you do."

Despite the artificial, flat voice, Louise heard the hatred.

He walked behind her, just out of her line of vision, and grabbed the roped that stretched from the back of her neck to her wrists.

Louise saw only red as she was yanked off the floor. The rope bit through her skin as she writhed, gasping for breath. Her shoulders felt like they were being ripped from their sockets, yet she couldn't stop struggling. The more she twisted, the deeper the binds cut. He let go.

Louise landed hard on her ribs. She tried to gulp air, but for a moment nothing would come. Then the precious oxygen rushed into her lungs. She couldn't stop coughing as uncontrollable tears poured down her cheeks.

The man walked back around and squatted in front of her.

"That was fun," the metal voice rang.

Anger, fear, and panic burst inside. Louise snaked and coiled and contorted her body to free herself. The pain and the fruitlessness drained her and all she could do was gasp.

"Feel better?"

How she wanted to grab that voice box and shove it down his throat, or up his ass. Any orifice would do.

"I didn't really know how I was going to kill you when I came in. Being the pig that you are, all trussed up with your neck exposed, I thought maybe slit your throat."

Something new fit in his hand, and he held it in front of her. His thumb pushed a button and a razor blade slid out. The edge brushed down her cheek and caressed her throat without breaking the skin. Then the blade instantly disappeared back into its holder. "But I really wanted something special, you know? Now I got it. He walked behind her and lifted her again. "I do this until you die." He dropped her and then came back where she could see him.

Louise tried to speak, but couldn't. Sweat stung her eyes.

"I figure I can hold you up for maybe thirty seconds per round. You could stand to lose a few."

You better hope you kill me, you son-of-a-bitch.

"I don't think you'll last more than round three." He walked behind her and twanged the rope. "Ready?" the metallic voice rang.

Instinctively, Louise tightened her neck muscles and held her breath as she was lifted off the floor. It was only a second before the pain took over and the gagging resumed.

Bliss came from nowhere and enveloped her body. Louise stopped struggling, suddenly feeling at peace with the world. Everything seemed so clear. From the kitchen, a drop of water dripped from the faucet. Next to the sink she noticed a corner of the wallpaper had started to peel.

Her nirvana snapped when an explosion crashed into the front door. The blinds clattered on the windows from the force. Once again, Louise landed hard on her ribs.

"What the fuck!"

Something sounded odd about the voice. Still gagging, Louise twisted.

The ninja peeked through the blinds. "Oh shit!"

He tore past Louise and into the kitchen as another blast rattled the door.

That's a real voice. I have to remember that voice.

The front door flew open and four silent paws galloped past. Somewhere on a cloud far away, Karla screamed.

Chapter 15

Gordon Grant's face filled Louise's vision. She shut her eyes hoping the sight would go away. When she opened them again, he was still there, unsmiling and staring down on her.

"Looks like someone gave you an ear-to-ear hickey."

Louise put her hand to her throat and felt a cool damp towel. She tried to lift her other hand but it wouldn't move, like it was locked in a vise. She painfully rotated her head. Karla was grasping her hand in a death grip. Her eyes red, probably from a crying jag that ended not long ago. Past her and out the bedroom window, orange clouds streaked an azure sky. Louise felt the familiar comfort of her mattress. Straining, she glanced at the clock. Six-thirty. *Morning or evening?*

"Did you get him?" The question came out in a raspy whisper and the effort drained her strength.

"That would make my life too easy," Grant said. "Escaped out the back door. Too bad he had the foresight to close it behind him or your dog would've shredded him."

Visibly shaken, Andrew walked into the room and stood next to Grant. He sat on the edge of the bed opposite Karla and gently brushed the hair from Louise's face.

"The EMTs are waiting in the other room. You ready to go?" Andrew asked.

Louise had a vague memory of taking a swing at one of them when he tried to put her on the gurney.

"I promised them you'd be good," he added.

"I'm not going anywhere," she croaked.

"Don't be an idiot," Grant butted in. "Get yourself checked out, relax overnight and you'll be home tomorrow."

Louise glared at the detective. "Other than a sore throat, I'm fine."

"You sound like you're belching." He asked Karla, "Can you convince her to do the smart thing?"

"How about I drive her over later today?" Karla asked.

Louise tried to squeeze Karla's hand but the grip was too tight from her partner.

Grant shook his head and left the room. Louise brought Karla's hand to her mouth and kissed her knuckles. "Thank you." She mouthed the words and then painfully twisted her head toward her brother. "Thirsty."

Instead of leaving the room like she'd hoped, to give her and Karla a moment of private time, Andrew reached over to the bed table and picked up a glass. With one hand he propped up Louise's head and held the glass to her lips.

"Small sips," he said.

Louise took enough to get rid of the cottonmouth. The coolness eased her throat, but a tinge of fear gripped her when she swallowed. A tight fit, but the water slid down. He gently placed her head back on the pillow.

"Can you talk enough to give me a description?" Grant plodded back into the room. He turned his attention to Karla. "I told 'em they could take off. I'm leaving it to you to get her to the hospital later today."

Karla nodded.

With that piece of business taken care of, Grant took out his pen and writing pad. "Well?"

Louise took a deep breath. "A blind ninja with throat cancer."

Grant didn't laugh.

"There shouldn't be too many of those around," Karla said.

"Ninja costume, dark shades, and a voice box," Louise whispered.

This time Grant wrote.

"And he was at the casino."

Grant stopped. Andrew gaped and Karla squeezed Louise's hand so tight, Louise thought her fingers might break. She jerked her hand out of Karla's grasp.

"The bones in my right hand are still healing. I don't need a matching set."

Karla choked back a sob.

"Sorry," Louise said.

She put her hand on Karla's thigh. Karla placed her hand on top.

"He heard Karla ask Andrew if she could stay with him."

"Oh my god," Karla whispered, squeezing Louise's hand again.

Grant resumed his writing. "Why did Karla ask to stay at Andrew's?"

"None of your business," Louise answered a little too forcefully. She started to cough. The burning traveled down her throat as the muscles in her neck spasmed.

Andrew quickly propped her up and held the glass to her lips. When the coughing subsided, Louise took another sip. Grant had his pen poised on his notepad.

"He was about five-ten, maybe one-eighty, slim build, and in shape. He lifted me up with no trouble."

"And you're what, one-forty-five?" Grant asked.

Louise glared. "One thirty-five, asshole."

"That's Detective Asshole." Grant flipped his notebook closed and shoved it in his pocket. "Well kids, I'd love to sit and chat but I have a few errands I need to run, including a drive out to the casino to chat with security about getting a tape. You got a DVD or VHS player?"

Louise nodded. "Both."

"Good. I'll be back this afternoon. This evening if they demand a warrant."

"One more thing," Louise choked out. "I heard his real voice. Something crashed into the house and he panicked."

Karla beamed. "That was Peanut."

Andrew followed up. "Damn Wing Nut jumps out of the car, freezes for half a second, then charges at the house. I thought he was going to smash the door in. Never saw anything like it in my life. I take back every bad thought I ever had about him."

Louise leaned to the side of the bed and searched the floor. "Where is my hero?"

"In the back yard," Karla said. "Didn't want him getting in the way when the ambulance guys were here."

Grant put a hand on Louise's shoulder but directed his attention at Karla. "Give me your cell number. I'll call first in case you're still at the hospital." He bent down and whispered into Louise's ear. "Might be a good idea to keep your gun within easy reaching distance."

Louise rolled her eyes. "Yes, Dad."

"Later." Grant left the room.

Already, the sky had faded to a lighter shade of blue and it wasn't even seven yet. Under her own power, Louise grabbed the glass of water. The first sip was tough, but after that the water slid right down.

"Andrew, will you check on the dog, please? From now on, I don't want him outside unless one of us is watching."

Andrew leaned over and kissed his sister on the forehead. As soon as she heard his footsteps on the kitchen floor, she grabbed Karla's arm and eased her down. Locking her fingers behind Karla's head, Louise brought her face to hers and kissed her hard on the mouth. The urgency shifted to sensual and Louise easily parted Karla's lips with her tongue.

"You came back," Louise whispered as they parted.

Karla's lower lip trembled. "I just…"

"Shhh." Louise kissed her again.

They stayed embraced until one hundred-twenty pounds of rottweiler leapt up onto the bed and joined the party. He licked Louise's face and she let him. Peanut's drool rolled off her chin onto the towel around her neck.

"That's just gross," Andrew said from the doorway.

Karla laughed and Louise let out a horse chuckle as she tossed the towel at her brother.

Andrew shook his head as the towel barely cleared the bed. "I've got to get ready for work. Call me and let me know what the doctor said."

Karla sprang up from the bed. "I'll walk you to the door."

The dog followed them out.

Alone, Louise felt almost good, considering the circumstances. At least she and Karla were back on. *Maybe this is a wake-up call.* Louise vowed to never let down Karla again.

Satisfied with her new outlook, Louise rolled out of bed. Every muscle ached as she made her way to the bathroom. A long, hot bath was what she needed. Her shoulders burned as she leaned over the tub and twisted the handle. A shudder ran through her body as she noticed the rope burns around her wrists. Hot water burst from the nozzle. As steam filled the room, Louise studied herself in the fogging mirror. Grant was right. It did look like a giant hickey.

She stripped off her clothes and stepped onto the scale. The needle stopped on one-forty-four. "Grant, you asshole. Aren't you sick of being right all the time?"

--

Standing naked in front of the mirror, he scowled at the reflection of his ninja suit stretched out on the bed. He'd fucked up.

"I should've slit that bitch's throat like a pig!" He banged his fist against the glass. The mirror held. "But you just had to be clever. You stupid jerk! Now she heard your voice."

No more playing, he promised himself. If she hadn't been on high alert before, she would be now. *Maybe a sniper shot to the head?* No, whatever he came up with, it would have to be quick, but she'd have to see it coming. The dog would have to go too. Just because. That would be easy, a piece of meat with shards of glass and a touch of poison, or a bowlful of antifreeze.

Maybe the dyke lover would have to go, too. And might as well throw in the brother.

Once Louise Miller was dead, the brother would never stop searching for her killer. But if he were dead, every cop and deputy would make it a top priority. Things were getting way too complicated. He had to think this out. Let things go for a couple of weeks, maybe a month. Let them start feeling secure again. He knew that they wouldn't. Hell, probably just the opposite. They'd go crazy waiting. Even better.

He stepped away from the mirror feeling almost giddy. Except for the surprise at the end, it had been a wonderful night. Neatly folding his black uniform, he put it in a box and slid it under the bed. More pressing needs now entered his mind.

      With no sleep, he popped a couple of caffeine tablets and hit the shower. In only a few more hours he'd finally get to read that bastard's will.

Chapter 16

Stanley Fettig greatly admired his multicultural office. After setting up two rows of four folding chairs, he took a seat behind his seventeenth century oak coffer desk and patiently waited for the Farkos family and Walter's business partners. None of them had ever been in his office before. Stanley knew they'd be impressed when they walked in. The first thing they'd notice was the beautiful view of Minneapolis behind him. Because the building was situated by the river on the outskirts of downtown, there were no skyscrapers to mar the view.

To the left stood a wet bar, complete with a black marble countertop. Above it hung a dream catcher, and next to that a Navajo sand painting. On the opposite wall were two African masks he picked up on his safari vacation last summer in Kenya. Below them sat a hand carved table from Thailand with a brass Shiva on top. Behind the conference table hung a watercolor of the Kremlin that he picked up three years ago on his trip to Moscow. In the corner sat a curio cabinet with Russian nesting dolls of the Imperial family.

The intercom clicked on his phone. "They're here, Mr. Fettig."

"Thank you, Jan. Send them in please. Give me five minutes then bring in some coffee."

Stan waited until the door opened before he got up from behind his desk. He had planned their entrance, meeting them just inside the door and shaking their hands as they ogled his collection of art.

Muriel was the first to enter. She seemed amazingly rested for the day after her husband's funeral. Following her, Elissa walked in arm-in-arm with her husband. Bringing up the rear were the twins, Jessica and Walter Jr.

Muriel headed straight to the bar and opened the mini-fridge.

"Got anything to drink?" She found a bottle of tonic without waiting for an answer, then searched under the bar and found some gin. "Oh, Beefeater Wet. Good stuff."

Feeling uncomfortable, Stan told her to make

yourself at home. He instantly believed all the stories Walter had told him of his wife. He turned his attention to the other four. His smile became genuine as they perused his treasures.

"Looks like a damn U.N. garage sale in here," Walter whispered to his sister.

She shushed him and elbowed him in the arm.

The smile vanished from Stanley Fettig. "Why don't you take a seat? I'm sure the others will be here momentarily." He didn't mean for his voice to come out so cold and tried to recover. "Can I get anyone else anything to drink?"

The door to the office swung open and the rest of the contingent stepped in. George Jeffers led the way. Stanley recognized Carp and Spender, but the woman with them was a stranger. He hurried over and introduced himself.

"Stanley Fettig. I'm Walter's attorney." He held out his hand.

"Beverly Wimpole. I'm the new partner."

Her hand was moist and limp. Stanley gave a slight squeeze and she made no attempt to apply any pressure back.

"Fettig, good to see you again."

Stanley let go of the woman's hand and grasped Jeffers'. This man had a good firm handshake. He wondered how hearty it would be after he heard the will.

"Ms. Wimpole, I'm afraid I didn't set up enough chairs. Being that you're not involved in the will, why don't you have a seat at the conference table?" He pulled out a traditional black leather visitor's chair with a padded seat, back, and arms. She'd be the most comfortable visitor in the room.

"Now that everybody's here, shall we get started?" Stanley went back and sat behind his desk.

Muriel took a seat at the end. Walter Jr. sat between her and Jessica, while Elissa filled in the other end. Her husband sat behind her. Jeffers sat behind Muriel, and Spender and Carp filled in the middle.

Stanley cleared his throat. "First off, I want to thank you all for coming and sharing Walter's final wish. When he asked me to be his executor, he was adamant that this is how he wanted it done. I must say that in my twelve years of practicing law, this is the first time I've ever done a reading of the will."

Looking at his audience, the family seemed comfortable while the partners looked confused.

"You mean we didn't have to be here?" Jeffers asked.

Stanley shook his head. "Ninety-nine percent of the time I just mail out a copy to all involved. This was strictly a non-enforceable request by Walter."

"But they do it in the movies all the time," Jeffers protested.

"I don't think it would be nearly as cinematically effective to have the actors just opening an envelope instead of all sitting in a room together, I'm afraid."

Once again, the office door swung open. All heads turned as a man Fettig had never seen before stepped in. "Sorry I'm late." He closed the door.

He wore a black overcoat, unbuttoned, and beneath it an off the rack suit.

"I'm sorry, this is a private meeting," Stanley said.

The man opened his coat and displayed a badge. "Detective Gordon Grant. I'm investigating Walter's murder."

"It's okay," Muriel butted in before Stanley could respond. "I told him he could come."

Walter Jr. arched his eyebrows at his twin. She shrugged. He turned to Elissa and she shook her head. Jeffers whispered something in Muriel's ear, and she chose to ignore his comment.

"Why is he here, Muriel?" Walter asked.

"Because I think somebody in this room killed your father."

Walter leered at Jeffers.

Jeffers scowled back. "How do we know you didn't kill your old man?"

Stanley wanted to scream. They were in his domain, dammit. They were his guests. It occurred to him that he hadn't really been in control since Muriel first entered his office. *Calling this family dysfunctional is like saying that the atomic bomb went 'pop.'* Stanley smiled to himself. *That was a good one. I'll have to remember that.*

"Are you going to draw out the murderer, Detective?" Drew Jarvis asked.

Those were the first words Stanley heard Elissa's husband speak. The way Elissa bore into him, they'd probably be his last.

"It is just like the movies," Jessica said.

"Enough!" Stanley knew he had to take control of the situation. "Detective, it's obvious you're going to be a distraction. I'll have to ask you to wait in the reception area."

"Let him stay." Walter pointed at Jeffers while the man had his back turned, facing the cop.

"Does anybody care if he stays?" Jessica asked.

Nobody raised their hand.

"This is better than the movies," Carp whispered to Spender loud enough for them all to hear.

Stanley watched the Detective take everything in. Like himself, this man was an observer of human behavior. "Fine. Can we just get started, please?"

They refocused their attention to the front of the room. Stanley was once again in charge. He opened a manila folder and took out the will. "You'll each get a copy of this at the end of the meeting."

"Why didn't he do it on video tape?" Walter asked.

Stanley buried his face in his hands and silently counted to ten. When he finished they were all obediently staring at him.

Stanley cringed. "I don't know. Can we get on with this please?"

"Does the detective get a copy?" Jessica asked.

"Enough!" Muriel sprang from her chair. "This might be a joke to you but he was my husband and I ask – no, I demand – you treat him with respect! God knows you never did when he was alive." Tears escaped her eyes as she crossed the room and poured herself another drink.

Walter opened his mouth but a subtle glance from his sister kept him quiet.

"Thank you Muriel." *I think that will be the last time you ever defend him.* He waited until she returned to her seat. "Anyone else have anything they need to get off their chest before I begin?" They all sat unexpectedly quiet. "You're sure?" No one made a sound. "Fine, let's get started."

The office door swung open and all heads turned once again. Jan walked in carrying a tray with an urn of coffee and ten cups. Her eyes met with her boss and she almost dropped the tray. Her cordial smile disappeared as she placed the coffee on the conference table and, as professionally as she could, high-tailed it out of the room.

Closing his eyes, Stanley reined in his temper and counted to thirty before moving forward. He opened his eyes to find nine astonished faces staring back. The Detective had poured himself and Ms. Wimpole a cup of coffee. His face registered no emotion at all.

"Dude looks like a heart attack waiting to happen," Drew whispered to his wife.

Before any more interruptions, Stanley came close to shouting. "I, Walter Farkos Sr., being of sound mind and body…" He settled down as he read through the boilerplate language naming himself executor and pouring past the legalese, then paused before he got to the part that everyone had come to hear. "To Muriel Kathryn Farkos, the slut that called herself my wife, I leave this backpack." Stanley lifted a hiker's backpack from behind his desk. "She can fill it with her jewelry, mink coat, and whatever else she can carry on her back, and nothing more. She has so many lovers, I'm sure at least one of them might take her in."

As hard as he tried not to look, an invisible force pried Stanley's head upright. From behind, George Jeffers had a hand on her shoulder. Muriel's jaw hung open, her eyes pierced into Stanley's, but he was sure they weren't seeing him at all. The glass fell from her hand, bouncing off the authentic Persian carpet. Fortunately, the glass didn't break and the liquid was clear. She gained her senses long enough to take in all the other faces in the room. No one, not even Walter or Jessica, was smiling.

Muriel got up from her chair and walked as gracefully as she could toward the door. Grant opened, and quickly closed it behind her.

After taking a deep breath, Stanley continued. "To my eldest daughter, Elissa Jarvis, I leave my home and all possessions inside it. Along with that I leave you two million dollars, which should handle the taxes and any other incidentals. I also leave you in charge of a police escort so Muriel doesn't take more than she can carry. I give you veto power to take back anything Muriel might want that belonged to your mother, or that may have any sentimental value to you. I know you never cared for Muriel, and you've always been smarter than I when it came to reading people, which is why I'm giving you the benefit of a doubt regarding your bleeding heart liberal husband. Maybe now that you've got money, you can turn him into a republican."

"Never," Elissa said.

Stanley paused, letting it sink in that Elissa was a new millionaire. She dabbed her eyes before she twisted around and embraced her husband. Drew looked ecstatic.

"To my daughter, Jessica. I wish we could have known each other better. For that I am truly sorry. Still, there is not one day that I haven't been proud to call you my daughter. I know you're going to be a great lawyer one day. And so you don't have to worry about pesky little things like student loans and a place to live, I leave you the sum of three million dollars."

"You were right," Jessica whispered to her twin.

Stanley paused again and saw her arms entwine her brother's arm.

"And to my son, Walter Jr., I can't count the number of times I've tried to turn you into a man. And each time I've failed. This is my final attempt. To you, Walter, I leave the company of Farkos Jeffers Spender and Carp. I give you my fifty-one percent of the stock. You now control the company. You can either drive it into the ground, sell it, or for once in your life you can follow my advice and learn the trade. You can amass a fortune. I'm sure my partners will be happy to show you the ropes."

Walter's color became ashen as he gulped for air. His hands shook in his lap with his sister's arms still around his. Behind him, Carp nodded his approval while Spender gaped open-jawed at Jeffers. Jeffers glared like he wanted to plant an ice pick at the base of the young man's skull.

"Are you all right, young man," Stanley asked.

Walter nodded and took slow, deep breaths.

Stanley took his own deep breath and kept reading. "Now to my ten percent partners Joel Spender and Leo Carp. Leo, you've kept hounding me about a buy/sell agreement, and I've always put you off. Here's the reason why. As of this writing I have one hundred and twenty-six clients. I've known you and Joel to be able to work amicably together. With that knowledge, I empower you to divide my clientele between the two of you."

A gasp came from George Jeffers.

Stan quickly resumed reading. "To my fifteen percent partner, George Jeffers, I leave nothing. My lawyer advised me that I had to mention your name to avoid any confusion as to whether I'd forgotten you. George, as hard as I tried, I could never forget you."

"This is bullshit!" George yelled at Stan and then faced Carp and Spender. "This isn't over by a long shot!"

He stormed toward the door, but Detective Grant blocked the exit. "Get out of my way!"

Grant made no move to do so. Jeffers grabbed the detective's lapel, but before he could shove him away from the door, Grant yanked his wrist and twisted. Jeffers yelped as his arm bent at an unnatural angle and he dropped to his knees.

"We need to have a little chat. You got a conference room we can borrow for a few minutes, Counselor?" Grant held tight onto Jeffer's arm.

It took a moment for Stanley to recover from what he had just witnessed. "Uh, talk to Jan, she'll show you where it is."

Grant led Jeffers out of the room. Stan continued to read the will as best he could. "The rest of my estate will be donated to the United Nations Health Organization. It's not a Ted Turner sized donation, but still, I think it will make a difference."

Stanley stopped reading. "The remainder of the will just goes into specifics which I won't bore you with. Jan, my assistant, will give each of you a copy. You can read it at your leisure." He saw relief on their faces. "With that, ladies and gentlemen, the reading of Walter Farkos' will is concluded.

"With Mrs. Farkos and George Jeffers safely out of earshot, I recommend that you each procure your own lawyer. I truly believe Mr. Jeffers when he says this is not over. And once Mrs. Farkos gathers her wits about her, I'm sure she will be talking to an attorney also. Because of possible conflicts, I'll be unable to represent any of you, but if you'd like I can give you some recommendations."

--

The table could easily sit twenty people. Grant uncomfortably placed Jeffers at the head. He took a seat around the corner. Their knees bumped.

He wasted no time. "Sounds like you've got a pretty good motive to kill Walter Farkos."

"That's ridiculous," Jeffers spat. "How could I have known what was in the will?"

"Good question." Grant studied his face. "How did you?"

Jeffers shifted his position, looking away. "I didn't."

"Is that right?"

"Yeah, that's right." Jeffers stood up. "Any more questions and it'll have to be with my lawyer present."

"Sit down, Jeffers, you're not under arrest. Not yet."

"Then we've got nothing more to talk about." He walked to the door and grabbed the handle.

"I can place you under arrest and hold you for thirty-six hours before I decide to charge you. Any plans for the next couple of days?" He assumed Jeffers wasn't knowledgeable enough to catch the lie. Grant had no probable cause at all to place this man under arrest.

The door was ajar when Jeffers froze. He slammed it back shut. Still, he refused to sit, preferring to stare down on the cop.

Grant was not intimidated. "According to Walter Jr., you seemed to know a lot about the will before it was opened."

Jeffers sneered. "Now that little shit deserves investigating. Did he also tell you he hated his old man?"

Grant kicked out chair and motioned for George to sit. "Let's talk about young Walter." Jeffers relaxed and took a seat. "But before we get to him, I want to know how you knew about the will before everyone else."

Jeffers scanned the room as if someone could actually be hiding. "Off the record?"

Grant studied his suspect's eyes. He could lie to him one more time and say yes. He decided one lie per interrogation. "Probably not. But if it turns out to be a non-issue, it'll go no farther than this room."

Jeffers swore under his breath. "Hell, it's probably not even illegal. I just find it a little bit beneath me."

Trying to keep his face stoic, Grant broke eye contact. It had to be awfully low to be beneath this guy.

Staring at the floor, Jeffers spoke, "At the end of the day I was getting ready to head out. Walter and I were usually the last ones to leave. Anyway, I heard Walter talking. I peeked around the corner and saw him go into his office with his lawyer."

"Would that be Fettig?" Grant asked. He had his notepad out and was writing.

"Yeah, Fettig." Jeffers gazed at the carpet. "They went into his office and closed the door." His eyes locked on Grant. "Who the hell closes the door when they think they're the only ones there?"

Without any prodding, Grant waited for George to continue.

"I took a cup from the break room and held it to his door. It's amazing, that really works."

"What did you hear?"

"I heard them mention my name and laugh. Then Walter told him he wanted his son to own the company. I tell you, I was ready to burst in there and kill him right then. Then he told the lawyer he wasn't going to bother with chemo, the cancer already spread to his liver. I realized what I was doing and got the hell out of there."

"You caught a case of morals, huh?"

Jeffers sighed as he pushed his hand through his hair. The fight had drained from him. "I'm not denying we had our differences, but when I heard cancer, it hit me, you know? The whole timing of the will thing started to make sense."

"You knew absolutely nothing about his illness?"

Jeffers shook his head. "He was a very private and a very egotistical man. He'd never let out anything that would make him appear weak."

Grant wrote 'autopsy – cancer' in his pad. Next came the question he really wanted to ask. "How do you know Louise Miller?"

The man's face went blank. "Never heard of her."

Good answer. "She had some dealings with Walter. I thought you might know her."

Jeffers gave it more consideration. "If it were business, I would've thought so, but if he was having a sexual relationship with her, I'd never know. He had many, shall we say, liaisons."

Grant concluded that George Jeffers probably, or at least maybe, had nothing to do with Walter Farkos' death, but certainly nothing to do with the terrorizing of Louise Miller. He flipped his pad closed and shoved it in his pocket.

"Don't you want to know about Walter Jr.?" George asked.

Tired, and still needing to drive out to the casino, then to the coroner, then head back to Miller's, Grant tried to dismiss it. "He and the old man didn't get along. I got that part. You really think he hated him so much he'd want to kill him?"

"Yeah, I do." Jeffers answered without hesitation.

Grant sighed and got out his note pad again. "What makes you think so?"

"The kid's a psychopath!" The man was getting himself worked up.

"How so?"

"I went there the day after to pay my condolences, ask if there was anything I could do. The only thing that seemed to bother Walter Jr. was having me interrupt his day. He was so busy making goo-goo eyes at his sister he literally threw me out of there."

That did catch Grant's attention. "Jessica?"

"No, the other one. From Walter's first wife."

Grant wrote the word 'incest' along with a question mark in his note pad. "That kind of makes him more of a pervert than a psychopath."

George leapt up from his chair, slamming his fists on the table. "That's it! Walter Jr. discovered that his dad found out that his kids were having an affair. Then he killed him."

Calmly getting up from his chair, Grant stepped to the door. "Let's make a deal, Jeffers. I won't tell you how to invest, and you don't tell me how to investigate."

Grant held the door open as a deflated George Jeffers stepped out. The detective reached into his pocket and pulled out one of his cards. Thinking about it, he stuck it back. "I'll be in touch if I need anything else."

Chapter 17

Holding the gun behind her back, Louise cracked open the door. She relaxed as Grant squeezed his way past. Closed and locked, she followed the detective into the living room. It still looked tacky with the beanbag chair replacing the couch, and she thought to ask him about when they might return it but decided to let him speak first.

Without taking off his coat he sat in Karla's chair by the stereo as he eyed the gun at Louise's side.

"You really think that he'd ring the doorbell first? It's my impression that so far he hasn't had any trouble getting in here at his leisure."

Louise twirled the revolver like Annie Oakley before placing it on the table.

"What did the doctor say?"

"Physically I'm fine. Watch the solid foods for a couple of days and if I have any problems, call him immediately." Her voice still sounded raspy, but not too bad. She fell onto the beanbag chair.

Grant scanned the room. "Where's the rest of your brood?"

Louise grinned at his choice of words. "Karla took Peanut for a walk. Introduce herself to the neighbors, do a little damage control. We decided it would probably be best if I didn't tag along. It seems the neighbors have a wee bit of a problem with me. Also, when I try to talk to strangers I seem to come down with a nasty case of foot-in-mouth disease."

She expected Grant to at least smile, but he just nodded thoughtfully.

"So, you want a beer or anything?"

Grant shook his head. "Still on duty." He reached into his pocket and showed her two compact discs. "I would like you to take a look at these, though."

Her pulse quickened. Louise hoisted herself out of the chair and strode across the room. She tentatively reached out. Grant handed her one. "Play this one first."

Flipping on the TV, Louise then slid the disc into the DVD. The television screen blanked for a moment, then the casino parking lot came into view.

He got up and they both stood in front of the set, Grant pointing his finger. "That look familiar?"

Security had placed the camera high up on the light pole, but still Louise recognized her car.

"Right here." Grant pointed to another car a few rows behind hers.

From a distance the picture was grainy, but as the door swung open, she could plainly see a man with blond hair tied back in a ponytail. A beard, mustache, and sunglasses camouflaged his entire face. Her jaw dropped as he popped the hood on her Saturn, easily took off the distributor cap and sauntered back to his car.

Grant pressed fast forward on the remote until Louise entered the picture. The date and time stamp at the corner of the screen showed that she missed the son-of-a-bitch by less than ten minutes. She saw herself get into the car, get out, and check under the hood.

"Here's where it gets good," Grant said.

The car backed out of its space and cruised to Louise's lane. As it slowly drove by, Louise on the TV screen glanced in its direction, giving it no more thought than a stranger's car in a crowded parking lot.

"We've got him," Louise said.

"You'd think so, wouldn't you?"

The excitement faded. It took about two seconds for her to figure it out.

"Stolen?"

Grant nodded. "The owner is about twice the size of that guy, and his alibi checks out." He popped out disc one and replaced it with disc two.

The scene switched to inside the casino. It started with Andrew and Karla stepping up behind Louise while she was oblivious to their presence. She was trying to act cool while raking in a giant pot. Watching now, Louise's stomach churned as in the picture she twisted around and faced them. Her hands trembled as she watched herself get up from the chair to go after them.

Grant paused the disc.

Louise's first reaction was to punch him, thinking he

was just being cruel, until he pointed to the screen. Blond hair in a ponytail under a wide brim hat, beard, mustache, and shades, the same man stood leaning against a pillar pretending to watch the action at the table behind Louise.

"Does he look at all familiar?"

Louise focused all her attention at the frozen picture. She thought back to as many arrests as she could remember, but could not connect that face to any of them. She shook her head.

"Two o'clock in the fucking morning and half the people in there are wearing sunglasses. He fits right in."

"It's so people can't read their eyes," Louise said, absently, still trying to recognize the face.

"I get it. Back in my day we knew how to wear poker faces."

Louise finally broke her gaze from the screen." Someone had already invented poker back in your day?"

Ignoring the dig, Grant resumed play. A dejected Louise gathered her chips and cashed them in. The man ambled out as Louise stood at the cashier's counter.

"He made a beeline straight to your house. He knew no one would be here."

Louise shuddered and glanced over at the table where she placed the gun. "I don't know what to do." Her voice sounded distant.

"We'll have patrols cruising around here constantly. That should ease the neighbor's fears somewhat, too," Grant said.

"You don't think it's a cop anymore, do you?"

Grant put the discs back into his coat and headed for the door. "I'm going to get these to the techs and let them do their magic. They might be able to pick something up."

"You didn't answer my question, Detective."

Grant unlocked and opened the door. "I don't think it's George Jeffers anymore."

"Who's George Jeffers?"

"He said the same thing about you. As for a cop, I'm still not counting it out. Take away the ponytail and the beard, who knows?" He gave her a half-hearted salute and strode out. Louise quickly shut and locked the door. *Take away the ponytail and the beard.* She was off of her game. The idea of a wig and fake beard hadn't occurred to her. She peeked out of the blinds and watched Grant get into his car.

"And you think I could be a detective?"

Where's Karla, she thought, frowning at the empty sidewalk. Across the street, cars were lined up in the Harper driveway and parked at the curb. Friends consoling the grieving widower, no doubt. Part of Louise wanted to go over there and explain. Fortunately, the sane part overrode that and told her to stay put.

Neighbors whom she hadn't yet met were walking over, more than one woman carried a casserole. Thinking about an afternoon of mindless TV, Louise caught sight of a car cruising down the block. An unmarked white Ford Victoria turned into her driveway. Louise knew it was a cop. She wondered if any civilians ever bought white Crown Vics.

Detective Hanson stepped from the car carrying her purse strapped over her right shoulder and a manila folder in her left hand. Louise greeted her at the door before the woman had a chance to ring. Hanson tucked the folder under her right arm and held out her left. Louise gave it an obligatory shake wondering why the left hand. Then she noticed the right. Alabaster skin stretched taut over bone. Pink scar tissue marred white background. The tip of the detective's pinky was gone. Louise wondered why she hadn't noticed it before, and then remembered the circumstances of their meeting and her state of mind. If clowns had been riding unicycles down the sidewalk while juggling, she doubted she would have noticed.

"What brings you out here on such a lovely day, Detective Hanson?"

"Please, call me Kate." She laid her purse on the table and handed Louise the folder. "Our report."

Louise thumbed through the pages. Nothing leapt out at her.

"No fingerprints on the gas can, or the outside back wall of the house. I'm pretty sure he never went into the next door neighbor's residence. He just splashed gasoline in through the broken window. Any chance of finding a footprint went nil when the fire department obliterated the scene.”

“Damn those bastards for trying to save the house.” Louise handed back the folder and saw the same expression in Kate that her sergeant and captain used to give her.

“That’s not what I meant. It just would’ve been nice to have one to compare with the one you found in the Harper back yard.”

“I’m impressed. Since when did departments start sharing information?” Louise couldn’t understand her own sarcasm, and yet couldn’t turn it off. Still, she motioned for Kate to come into the living room.

Today the detective wore a gray dress, cut at the knee, and a gray blazer. Her shoes were a simple black with comfortable one-inch heels. Tempted to offer the beanbag chair, Louise thought better and led her to Karla’s chair.

The detective sat and suddenly looked tired. Maybe it was the changing direction of light, the way the shadows made her eyes darker.

“Urban myth,” Hanson said. “We’ve always been good about making sure everybody was up to speed. I know you’re cynical, but all the departments really do want to work together to solve cases.”

Louise thought back to her days trying to do her job. Too many times she’d been impeded, by her fellow officers and also by her sergeant. But that was then and it wasn’t worth debating a dead subject.

“Can I get you anything? Coffee? Tea?”

Hanson waved her good hand and shook her head. “Don’t have that much time.”

Louise sat in the beanbag chair. “So, Kate, what really brings you out here? You didn’t come all the way here to show me a report, especially one that doesn’t really say anything.”

“I won't waste your time. I read your file.”

Louise closed her eyes. *Why didn't they just burn the damned thing?*

“Didn’t make a lot of sense. On the surface it said you were insubordinate –”

“Guilty,” Louise interrupted.

"…had a bad attitude –"

"Strike two."

With a disproving stare, she added, "And you don't play well with others."

Louise had to grin at that one. "It actually said that?"

"I'm paraphrasing. But when you read between the lines and see what you accomplished, your number of arrests, how many times you were asked for on domestics, it sounds like you could've – scratch that – should've been a great cop."

Louise shrugged and went into robotic mode, a defense mechanism to hide any and all emotions. It worked great on the force, not so much at the poker tables. "They did what they did, and I did what I did. No point crying over it now."

The detective studied her face. "Mm hmm. What would you say if you could start from scratch?"

Louise arched her eyebrows to feign interest. Hanson had to have been talking to Grant. They had formed a tag team to bully her into asking for her job back.

"I have an opening on my arson squad. I'd like you to apply."

Louise's jaw dropped. This time she wasn't faking. She tried to speak but the words never made it as far as her mouth.

"I'm sure I can get you reinstated at your current level of pay. You'd have to take a couple of courses, but that shouldn't prove to be any problem."

"Right now my current level of pay is zero." Louise didn't want to be flippant, but it was the only way the words would come out.

"You know what I mean. The same pay grade as when you left the force."

Louise stood up, not sure what to do. She had to hold her hands together to keep them from shaking.

"You'll have a female boss, someone who won't hold your previous record against you. And someone who will show you the respect you deserve. Hopefully, you'll knock off with the attitude and reciprocate."

"I don't know what to say."

Hanson also got up. Louise hoped the detective hadn't taken Louise's standing as a signal to leave.

"You don't have to say anything right now. Talk to your partner. Think about it…but not too long. I'll need your answer in a day or two." Hanson picked up her purse and walked to the door.

Louise didn't know if she should hug the woman or just shake her hand. The ringing phone saved her from making more an ass of herself.

"I'll see myself out. I expect to hear from you one way or the other."

Louise nodded as her future boss walked out the door. In a daze, she strode to the phone.

"Hello?"

"Louise Miller?"

She didn't recognize the voice and checked the caller ID.

"Yes," she answered cautiously.

"This is Sergeant Ronald Crabtree. I'm head of security at Hiawatha Casino."

With her heart beating double time, Louise clutched the phone tight. "Did you catch him?" She hoped she spoke loud enough for him to hear.

"Excuse me? I'm calling about your job application. If you're still interested, I'd like to set up an interview."

Elation mixed with disappointment. "Uh, yeah, sure." *You've got to be kidding!* How long had it been since things had gone right? She couldn't remember.

"That's great. We've got an opening at ten tomorrow morning. Can you make that?"

"Perfect," Louise said, her mind still in a fog.

"Excellent. We'll put you down for ten. Look forward to seeing you."

"Mutual." Louise hung up the phone.

Before anything else, Louise searched her purse for the number of the temp agency. She called to let them know she wouldn't be returning. Her one day as a floor walker had been enough. Wandering to the window, she searched for Karla. She couldn't wait to see the reaction of her partner when she told her the news. Two job offers! Well, two interviews and one job for sure, probably both. Maybe she should invite Andrew over too and they could celebrate together. They could go back to the Asian restaurant and all hit on that waitress.

A pang of guilt hit and instantly ruined her playful frame of mind. Condolence wishers were still filing into the Harper house, but that had nothing to do with her change in mood. She had no intention of accepting the security job, but it gave her the perfect opportunity to get in a couple hours of cards.

Louise knew she shouldn't, but also knew herself well enough to know she'd be unable to stop the urge. Not if she was going to be at the casino anyway. Still, that wasn't the worst of it. The hardest part would be lying to Karla one more time. *It's not exactly a lie. Well, a lie through withholding information. That's not so bad, is it? It's not like a real lie.*

She viewed the street one more time. A huge rottweiler rounded the corner, gently pulling his human. Karla didn't seem to be straining too hard to keep up. They both looked happy. Much happier than when they left the house. Louise knew she could act. She could keep one more secret. Hell, she'd had a lot of practice over the last couple of months.

Louise thought of how excited Karla would be over the news. But in the back of her mind, all she could think of was playing Texas Hold 'em tomorrow.

"Just one last time. Get it out of my system."

Not even Louise believed those words.

Chapter 18

The sun rose just high enough above the horizon to make the car visor worthless. Gordon Grant snarled as he tried to sit higher up in his seat to block out the blinding orange orb that grew brighter yellow by the minute. Of course Douglas Harper had to live east of Grant's house.

Grant had gotten a wake-up call at six a.m. to report to Harper's residence. Dispatch didn't know why, only that Douglas Harper asked for him personally. "I'm not his goddamn grief counselor." It had been a bad start to a day that had followed a bad night.

The evening ended in an argument with his ex – nothing new there. She wanted to send their fifteen-year-old son away to a two-week baseball camp and thought it only fair that Gordon pay. After his unsuccessful attempts at negotiation, and her threats of, "I'll see you back in court," Gordon finally relented. When he hung up, Grant was grateful the dregs he arrested didn't have the balls of his ex. He'd tossed and writhed in bed until three wondering if he'd be able to survive financially until his kids turned eighteen.

The only saving grace of the morning was sports radio. The Twins were off to one of their best starts in years, the Wild were in the play-offs with home ice advantage at least through the first round, and the T-wolves season was mercifully over.

Now that the sun had finally risen to above visor level, Grant had to turn north to get on Harper's street, so serene at this hour of the morning. He understood why people would want to live in this neighborhood. His previous visits were when the street was blocked off with police cruisers and fire trucks, or after dark. Now, with no trace of dead bodies, and a torched house one could easily miss, it looked downright inviting.

Grant turned into Harper's driveway, blocking the man's tow truck. Getting out of his car, he observed Miller's house across the street and wondered if she was up yet, if she'd gotten any sleep at all, and how she was holding up mentally. When he last saw her she seemed to be on the verge of unstable. Hell, maybe they could do breakfast and compare notes on whose life was worse.

When Louise Miller first joined the force, it had taken about a year for Grant to get over her being gay. He'd met a couple of homosexual guys before, even a few that weren't under arrest, but never a homosexual woman, as far as he knew. At first he figured her as a girl who never got over being a tomboy, but then he noticed her work, and unbeknownst to her, he began to review her files. He liked what he saw and wondered if she might be a protégé he could mentor. Her sexual preference stopped being an issue. He kept his feelings secret, but felt betrayed when she quit the force.

Before Grant rang the bell, the front door opened. The way Douglas Harper jumped around, Grand wondered if he might be on some drug. He had a bad feeling.

"I need to show you something." The man jittered with impatience waiting for Grant to approach.

When the detective reached him, Harper held out his hand. "Thank you for coming. You have to see this."

The man gave Grant's hand one good shake, then hurried into the house. Grant slowly followed. By the time he caught up they were in the kitchen. Douglas Harper picked up a camera off the kitchen table and dangled it from its black cord in front of Grant's face.

Grant carefully took the camera. It was one of those digital ones that he had no idea how to work and no desire to touch in fear of breaking the damn thing.

"Sit down," Grant said.

Like a new recruit, the man sat.

"It was a suggestion, not an order." Grant calmly took a seat across from him.

"I've got to show you this."

Harper snatched for the camera, but equally as fast, Grant moved it from his reach. He was impressed his reflexes were so fast for that early in the morning. It was still before eight. Hell, fast for any time of day.

"Close your eyes, take a deep breath, and count to ten."

Grant thought Harper might leap across the table. But in a flash the anger disappeared and the man did as he was told. When Harper got to ten he looked fifty degrees more relaxed.

"Sorry, I'm just excited," he said in a rational voice.

Grant carefully slid the camera across the table. "Before you show me anything, start from the beginning."

Harper closed his eyes and took another deep breath. When he opened them he spoke calmly. "I was going through our pictures. I just wanted to look at her again." Doug's voice cracked. "Then I remembered the camera. We went to the zoo a couple weeks ago with the kids. I took some pictures but never got around to downloading them on the computer. There were a couple of great ones of Em."

Grant waited for the man to get to the point. He didn't have to wait long.

"I found these."

Harper pressed a button on the camera and a small screen on the back lit up. He came around the table and held it in front of Grant's face. In the picture there was a man walking into Louise Miller's garage. For a two-inch photo, and considering it was obviously taken from inside the Harper's kitchen window, the clarity was amazing. Grant easily made out a blond ponytail and the gas can in his hand. In the garage sat a car but the shadows were too dark to see the make and model, let alone the license plate. Grant hoped the guys from the BCA could enlarge it and lighten the picture enough to make out the numbers. Even after all these years, he was still amazed at what they could do.

Harper pressed a button and a new photo appeared. Again the man was walking into the garage, but this time without the can. In this one there was a partial profile. Grant felt ninety-nine percent certain this was the guy from the casino.

Another press of the button, and another photo appeared. *Hell with the BCA.* This one showed a maroon Chevy Impala backing out of the driveway. He could almost make out the license with no enlargement at all.

"This keeps getting better and better," Grant mumbled.

Harper pressed the button one last time. This picture showed a side view of the Impala driving past the house.

Even though he was wearing sunglasses, they could see the driver was looking right into the camera.

Harper switched off the screen.

"Wow," Grant said. *Ninety-nine percent nothing. The only way this isn't the same guy is if he's a clone.*

"Do you think he saw my wife taking pictures, and that's why he killed her?" There was a lot of pain in Douglas Harper's eyes.

"I wouldn't bet against it." He guided the camera out of Harper's hand. "We're going to need this." Grant slid the camera in his pocket.

"All you need is the memory chip," Harper said.

"Just to be safe, why don't I give them the whole kit and caboodle?" Grant knew nothing about digital cameras and had no reason not to believe him. Still, he didn't give it back. "I'll make sure they don't ruin any pictures of your wife." He really had no idea if that was possible, but hoped so.

"Doesn't matter. I already downloaded them onto my computer while I was waiting for you to show up."

Grant tried to hide the anger from his voice. Maybe he should confiscate the computer too. "Did you download what you just showed me, too?"

Harper nodded.

"Can I see those, please?"

Without a word, Harper led him to the den where a computer sat on a roll top desk. It was already on. On the monitor was a picture of a smiling, young Emily Harper wearing a wedding dress. With just a few clicks from the keyboard, there were the photos.

"Show me the one where the car's backing out of the garage."

The Impala flashed on the screen.

"Can you make it bigger? I want to see if I can read that license plate."

Harper zoomed in the plate and Grant punched the numbers on his cell phone. It took him less than a minute to confirm the car had been stolen. "They never make it easy for us," Grant said when he saw the dejection in Harper's eyes. "Don't worry, we'll get him. We'll plaster his picture on the news and in the papers. Someone will recognize him."

Douglas Harper's spirit lifted just a little. "There's one other thing. I'm not sure that it's important. It's probably nothing."

"Only way to find out is to tell me," Grant said.

"Again, it's probably no big deal, but I can't find my wife's camera. We have a 'his' and a 'hers.' We kept them in the same drawer, but I can't find hers anywhere."

Grant opened his notepad and clicked his pen. "It might be very important. When did you first notice it was missing?"

"This morning. I opened the drawer and mine was the only one there. The only reason I noticed it is because she's so anal about it." Doug stopped, his right hand grabbing his left wrist. "Was," he whispered. The man fought back tears. He was obviously one of those who thought it unmanly to cry in front of other men.

"Same kind of camera?"

"Except hers had a blue cord."

The detective put his hand on Doug's shoulder. "Call me right away if you find it."

The two men walked to the door and shook hands.

"Promise me one thing?" Doug asked.

"If I can."

"Promise that if you catch him, you'll give me ten minutes alone with him."

Grant smiled sympathetically. "You might have to get in line. The lady who lives across the street, if she finds him first, well, there won't be enough left of him to share."

A sneer spread across Harper's face. "Maybe we can team up."

"Actually, I think she'd like that."

If the morning temperature was any indication, one long, hot, miserable summer was coming. Sweat already beaded on Grant's forehead just walking to the car. It's not that he didn't enjoy the warmth of the sun on his skin, but hot weather was a sure indication it would be a violent summer. He had the stats to prove it.

The detective backed his car out of Harper's driveway, and with very little maneuvering, reversed it into

Miller's. He had no real reason for visiting, other than he enjoyed her company. Even though they only knew each other for days, she asked the right questions, wasn't afraid to disagree, and kept him sharp. He hated himself for thinking it, but on a number of occasions he'd wished she was his daughter instead of the one he got stuck with. He loved Jenny with all his heart, but what a fucking drama queen. Just like her mother.

On the drive over to Harper's he'd tried to think of an excuse to visit Miller and concluded that if he couldn't think of one he'd let it go and drive back to the station. As he got out of the car he patted the outside of his pocket that held the camera.

The door opened and Grant didn't know who looked more surprised. My God, was she wearing make-up? Eye liner for sure. It was the first time that he'd ever seen her hair not tied back in that rat-tail. The red looked lighter hanging loose and resting on the shoulder. She wore a white cotton blouse and neatly pressed gray slacks.

"Is this the Miller residence?" he asked.

She did not look amused. "Unless you came here to tell me you caught the guy, I really don't have time."

"You got a date, or something?"

"I heard that," Karla called from the kitchen.

"Or something," Louise said.

Turning professional, he took the camera out of his pocket. "I was across the street talking to your neighbor. By the way, I think I smoothed it over between you and him. Anyway, I want to show you something." He handed it to her hoping she knew how to work a digital. If she left it to him, he was pretty sure he'd break it. "Look at the last four pictures."

Louise raised her eyebrows but invited him in. The two stood in the living room with the TV news quietly playing in the background. Louise flipped on the miniature screen of the camera and pressed a button. Grant silently felt relief.

"Holy shit," Louise whispered.

"I guess I can finally take you off of my list of suspects," Grant said.

"Very funny." Louise handed the camera back, but held a large amount of satisfaction at his find. This was huge. "Now if you'll excuse me, I've got a job interview to get to."

It was a strain for Grant to keep his face noncommittal while he beamed on the inside. "Tell Detective Hanson I'll be a reference."

Louise finally flashed a genuine grin. "You think you know everything. Well you don't. I'm interviewing for something else."

Grant didn't let the disappointment show. "Do tell."

"It's not really any of your business," she said with a smirk.

"I understand. You're embarrassed to tell me. Bouncer at a strip bar?"

"If you must know, it's for a security job at the casino."

He had overestimated her. No way did he think that she would fall for that one and open up. "You're not interested in the arson squad? I bet it pays a hell of a lot more. And not nearly the commute."

"It's nice to have options," Louise answered. "Besides, money isn't everything. At least with this one it won't be like I'm crawling back begging for forgiveness."

Grant couldn't come up with any answers for that logic. Instead he changed tactics.

"How about I give you a ride? I really need to go back there. I've got a few follow-up questions I'd like to ask."

Louise's body language instantly changed. She acted edgy, if not downright nervous.

"I appreciate the offer, but I don't think so. I've got a few errands to run afterward."

"I think that's a great idea." Karla walked out of the kitchen carrying a cup of coffee and wearing a pink terrycloth robe tied at the waist. Her blond hair stuck out with that just-got-up-and-haven't-looked-in-the-mirror-yet style. "It's not like the store is out of the way if he drops you off back here to get your car."

For a very brief moment their eyes locked, invisible lasers shooting into each other. To Grant's shock, it was

Louise that bowed. His estimation and respect for Karla shot up tenfold.

Another transformation overtook Louise. The edginess vanished, overtaken with relief .

"What the hell. Maybe you can tell me what you know and I can solve this case for you. All the clues you've got, and you still haven't done squat. Let's go."

Karla set down her coffee and gave Louise a hug. "Good luck, babe."

The women kissed and Grant uncomfortably turned away. He wasn't repulsed by the action, but unlike a lot of guys he knew, it did nothing to excite him either. He just felt like an intruder during a private moment that he had no business witnessing.

Karla closed the door behind them. It wasn't until Grant put the key in the ignition that Miller spoke. "We're going to be quite early for my interview," she confessed. "I wanted to case the joint first. See if I could spot any holes or weaknesses in their system that I could impress them with."

In the short time he'd known her, Louise Miller had tried to outthink him, tried to rile him, pressed buttons to piss him off, she even swore at him. But to his recollection, this was the first time she ever flat-out lied to his face.

Chapter 19

Not even the clouds blocking the sun could brighten Louise's day. The trepidation kept building the closer she got to the entrance. Once inside she stopped, feeling overwhelmed by the familiar sights of the tables and the dealers she now knew by name. Hell, she even recognized some gamblers, and knew their names too.

"You're here for an interview, remember?"

Louise jumped, forgetting that Grant stood beside her. "Am I that much of an open book?"

She no longer tried to hide her ulterior motive, nor wait for an answer. Instead, she walked up to the front desk and told a guard she'd never seen before that she had an appointment. Right behind her, Grant laid his shield on the man's desk and said he had a few more questions for Sgt. Crabtree.

Unable to find an answer as to why, Louise had hoped Chuck would've been sitting behind the desk. He had seemed fond of her. Also, he had seemed so intent to cover her back. She certainly wasn't all that fond of him, other than maybe in that kind of cute hetero-dufus sort of way.

"Louise Miller? You're early."

Louise spun around, almost bumping into Sergeant Crabtree. A lump caught in her throat as she tried to swallow. This was the same jerk that wouldn't let her see the surveillance tapes.

"I'll be conducting the interview." He focused on Grant. "I understand you have some questions for me. Which one of you would like to go first?"

Before Grant could open his mouth, Louise told him to go ahead. "I'll peruse the joint and see if your security could use a little sprucing up."

Both Crabtree and Grant appeared downright angry.

Foot in mouth nothing. I just stuck in my whole leg. "Seriously, I'm sure I'll be very impressed."

The two men disappeared through a side door without a word. Embarrassment spread across her face as the seated security guard tried unsuccessfully to hide an impish grin.

"You didn't really want this job, did you?"

Louise buried her face in her hand and shook her head. When the red faded to pink she peeked through her fingers. The guard was held back his laughter.

"Any way to redeem myself?"

He shook his head. "One thing about Sarge, he takes his job very seriously, and he has no sense of humor." He paused. "I guess that's two things, isn't it?"

His brown eyes gleamed and his smile showed a space between his front teeth. "Robert Starkey" He held out his hand.

The son of a bitch is flirting with me! "Louise Miller." She held out her hand half expecting him to jerk his back and smooth out his hair, but instead he gave hers a gentle squeeze. *Well, two can play at that.* "So, what do they call you security guys? Officer? Deputy?"

"Friends call me Ringo." He waited. "Richard Starkey. Get it?"

She got it. "Wasn't he a serial killer?"

That got him off kilter, but only for a second. Richard Starkey? Ringo Starr? Drummer for the Beatles?"

Louise put on her best bewildered face.

"You're probably too young."

Bewilderment changed to coy. "Thank you, I think. So, can I call you Ringo?" Louise was enjoying herself a little too much.

"I don't know. What can I call you?"

Good lord. Pump 'em full of steroids, give 'em a uniform and they're god's gift to women. You're attracted to a dyke, Bob.

She imagined the fun she'd have telling him her partner's name was Karla. Then it occurred to her that he'd probably take it as an open invitation to a three-way. When that thought popped into her head, the fun stopped.

"You can call me already taken."

He didn't even cause a ripple in the flow of conversation. "We can still have some fun."

Before she could ruin his smile by uprooting a few teeth, the door opened. Grant and Crabtree walked out. "If you'll come with me, Ms. Miller." Crabtree already sounded bored.

Before Louise followed him to the door, she winked at Starkey. "I always thought Pete was Best. Get it?"

She followed the sergeant down a white hallway and into a conference room. Disappointed that she didn't get to sit in the room where the action was, Louise took a seat at the empty table and waited. As the seconds of silence passed, she wondered if there might eventually be an interview. Finally, with no prompting, Louise spoke. "I believe it's supposed to go you ask questions and I answer them."

Crabtree's lips cracked into a slight grin – or possibly gas. He took a seat across from her, clasping his hands and resting them on the table. He spoke slowly and deliberately.

"Detective Grant thinks very highly of you."

"Is that right?" Not only was she surprised that Grant thought so, but also that he'd ever mention it to anybody.

"He also said this might not be the best environment for you."

Her wispish grin disappeared. "What else did Detective Grant have to say?"

Crabtree shook his head. "I also talked to your captain."

"Ex-captain," Louise interrupted.

"Whatever. He played it safe. Just verified you worked there. Wouldn't talk about your job performance."

Louise bit her lower lip. No lawsuit there. With no windows in the room, Louise hoped something, anything, might catch her attention. The walls were bare, no artwork. Only Crabtree. He sat calmly observing her.

"Why do you want this job?" he finally asked.

Louise had rehearsed the answer in her head. She decided on the bullshit boilerplate language about how being in law enforcement made her the perfect candidate. She liked people, she liked the atmosphere, the excitement of the casino. But when she opened her mouth the words came out garbled.

"I was a policeman – police woman. No, I mean an officer of the law…a law enforcement officer."

After about ten seconds sounding like a fool she closed her mouth and her eyes and visualized herself sitting calmly. When she opened them Crabtree was still staring. He hadn't flinched.

"I've gotten to know a lot of the employees." She enunciated each word. "I like them, even respect them. I'd like to be there for them if they ever need me."

Crabtree rubbed his chin, weighing her words. "You've spent a lot of time here, haven't you?" Before she could answer, "And lost quite a bit of money."

The words stung. He had no right to bring that up.

"How does the casino know that you don't just want this job for some revenge scheme?"

Blood pounded against her temples as her hands formed into fists.

"You son-of-a-bitch. Is that what you think this is? Trust me, Sergeant, if I had wanted revenge, I'd be behind bars right now, and a few of your men would be in the hospital. This casino would probably be closed for repairs." She stormed out of her chair and reached for the door.

"Sit down, Ms. Miller."

The authority in his voice made her stop. "If you're this easy to rile, maybe the detective is right. Maybe this isn't the right environment for you."

Stupidity struck. She had failed the first test and probably the simplest. She sank back in the chair and realized that even though she didn't care about the job, she would at least like to have been asked. She figured her chances of that happening just went from slim to nil.

"You realize," Crabtree continued, "that if you did get the job here you wouldn't be allowed to gamble. Get caught gambling here would mean instant dismissal."

She didn't know that. *Then what the hell am I doing here?* "That wouldn't be a problem."

The rest of the interview was a blur. He asked the standard questions, she gave the standard answers. No way would she accept the job now, and these bastards had better offer it so she could tell them so.

Louise shook hands with Crabtree and came out to see Grant leaning on the front desk chatting with the guard.

They were talking about baseball and whether the Twins could take the division this year. When he saw her he stood up and straightened his coat.

"You ready?"

Louise glanced back at the tables and a momentary rush faded into guilt. "Yeah."

She led the way back to the car.

--

Grant pulled into Miller's driveway. The ride back had been uncomfortably silent. Other than the detective asking how the interview went, and Louise answering "fine," they hadn't said twenty words between them. Louise had asked what he'd said to Crabtree. When Grant dodged the question by saying he had just wanted to follow up on the other day, that ended their conversation.

Louise mumbled a thank you and headed to the house. On the one hand she figured out they probably wouldn't offer her the job. On the other she succeeded with a minor victory in that she avoided the tables. She wondered if she could've done that had Grant not been there. And what would she have told Crabtree if he caught her? *You didn't offer me the job yet. Give me the job and I quit playing.*

Louise opened the door just in time to catch Peanut as he jumped into her arms. Smiling, she dropped to her knees as the dog's front paws rested on her shoulders. "Care to dance?" Louise nestled the side of her face into his. Out of habit she made sure it was the side of his face where he could see her.

Peanut licked her cheek. Louise didn't even mind the drool slithering down to her chin. He had the magical ability to make her forget her daily woes for those brief seconds while he said his hellos. For that moment the world took on a healthy glow.

From out of the kitchen, Karla appeared. A smile lit her face as she walked over to Louise. She stooped to give her a kiss on the cheek, saw the rottweiler's spit-glaze and changed her mind, instead giving her a peck on the top of the head.

"How did it go?"

"Why aren't you at work?" Louise eased the dog's paws off her shoulders.

"Mental health day."

Louise nuzzled the dog, wiping off the saliva he left on her cheek onto his. "Hard to say. I think I impressed him, but who knows? I made a couple of bonehead remarks, but I also think I dazzled him on a couple of questions, too."

Karla studied her for a moment then dropped onto her knees joining the pair on the floor. Peanut squeezed himself between them.

"I know I should be more supportive, but I really hope they don't offer you that job. It's not that I don't think you'd be great at it, I just don't think you need the temptation."

Louise leaned over the dog and kissed her partner hard on the mouth. "I know. And thank you for not being a bitch about it."

"Well, aren't you Miss high and mighty?" Karla playfully pushed Louise onto her back, leapt over the dog, and pinned her. Louise laughed as she battled to get free.

"I have no intention of taking that job. I just want them to offer it so I can tell them where to shove it." Using cop training, she slipped out from beneath Karla and maneuvered herself on top.

Karla joyfully struggled to free her arms, but Louise had a tight grip around each of her wrists as she seductively wriggled her way up to planting her knees on Karla's shoulders. With her knees rendering Karla helpless, from there she'd reach behind unzipping her own pants and the sexual games began.

A throaty growl sent a warm whiff of air into their faces. Both women observed the dog, stopped playing, and froze. Peanut appeared almost rabid. Hair bristled from around his collar and down his back. He tried to bark but with severed vocal chords, only a raspy cough came out of his mouth. He crouched, ready to attack.

Goosebumps sprang up as Louise froze at one hundred-twenty plus pounds of tensed muscle ready to attack.

"Look away," Karla whispered. "Don't challenge him."

Louise lowered her eyes and slowly held out her hand for the dog to sniff, not sure as to why. The rottweiler broke the silence with a throaty growl, peeling his lips back even farther, exposing glistening fangs. The broken tooth had been filed down but there were still three more that could do plenty of damage. A silent bark showed the strength of his jaw as it clamped shut. Like a loaded spring, it snapped open once again. Spittle sprayed Louise's fingers. A string of drool hung from his chin, bobbing an inch from the floor.

Louise had no idea why at this time, or where it came from, but all she could think of was bungee spit. She hoped one-day she'd think that was funny. She then prayed her reflexes were quicker than his or she might be missing a finger or two in just a moment.

"Peanut?"

The lack of emotion from Karla's voice masked her fear. The dog cocked his head and the string of spittle broke from his chin, splashing onto the floor.

"It's okay, sweetie," Louise added, her voice matching Karla's calm.

The rottweiler looked at Karla, then back at Louise. Rage faded, turning into confusion. His fangs receded back into his mouth while attack slowly drained from his posture. His fur lay back and muscles eased as both women cooed and whispered. If dogs could show embarrassment, that was Peanut.

Neither woman took her eyes from the dog, but they were careful not to look him in the eye. As Louise got up off Karla, she created an impressive balancing act while at the same time gently scratching the dog's inner ear. With her free arm she helped Karla to a sitting position.

"You all right, boy?"

The dog purred while pressing his head harder into Louise's fingers, as if asking for forgiveness. By now the threatening menace had returned to affectionate pup.

"What the hell was that?" Louise whispered, her breathing still labored.

They sat, sandwiching the dog, petting his fur and feeling an occasional spasm.

"I don't know," Karla finally said. "He's been so good for so long, I think maybe we forgot where he came from." With deliberate movement for the dog to see, Karla reached across and scratched the top of his head.

"It's not like he's never seen us get a little frisky before."

Karla continued scratching his head while Louise stroked the fur down his back. All was forgiven.

"I don't know. Has he?" Karla softly spoke. "He's seen us be tender with each other, but every time we've gotten playful we've always kicked him out of the room. I don't think he's ever seen us get that physical before."

"That fucking son of a bitch," Louise sneered.

"Who?" Karla asked.

Louise closed her eyes and shook her head.

"Oh, him."

Louise took a few deep, relaxing breaths while fantasizing a hell where the Peanut's previous owner was being mauled and shredded by a pack of wild dogs for eternity. Five minutes every hour they would stop so a demon could pour salt in the wounds, then it would start all over again.

"New rule," Louise said, breaking away from the fantasy. "From now on no more wrestling around the dog."

"I'll sign him up for obedience school tomorrow," Karla added.

Goosebumps broke out on Louise's arms. "What if we're taking him for a walk and he sees some kids wrestling in the park? It breaks my heart to say it, but I think we might have to consider putting him down. Can you imagine what would happen if he attacked a kid?"

"No!" Karla was vehement and answered with no hesitation. "I'll get him a muzzle. He won't hurt anybody."

Louise shook her head. "It'll take years, if ever, to dig deep enough to fix whatever that monster did to him."

With a pleasure grunt, Peanut stood up, shook off the women's hands and trotted to the back door.

"Then he can be in obedience school for years. Hell,

he can graduate with a goddamn PhD."

Louise hoisted herself up with the help of Karla's shoulder and followed the dog, grateful for the distraction. "All that lovey-dovey makes him gotta pee."

Karla laid back and closed her eyes. "Which one of us do you think he was going to protect?"

Louise shivered, and stopped. She had been on top, in total control and no need of protection. *Who do you think? And I was the one that saved him. You weren't even sure that we could keep him. He's my dog, goddammit.* That hurt.

Chapter 20

"YOU CUNT!"

He hurled the camera. It bounced off the wall, specks of plaster and dried paint showered the floor. The camera ricocheted and almost made it back to the bed. Almost. The camera mocked him, undamaged. The goddamn whore had tricked him.

"How could I have been so stupid?"

On the television set they replaced the picture showing his car backing out of Miller's driveway with another one of himself staring right into that bitch's house. He knew exactly when it happened. The flash from the camera gave it away and cost that skank her life. The anchorwoman asked anybody with information to please call the Minneapolis Police Department. After a little chit-chat with her co-anchor, the news broke for a commercial.

He sat on the bed trying to calm down and think rationally. The stolen car had been ditched, all fingerprints wiped off. That was good. The wig and beard sitting on the Styrofoam head on top of the dresser were now worthless. Maybe not totally worthless, but he'd have to be very careful if he were to use them again. Fuck it. He couldn't use them again. Hell, even in the disguise he'd recognized himself. He shuddered at the thought of maybe someone else doing the same.

Flopping onto the bed, he became entranced with the ceiling fan, watching the blades spin in lazy circles. A slight breeze caressed his face as he waited for the police to crash through the door. Well, he envisioned it, but didn't really expect it. After sucking up some self-doubt, he convinced himself he would not be recognized. Now he had to put it behind him. A new idea popped into his mind and he sat up with a self-satisfied grin. There were things that needed to get done, people that needed his attention. He had to move quickly.

--

Leo Carp and Joel Spender sat at the conference

table, each with his own list of Walter Farkos' clients. George Jeffers peeked through the glass partition next to the door. His demeanor had become even more rigid since the reading-of-the-will debacle. Joel whispered to Leo, turning red as he fumbled with a list, hastily looking for a folder to cover it up. Leo smirked, making no intention of hiding their actions.

"Et tu, Joel?" George asked as he parked himself in the doorway.

Joel couldn't look him in the eye. Leo did not have that problem.

"You can fight us in court if you want to, but you'll lose," Leo said.

"This isn't over. I'm still the senior partner here."

"How about we take you to lunch, George?" Joel asked, his voice pleading. "I'm sure we can work this out."

Jeffers tromped down the hall. "This isn't over by a long shot," he mumbled.

He stopped at Beverly Wimpole's new office. Even with boxes littering the floor, the office still had a neat and orderly feel to it. Beverly sat behind her desk, crouching and carefully lifting something out. George had a clear view down the front of her blouse. Two white bra cups, probably an A size, held up breasts small enough that she showed hardly any cleavage. Still, he felt himself stir.

"Oh, Mr. Jeffers." She sounded startled.

George smiled. His eyes shot up to meet hers. No way had she caught his gaze. He was too quick. "You're a partner now. Call me George." The venom from his previous encounter with Carp had left. "How's the unpacking going? I see you're making yourself at home."

Beverly laid her MBA degree on the desk. It was matted in a simple black frame. "Everything is happening so fast. I feel like I'm drowning."

George struck a pose placing his elbow in the doorjamb and resting his chin on his fist. He crossed his left leg over his right and gave a flirtatious smile. "I wouldn't have recommended you for the promotion if I didn't think you could handle the job."

Her reaction hinted he scored some points. "How

about some lunch?"

Even though she wasn't his type, small breasts, a butt with a bit too much padding, and she was a little frumpy looking – still, he wondered if he might possibly talk her into a nooner. The unassuming ones were usually wild in the sack.

A long sigh escaped past Beverly's lips and she shook her head. "I'm sorry, I've got so much to do. How about a rain check?"

She bent over, picking something else out of the box. George took another long glance down her blouse.

"That stuff's not going anywhere." He jerked his eyes to hers as she sat up. "Besides, I'd like to apologize for my behavior in that lawyer's office." George switched to his puppy dog face.

Beverly placed another framed certificate on her desk and rubbed her eyes. "I guess I could use a break." Her posture straightened. "What the heck. Let's go." She opened the desk drawer and reached for her purse. "Are Leo and Joel joining us?"

"No!" George spat out a little too quickly and too forcefully. "Uh, they're sorting through Walter's client list." He kept his voice steady. In fact, he impressed himself that it came out sounding like it didn't matter to him in the least.

Still, Beverly made a tiny jump as she reached for her purse.

"It's all right," George said. "Just a little in-house squabbling that I'm sorry you got caught in the middle of. It'll be fine."

Beverly blushed.

"I'd also like to use this lunch as an apology to how I acted at that lawyer's office. My conduct was inexcusable."

Her cheeks faded to a rosy pink.

"Am I repeating myself? Sorry. I guess it just really affected me." George could almost see the wheels turning in her head trying to come up with something conciliatory to say.

"Let me get my coat," were her words of wisdom.

--

They left the building; George's arm rested loosely

across Beverly's shoulder, guiding her to the left. The outside air smelled heavily of cigarettes as the smokers huddled by the door, ignoring the sign that ordered them to be at least forty-five feet away from the entrance. She felt a headache coming on from the stench, and was also uncomfortable with him touching her. Doing her best to show no ill effects, Beverly smiled at Jeffers.

He seemed to take that as encouragement, giving her shoulder a little squeeze. She sagged her shoulder a bit, hoping his arm would drop. Instead, it had the opposite effect – he held on tighter.

"My car's right in here." George led her into the parking ramp and to the elevators.

Every red flag in Beverly's defenses shot up. Downtown had everything from fast food to martini lunches, and all within easy walking distance. She twisted her body reaching into her purse and forcing his arm off her shoulder. She blew her nose into a tissue, making sure it was as undainty-like as possible.

"Oh, Mr. Jef—"

"George," he corrected.

"George, do we really have time for a long lunch? I've got so much work to do."

She hated coming down so forceful, but she didn't want to spend time alone with him, and she really did have a lot to do.

"Nonsense, I know a place with great service. In and out." He gave her a wink. "I'll have you back here before Carp and Spender even get served at one of the overpriced joints they like to go."

The elevator door opened. George stepped in, Beverly didn't. A chill tightened around her skin that had nothing to do with the cool spring air.

"I thought you said they were working."

George stood silent as the doors began to close. He stuck out his foot and the doors bobbed open. As frightened as she was about defying her boss, she had no intention of joining him.

"Um, well, actually," he sounded like a little boy. "Uh, the truth of it is, they didn't want me to join them. Ever since Walter's will I've kind of been an outcast in their eyes." He lowered his head and turned his back to her. "I think they're trying to force me out."

The chill and red flags disappeared as Beverly stepped into the elevator. *You poor man.* "I'm sorry. It must be very hard. That had to have been quite a shock." She laid a comforting hand on his sleeve.

"I thought I knew them," George said, his face away from hers. "I guess it all boils down to greed."

In the corner of elevator a mirror caught George's reflection. It must've been a trick of the light and the angle of the glass, because for an instant she could've sworn he smiled. But when he faced her, *it must have been a mistake.* The bell dinged and the doors whooshed open, rescuing Beverly from an even more awkward moment.

"Well, here we are" George said, his voice now cheerful.

Bev did her best to smile. *The poor man must be going through hell.* She followed him to his silver BMW taking up two spaces at the far end of the lot. Even with all the slush the past few weeks, the car was almost spotless.

Like a gentleman, George opened the passenger door. For the third time that day Bev caught him glancing down her blouse as she slid down into the seat. Unlike at the office, where she tried hard not to turn red, there was no way he could see anything now. Her coat pressed the blouse to her body. There was nothing to ogle at.

It had to be a guy thing. She knew that George was happily married – well, at least married – and that his wife had been a fourth runner up in the Mrs. Minnesota Pageant a few years back. She'd also seen pictures of his wife in George's office. Beverly considered herself cute, but certainly not in the same league as Mrs. Jeffers. After a little more thought about George's roving eyes…

How could I have just felt so sorry for that pig?

George got in the drivers side and buckled up. The engine purred to life and they took off.

Even a week ago there had still been patches of snow on the ground, and already road construction played havoc with downtown streets. Jackhammers pounded pavement and eardrums while cars and pedestrians tried to navigate new paths. George cursed under his breath while swerving to avoid a new pothole. Beverly clutched the door handle as the Beemer clipped an orange cone. Jeffers swore again, this time quite audibly.

"Where are we going?" Beverly asked, trying to conceal the fear.

George glanced over at her like he'd forgotten she was there. "What? Oh." A creepy smile slid across his face. "There's a great place on the 494 strip. Have you ever been to the Sofitel?"

A lump caught in Beverly's throat. She hadn't been to Le Hotel Sofitel since her high school prom. Her date had taken her there for dinner and afterward decided she *owed* him for the expensive meal. The night ended with a torn dress, broken glasses, her date's skin under her fingernails, and the label 'whore.' She still couldn't understand that last one. He hadn't even gotten to first base. Beverly had tried to think of herself as brave, but she knew better. The scratches were an accident. All she tried to do was push him away. He just happened to get his face in the way.

They were finally able to weave around the Target Center and get onto 394. Noontime traffic was light and George opened it up. The car smoothly crept above eighty miles per hour. To Beverly it felt like they were going fifty.

"Oh shoot!" George frowned. "We'll have to take a slight detour. There's a file on my desk at home that I forgot to bring in this morning."

Again, every red flag waved as Beverly grasped the handle even tighter and locked her knees together out of reflex. Part of her wanted to scream, TAKE ME BACK TO THE OFFICE - NOW! But another part, the part that had been instilled since childhood, told her to shut up and quit being stupid. George Jeffers was a man of authority. He had a beautiful wife. He must have bundles of files at home. Of course he might forget one occasionally. *Besides, what could he possibly see in me?*

She convinced herself and relaxed. George slowed and exited on Penn Avenue, driving the winding roads around Cedar Lake over to Kenwood. Bev relaxed. If this were a ruse he would have exited downtown by Loring Park, a much more direct path.

"I love this neighborhood," George said. "When I was younger I was a bartender at the old Guthrie Theater. I'd ride my bike past these mansions and promised myself that one day I'd live in one. I'm not quite there yet, but at least I'm in the neighborhood."

Releasing her hand from the door, the tension eased from her body. Nothing in the world beat harmless chit-chat. You could learn so much about a person. She had no idea Mr. Jeffers enjoyed the theater. Maybe he hung out at the Walker Art Center too. Who knows, they might've even bumped into each other there long before they met in the world of finance.

"Have you been to the Guthrie since they moved to the river?"

"No, I haven't."

"It's just beautiful," she beamed. "I saw Othello there. Not a bad seat in the house."

"Is that right?"

"Oh yes." She carried on about the lighting, the stage, the actors. But when she began lauding Shakespeare, the car instantly filled with The Moody Blues singing 'Ride My Seesaw' in surround-sound.

Now that is just plain rude!

Moments after she quit talking, the music disappeared.

"Sorry," George said. "There's a button on the steering wheel. My thumb slipped."

Beyond rude! Beverly peered out the passenger window. Soon the bare branches would sprout buds. In no time a canvas of leaves would spread high across the streets, making her feel like she was driving under a green sky.

"Here we are."

The BMW turned into the driveway of a two-story brownstone. A walkway curved up a small hill from the middle of the driveway to the front door. The garage door whirred as the panels went up. Other than a snow blower and lawn mower, the two-car garage was bare.

"Ten years ago I bought this place for four seventy-five. Today I could probably get three quarters of a mil, maybe more because of the attached garage. Rare in these kinds of houses."

Beverly wished she had a magic button that would drown out his voice with music. Preferably Bach.

The Beemer idled its way into the garage. George shut off the engine and closed the door before getting out of the car. Beverly remained seated, her seatbelt still buckled.

"C'mon in, I'll give you a tour."

"That's all right. I'm fine here." *How long can it take to get a file?*

"Don't be silly. The light's on a timer. When it goes out it'll be pitch black in here – and cold. Besides, I just remembered I have to call Joel. It'll probably take at least five, ten minutes."

"I'm sure I'll be fine." Bev's voice quivered.

George closed the driver's door and walked around to the passenger side. Beverly thought about locking the door, but that was stupid. He had the keys in his hand. George opened her door. Oh, how she regretted her decision to take him up on his lunch offer. He held out his hand.

"Ms. Wimpole, as senior partner, I insist you come with me."

Beverly couldn't shake the thought of her high school prom. *That's ridiculous, I'm an adult now.* Still, he was her superior. He could easily take away her partnership, maybe even fire her. *Nonsense.* Joel and Leo wouldn't let him. She wondered if it could be true what he said, about Leo and Joel trying to force him out. Well, if he didn't change his attitude quick, she just might join that conspiracy.

With a new resolve, Beverly undid her seatbelt and got out of the car. She made a statement by not taking his offered hand. Instead, she bunched up her coat around her neck, not giving her senior partner another opportunity to peek down her blouse. She didn't say a word as he closed the door behind her.

"Honestly Ms. Wimpole, sometimes I don't understand you at all. I've seen you around clients and you're a real go-getter. You throw numbers at them, answer questions, convincing them that your opinion is the only one that could possibly be right. Then I talk to you and you turn into a shrinking violet. I'm not a bad guy. I won't bite."

Beverly waited for the obligatory 'unless you want me to,' but Jeffers had the decency to let it drop. Again, she doubted herself as he unlocked the door to the house. Without a word Jeffers motioned for her to go in. Could she be so wrong about him? He seemed to be one giant contradiction. Sometimes he could be such a jerk, and then turn around and do something noble. A perfect gentleman one minute, then often ruin it with an off color remark. Her mother had taught her to always see the best in people, but he made it very difficult. This one last time Beverly would give him the benefit of a doubt.

He followed her in and closed the door behind them. A chill raced through her as she heard the deadbolt snap shut.

"This is the laundry room," George said.

He squeezed between her and the washing machine and climbed up the steps. She followed as he showed her the living room, dining area, kitchen, and den. Reluctant, but obediently, she went with him up to the second floor.

"Bathroom." He jerked his thumb straight ahead as they reached the top of the stairs. Pointing to the left. "Spare bedroom."

They walked down the hall past an open doorway. Inside, a sewing room that Jeffers didn't even mention as they walked by.

"And here –" He grabbed her arm and ushered her in. "The master suite."

He smoothly slid his hand up the arm of her coat as she stood numb, staring at the king size bed. The bedspread consisted of a quilt with a pattern of different color roses. The room had the flair of a woman's touch.

She tried to move but her legs froze while ice formed in her stomach. At the shoulder George gave a brief tug, yanking at the coat. Finally, Beverly was able to jump. In an instant she stood more than an arm's length away, her coat dangling off one shoulder.

"You're married," she mumbled, fighting back tears. She prayed he had some common decency.

"You don't need to worry about that. She's off organizing some charity thing. She won't be home for hours."

Beverly tasted a little bile.

"I've always found you to be very attractive, Ms. Beverly Wimpole."

Beverly raced out of the room, down the hall and into the bathroom, slamming the door and locking it. As she leaned over the toilet, she chided herself for stopping. She should've kept running, right out the front door. If she threw up on his fancy carpet on the way out, so be it. He deserved worse.

Her stomach settled before anything came out. With shaking knees, Beverly stood up, put the seat cover down and sat. Tears streamed down her cheeks. She took the last few sheets from the roll of toilet paper and dabbed at her eyes. Fortunately, she was a silent crier.

"I worked so hard," she whispered to herself. *Goddamn you, George Jeffers.* She'd never curse out loud. Now he'd fire her and she'd have to find a new company. *You bastard! I'm too old to start from the bottom all over again.* She could sue him, but it would be her word against his. The thought of testifying made her feel nauseated all over again. Maybe Leo and Joel would defend her. Leo would for sure. She'd seen how he and George got along. *Please make it true that they're going to force him out.*

A light rap on the door startled her back to the present.

"Are you all right in there?"

Beverly couldn't answer.

"I am so sorry, Ms. Wimpole. I misread your signals. My fault entirely."

Signals? What signals! Once again she questioned herself. *Did I send signals? Oh my God! I put my hand on his sleeve. Of course he'd think I was making a play for him. He must've thought I was playing hard to get after that, especially after I smiled at him. Oh Beverly, you are so stupid!* She thought that if only she could transfer some of her money skills into people skills, she wouldn't get herself into these kinds of misunderstandings. First it had been her one and only high school date, and now this. Of course he was still a philanderer, but what men of power weren't? He probably had women throwing themselves at him all the time.

"I promise it'll never happen again." His sincerity oozed through the crack under the door. "How about we just go back to the office and pretend this never happened? We'll do lunch another time. A real lunch. Business only."

"I'm all right," she squeaked and cleared her throat. "Give me just a minute."

She reached for more toilet paper to dab at her eyes before she noticed the empty roll. There were no tissues on the counter.

"I just want to guarantee you this will have absolutely no bearing at all on our working relationship. "I'm far from a perfect man, Ms. Wimpole. I have my weaknesses. But I give you my word, our relationship will be professional from now on. I solemnly swear."

Relief engulfed her as she bent down to open the cabinet under the sink searching for a tissue or more toilet paper. She couldn't understand, or explain, the blonde wig, mustache and beard pinned to the Styrofoam head.

Chapter 21

Walter Jr. lugged a case of champagne to the front door. He'd gotten the phone call that Muriel had left the house without a police escort. Despite the fifty-degree temperature, a rivulet of sweat rolled down his cheek. He wished he could've been there to watch, but Elissa made it clear he should stay away until his mother had gone.

Maneuvering the box with one arm, Walter tried to open the door, but it was locked. "What the hell?"

He set down the carton and rang the bell. After a few seconds the door opened a crack. "Yeah?" Drew smiled his asinine smile.

"I was told it's safe to come over."

"What's the password?"

Walter contemplated kicking in the door and knocking Drew on his ass, but decided to stay on the good side of his stepsister. "Assholes don't get any champagne," he answered.

"Get out of the way," came a familiar voice behind the door.

Drew's smile vanished, his body pushed aside. The door swung open and Jessica spread her arms wide. "Welcome, baby brother."

Walter hugged his sister while Drew seemed a little chagrinned.

"Nice hair. Don't think I've ever seen it down before. Now why don't you bring that in?" Walter jerked his thumb toward the champagne still sitting outside.

Drew shook his head to show off his thick tresses. Before he could say a word, Walter released his sister and they walkedaway arm-in-arm.

"What a fucktard," Walter whispered.

"Walter!" Elissa walked into the foyer and pecked her stepbrother on the cheek. "Let me take your coat. Did Jessica tell you?"

"Haven't had a chance." Excitement rang in her voice as she grabbed Walter's hand. "Muriel threatened to sue. Warned us we'd better not be cashing any checks, she'd be back with her lawyers."

Drew mule kicked the front door closed while carrying in the case of champagne. "Little help?"

The three ignored him as they made their way to the living room. Elissa took Walter's coat and threw it on the couch. Walter dropped into the recliner and pouted at his sisters.

"How come Jesse got to be here for the show, but you told me I couldn't come 'til after?"

"Jesse is staying here," Elissa said. "What was I going to say, she had to leave for a while?"

Jessica stuck her tongue out at her brother.

Drew followed them in and set the box on the coffee table. "Do we need to bother with glasses, or should we just each take our own bottle?"

"There's some flutes in the cupboard next to the fridge. Be a dear," Elissa said.

Walter sensed some aggravation in Elissa's voice. Maybe things weren't all hunky-dory. With a million-and-a-half dollar home and two million in cash, what did she need a husband for? Maybe there was a chance.

Jessica took a seat next to Walter's coat and opened the box, pulling a bottle of Dom Perignon, 2000 vintage.

"Damn, baby brother. Where'd you get the money for this?" She held the bottle up to the light.

"Got a good deal," Walter said.

Elissa scowled. "You didn't sell Dad's company to Jeffers already, did you?"

Walter chuckled. "I'd run it into the ground before I'd sell a share to that asshole."

Drew walked in carrying four glasses and set them on the table.

"Coasters," Elissa said.

Drew placed a coaster under each glass.

"I might just run it into the ground anyway. Could be fun."

"Bubbly?" Jessica asked.

Elissa held up her hand. "Hold on a sec. Honey, as long as you're up, would you go to the kitchen and get a towel? I don't want champagne spraying all over the room."

"What am I, a lackey?" Drew said it with humor, but

underneath, Walter heard tension.

"You know, I hear you don't have to split an inheritance in a divorce."

The glare Elissa shot Walter felt like a bullet between the eyes.

"Did I say that out loud?" Walter sank deeper into the chair. *Too much, too soon.*

"What's up, Lissa?" Jessica asked. "You get a big expensive house and all the sudden you're afraid of a little stain here and there? That's not like you."

Walter sent his twin a telepathic message. *Thanks for bailing me out, sis.*

Elissa closed her eyes and took a deep breath. She opened them and tears formed. "I'm sorry. It's stress." She used her sleeve to dab at her eyes. "Me and Drew have been talking. We might sell this house and keep the one in Edina. This is just too big for two people."

Walter was about to get out of his chair to comfort her, but instead, Drew made an untimely appearance. He had a white towel draped over his arm as he walked over to his wife and kissed her on top of the head. She took his hand and gave it a slight squeeze.

Maybe she got mad at me because that's what she was already planning. And I just alerted the Bozo. Walter, you're an idiot!

Drew sauntered to Jessica and held out his arm. "As long as I'm playing butler, may I?"

Jessica nodded gallantly and handed him the bottle.

"I don't know. You guys grew up here. Would you be okay with me selling the place? I want your opinions."

Walter and Jessica shrugged in unison.

"It's just a house," Jessica said. "Hell, I might just stay in Connecticut. You think fall here is something, go to New England. And the winter is so much warmer there."

"Your house," Walter added. "Do what you want with it."

"I think I just convinced myself," Jessica said. "And now I can afford to live in the suburbs instead of New Haven."

A muffled pop sounded from under the towel.

Careful not to spill, Drew filled each flute.

"What about all the childhood memories?" Elissa asked.

"Pfft. I wish I could forget most of 'em," Walter said.

Drew handed a glass to Jessica and to his wife, then took one for himself. He left Walter's on the table. "A toast." He raised his glass.

"Drew?" Elissa pointed at the glass still on the table.

"Oops. Guess I'm just a fucktard."

"Umm, you heard that, huh? Sorry."

Jessica laughed as she got off the couch. "It's okay, my brother deserved it." She brought him his glass. "A toast." She raised her flute. "To Walter Sr."

"May he rest in peace," Elissa said.

"While his soul burns in hell," Walter added.

Drew choked on a mouthful of champagne, spraying a mist past his lips while Jessica chuckled and Elissa gaped.

"Oh c'mon. It's not like he's ever been heaven material."

Jessica planted herself on the arm of Walter's chair. She still had her purse and expertly dug in with one hand, the other still holding the glass. The strap fell off of her shoulder as she retrieved her cell phone.

"Got to show you something." She held up the tiny screen in front of Walter's face, pressed a couple buttons and the screen came to life. Muriel was standing in her former bedroom with an open suitcase on the bed. Drew stood next to her like a guard overseeing a prisoner on leave. Both seemed unaware they were being filmed.

"Aww, where's the backpack?" Walter asked.

"She thought that was too demeaning," Jessica answered.

The phone showed Muriel as she loaded the suitcase with jewelry and some of her more expensive clothing. The show ended before she closed the suitcase.

"Only recorded thirty seconds worth, but thought you might enjoy it."

Walter clinked his glass to hers. "Thanks."

"You two are incorrigible," Elissa said.

"Except I had to help her close the suitcase, it was so stuffed," Drew added. "I actually felt a little sorry for her until she made the threat. And by then she was already on the front lawn."

"Enough!" Elissa said. "This is supposed to be a celebration remembering our father, not badmouthing your mother. Now who has something nice to say?"

"Thanks for making us filthy rich," Walter said, raising his glass toward heaven. "Oops." He lowered his arm and looked down.

Elissa groaned. "What about you, Jesse?"

Jessica thought for a moment. "I guess all I can say is, ditto. I hardly knew the guy."

"Consider yourself lucky," Walter piped in.

"Guys?" Drew nodded toward his wife.

A crack formed in Walter's heart. Elissa seemed to be using all her resolve to keep calm. Jessica's hand pressed his shoulder as a warning that they were both balancing on a very thin rope.

"I'm sorry," Jessica said. "You've known him a lot longer than we have."

"You probably knew him before he crossed to the dark side of the force," Walter said.

Jessica pinched the nerves between Walter's neck and shoulder.

"Oww. What?" Elissa broke into a slight smile. He wasn't sure if it was his witty comment or Jessica's Vulcan death grip. It didn't really matter.

"Maybe I did," she answered.

Drew refilled his glass and topped off the others, even Walter's. "So, Walter Jr., being that you're far richer than both your sisters combined, what kind of plans do you have for your fortune?"

Who the fuck are you? Walter thought.

"Who the fuck are you?" Jessica spat. "It's none of your damn business what he does with his money."

Drew backed away. Elissa seemed to be enjoying the scene. Jessica rested her chin on the back of her hands, her face just an inch from Walter's.

"So, baby brother, what are you going to do with

your fortune?"

Walter's eyes sparkled. "Drugs and whores." He leaned in and gave her a peck on the lips.

She stepped back and took a sip of her champagne. "You're right, he is incorrigible."

A seriousness transformed Walter and he became contemplative. "Actually, I have been giving it thought. I was thinking maybe we can split it. What's fifty-one percent of a company divided by three? Seventeen," he answered before they could. "I figure I'm going to need all the help I can get running it. But only if you all are very nice to me."

"Very generous," Drew said.

Walter drained his glass, giving an evil eye to his brother-in-law. "But if I hear one cent of company money going to Greenpeace, you're out." He winked at Elissa. "It'll be your responsibility to keep him out of trouble."

"What makes you think I need, or even want more money, let alone helping you run an investment company? You need to be really nice to us, or you're on your own," Jessica said.

"Then I guess it's back to drugs and whores."

"Let's not get hasty here," Drew said.

The three siblings broke out laughing.

Elissa set her glass down and stood up. "You all fight it out, I'm going to lay down for a bit. I've got a headache. Drew speaks for me when I'm not here."

"How much did she have to drink?" Walter mouthed the words to Jessica.

She shrugged and scrunched her face in an I-don't-know expression.

Walter twisted in his seat and ogled as Elissa climb the stairs. "I should probably get going too. I want to call Leo Carp. He left a couple messages for me yesterday."

"Who's that?" Jessica asked.

"One of the partners. I think he wants to get rid of Jeffers as much as I do." *What an ass on that woman.* Each step up Walter studied the curves of her body and he could almost feel his heart thump through his chest. His eyes followed, his stare glued to her frame until she was out of sight and the door closed behind her.

Smiling, and taking a gulp of champagne, Walter swiveled back to his audience.

Jessica gave him the strangest look. "What the hell was that?"

But the liquid froze in his throat when he saw the icy glare that Drew threw at him.

Chapter 22

Louise sank into the new sofa and purred with delight as she stretched. It had worked out perfectly. The deliverymen showed up exactly when they said they would, while Karla was away with Peanut at his first day of obedience school. Karla taking another day off work concerned Louise, but she was in no position to do any criticizing. She trusted her partner, and hoped one day the feeling would again be mutual. It didn't matter at the moment. Today would be a fun surprise day. Karla would love it. It resembled her old couch that she gave up, begrudgingly, siding with Louise's more conventional one when they moved in together.

Snuggling in the overstuffed cushions, Louise realized that getting rid of Karla's sofa had been the mistake. What hadn't been a mistake was letting the cops keep the one they took. Who wanted a couch that had had a dead body sitting on it? A murdered body at that, with blood stains – definitely bad karma.

Louise lit a cigarette and popped an old Karla Bonoff CD into the stereo. It was a first gift she'd bought for her Karla only because they shared the same first name. They even spelled it the same, not with a C. Louise had never heard of the artist before, but the instant they heard the music, they both fell in love with her.

For the first time in a very long while, Louise finally felt at peace. Smoke rings drifted toward the ceiling, but the ringing telephone interrupted her tranquility. Frustrated, she sat up, checked the caller ID and snatched the receiver. "This is Miller."

The message from Crabtree was short and direct. Louise didn't get the job. She uncharacteristically thanked him for the opportunity and his time, wished him a good day, and gently hung up the phone. She couldn't think of a more accurate mixed blessing. Could she have even told him where to shove the job like she originally planned as they were supposed to offer it? The reality hurt. Louise would've accepted the job, and more than likely been fired within a week or two. Worse, she'd probably be left alone with a house she couldn't afford. This definitely worked out for the best, but still it stung.

Louise settled back onto the couch, flicking her cigarette ash in the general vicinity of the ashtray as she went down. At least she thought she remembered seeing an ashtray on the coffee table. A growing crack grew in the foundation of her Zen mood as she took another deep drag from her smoke. Then "Someone to Lay Down Beside Me" danced melodically through the speakers. Louise hadn't heard the song for ages. It was "their" song, and she closed her eyes and began to feel whole once again.

The door swung open and the clawless rottweiler galloped across the hardwood floor dragging a leash behind him, skidding to a stop at the foot of the couch. While he sniffed a myriad of new smells, Karla stared, her jaw hanging.

"Oh my God! My couch!" Karla's hand trembled as she brought her fingers up to her lips.

"New and improved." Louise beamed back.

Karla walked over, unclasped the leash from Peanut's collar, and set it on the table. Carefully, as if the sofa might be fragile, she lowered herself onto the cushion at the opposite end of her partner, closed her eyes, and leaned her head back.

"Oh yeahhhh…this is nice."

Peanut leapt up and snuggled between Karla's leg and Louise's feet, releasing a pleasure grunt himself. They remained motionless until the disc ended. Louise finally sat up, to the annoyance of the dog. She quickly remedied the situation by sliding down making a dog sandwich. Peanut rested his chin on Karla's lap.

"How was school?" Louise asked.

"Star pupil," Karla answered, not moving. "Some yippy little Pomeranian with a Napoleonic complex thought he was going to run things."

Louise leaned down and scratched the dog behind the ears. "Not hardly even a snack for you," she cooed.

"Peanut totally ignored him. It was a bulldog that took a snap at the little mop."

"Oh my!"

"Everything was fine. The instructor was there in a flash. Had 'em under control in less than a minute." Karla lifted her head and looked at Louise. "Reminded me of that Dog Whisperer guy."

Louise snuffed out her cigarette in the ashtray and swept the previous ash on the coffee table into her hand, rubbing it into her jeans. Karla reached across the table doing her best not to disturb Peanut, reaching for Louise's smokes.

"Didn't get the job at the casino."

The relief on Karla's face couldn't be hidden. "Sorry."

"I still would've liked to have been asked so I could've told 'em where to go."

Louise beat Karla to the cigarettes and pulled out two. She lit them both and handed one to her partner. Karla inhaled and watched as a thin stream of smoke wafted up, quickly smothered by a cloud as she exhaled.

"I do think it's for the best, though."

Louise nodded. "I suppose."

"What about being a cop again, working with that lieutenant on the arson squad?"

Louise puffed at her cigarette, the tip turning bright orange. "She's a detective, and I suppose I'll have to." She was hoping for sympathy but it never came.

"By the way, are we doing anything tonight?" Karla asked.

"Why? What's going on?"

"I met a guy in class. He's got a chocolate lab, lives about a mile from here."

"He wants a play date with Peanut? That's adorable."

"Not hardly. He's having an AIDS fundraiser, asked if we might like to come over. There'll be a couple state senators, maybe a county commissioner. I gave him a definite maybe."

"What? You wearing your 'I'm a lesbian' sign again?"

Peanut lumbered off the sofa and trotted toward the kitchen and the back door. Karla got up and obediently followed. "His GAYdar must've been on."

"Did you tell him we don't have any money?"

"Yeah. He told us to come on over anyway. There'll be food. And just for your information, he mentioned it to everybody, not just me."

Louise waited until she heard the back door open and close. She raised her eyebrows. "I dunno. I was thinking we would maybe christen the couch tonight."

After a pause of about a half-minute, Karla stepped out of the kitchen. A cigarette dangled from her lips as she slipped out of her bra, her blouse already resting behind her on the linoleum floor. She smiled wickedly. "No time like the present. We've got two hours."

--

They knew they had the right house because of the rainbow banner and AIDS rally sign at the foot of the driveway. That, and the closest place to park was a half a block down. Other than a couple of small brown patches of dead grass on Lawrence Peters' lawn, the yard looked immaculate. Neatly pruned shrubs decorated each side of the front door. The door itself was a heavy security type, but ornately done.

Louise rang the bell and a tall, lank, bald man opened the door. He wore a diamond stud in one ear lobe, a small gold hoop in the other. The two-days beard growth was more for fashion than neglect.

"I'm so glad you could make it." He gave Karla a hug. "You must be Louise." He let go of Karla and greeted Louise the same way. "A pleasure."

"Mutual," Louise answered.

"This is Lawrence Peters," Karla said by way of introduction.

"Your timing is perfect. Senator Greenfeld is about to speak." He whispered conspiratorially. "Food is in the other room. We'll make sure you get a plate before she starts."

Louise had heard of Megan Greenfeld. Her district included parts of the southern suburbs. She even met her a couple of times at some GLBT meetings. Had she lived in Greenfeld's district, Louise would've actively campaigned for her. She had to remember to shake hands and say hello.

A throng of people clustered throughout the small house, a half dozen or so little cliques, mostly talking about the same thing. Claustrophobia grabbed Louise as she tried weaving between the bodies. She concentrated on things other than people. On the wall hung a Matisse of a woman in a short black dress sitting in a chair with her legs crossed. The background was a black and white checkered wall. On another wall hung a 55-inch flat screen. On the way to the food, they toured through rooms that were rather small, but Peters had maximized the use of space. Louise liked this Peters guy.

"So where's your pup?" Karla asked above the din.

"Buster is outside. He'd have too much fun with all these people."

Good to know. Louise might join the pup soon if she started feeling anymore boxed in.

--

He drove past the house after Louise and her lover went inside. Cars swelled out of the driveway and down the block in both directions. It must've been one hell of a party going on in there.

He drove well under the limit, but not too slow as to arouse suspicion. He had to be very careful. This time he wore no disguise and was driving his own car. What started as just a regular reconnaissance mission had grown into a jackpot. It was stupid, but the pull had been too strong. Just a quick drive past Miller's house to get the creative juices flowing and he'd be gone. He needed to come up with a new plan to harass and disrupt until the final blow. Something to make her totally miserable until her final breath.

By pure chance he had been at the stop sign ready to turn the corner and drive by the bitch's house when the Saturn backed out their driveway. Both lesbos were in it. To prove God was on his side, the entire way on their short trek, at least two cars had been buffered in between them making him almost impossible to spot.

Too bad I don't have a rocket launcher. I could take care of a good chunk of Minneapolis' faggot population. On the downside of that thought, the city didn't need a bunch of homo martyrs. But even more important, Miller had a lot more suffering to endure.

Chapter 23

George Jeffers woke in a splendid mood for the first time in months. He had a plan. Not only would that dried-up bitch, Wimpole, be gone from the company, but if he could sway Spender the right way, he might even be able to get rid of Carp in the same process.

He'd stepped over the line with Wimpole. A sexual harassment complaint would be more than enough fuel to land him out of a job and his marriage. Even if she promised to keep her yap shut, Beverly Wimpole had become a liability. He had to do something.

Last night had gone down as smooth as French silk pie. With a nod and a wink, and three hundred dollars cash, Hakeem, or whatever the hell that night janitor's name was, guaranteed there'd be an eight ball of coke under the file on Beverly Wimpole's desk, and her office door would be unlocked. Spender would find it.

George set up an early morning meeting only with Joel. He would tell him to get a file from Beverly's desk. Joel would find the coke and by the time she walked in, the cops would be waiting. If she had the gall to bring up their little misunderstanding… *'Officer, I had hoped we could've been discreet and not mention this. She made me promise never to tell, but now she gives me no choice. She asked for an advance and I said no. She propositioned me. I told her I was happily married. She broke down and told me she needed money to support her habit. I told her the company would pay for treatment. We hugged – that's all. She seemed so grateful.'*

George had smoked a little dope in college, but was unfamiliar with cocaine. The only things he knew about it were the drug was expensive, and a felony. He had no idea but figured that coke the size of an eight ball would be costly. Hakeem told him he was getting a bargain. Besides, the risk factors were high.

To make sure no fancy-assed lawyer would have the opportunity to pin it on George, he waited outside the building until Joel Spender showed up. They'd go up together so he'd have an alibi that he was never in the office alone. The cameras by the elevators would show he hadn't been inside earlier that morning.

Joel walked nervously out of the parking ramp and toward the building, constantly scanning the street like somebody might actually care. His hands were pushed deep into his pockets and his head down, shoulders bunched forward. Good. George wanted him off-balance. He'd be easier to control. When he called Joel last evening, he'd been very vague, just that he needed to see him early, and it was important. Both of their jobs depended on it.

"Good timing." Jeffers patted Spender on the shoulder. "Just got here myself."

"What's this all about, George?"

Joel reminded him of Lenny from Steinbeck's "Of Mice and Men." *Can I pet the rabbit, George?*

"I'll tell you when we get to the office. I don't want any prying ears."

Joel followed him into the building. At seven-thirty in the morning the elevator doors were wide open on the ground floor. The two men stepped in. George pressed the button and the doors whooshed shut. George enjoyed riding the elevators early in the morning and late in the evening. Those were the only times he could get a nonstop flight from ground floor to forty-two, and vice versa.

"What is it, George? No prying ears in here."

George kept his back to Joel. "It's about Leo."

"Oh c'mon. You dragged me in a half-hour early for this. I'm not stupid, George. I know you're out to get him. I've known that for a long time."

Jeffers whirled around, indignation on his face. "I'm out to get him? It's the other way around. He's out to get me. And it's not just me, buddy boy. You're on the list too."

"What are you talking about?"

"Believe it or not, I almost like the guy. Yeah he pushes my buttons, but he also keeps me on my toes. I had to respect him for that, until now."

Joel wasn't buying it. The elevator slowed to a stop.

"I also think he's having an affair with Beverly."

The doors slid open and Joel Spender's jaw sprang open. George stepped out and had he not held the doors open, the elevator would've taken Spender back to the ground floor.

"What they do with their private time doesn't concern me," George said. "Unless it concerns me. Know what I mean?"

"Do you have proof?" Joel stepped out of the elevator, still in a daze.

George spoke above a whisper as he fished out his keys and unlocked the office door. "When you and Leo were going over Walter's list…"

"I'm sorry about that, George. It's just that…"

"Don't worry about it. I'm not blaming you. You do what you have to do. I can handle it. I'm a big boy."

Joel walked down the hall like a boulder had been lifted from his psyche.

"As I was walking back to my office, I saw Beverly unpacking, thought I'd take her to lunch. You know, a little informal welcome to the team. She acted very suspicious when I came in."

"Well did you knock or just walk in? I'd be uncomfortable if someone just barged into my office."

"That's not important," George snapped. "Maybe she didn't know I could read upside down, but there was an open file on her desk."

A couple of clericals, George couldn't remember their names, walked in, nodded hello and headed straight to the break room to make coffee. He didn't expect them so early, but that was okay. When Joel discovered the cocaine on Wimpole's desk, witnesses would be a bonus.

George stepped into his office and motioned for Joel to follow. He closed the door and glanced at his watch. One thing he liked about Beverly Wimpole was that the woman had the punctuality of a human clock. She came in precisely at 7:50 every morning. Today that didn't give him a lot of leeway.

"I didn't see a lot of it before she closed the file, but one thing that stood out was all of our names were on the header, but yours and mine were crossed out."

"You're kidding! Why?"

George had him. "I also saw handwriting. It was

Leo's. I didn't have time to read much, but let's just say that I saw a little heart dotting the 'I' above her name."

"Uh, there's no 'I' in Beverly, George."

"But there is in Wimpole." *You moron.*

"Oh yeah."

"What I need you to do, Joel, is go get that file. It should still be on her desk. If you bring it to me, and if we stand together as a united front, maybe we can get her to tell us what the hell is going on, and before Leo gets here to even the odds. Divide and conquer."

Joel stood like a zombie, obviously trying to soak it all in. George held out his wrist and tappned on the watch crystal. "It would be nice to have a peek at that file before she gets here."

That seemed to bring Joel out of his reverie. "Good idea. I'll be right back."

Alone in his office, George clasped his fingers behind his neck admiring the view from his window. He felt like a king surveying his realm when a sudden pang of fear stabbed at him. Obviously there was nothing incriminating in the folder, just some schmuck's account portfolio. What if Joel didn't bother to pick it up, but just opened it and saw it was nothing? No. Joel could be an idiot at times, but even he'd notice cocaine the size of an eight ball.

Seconds stretched to minutes and still there was no commotion. *What the hell is he doing?*

George stood up and walked out from behind his desk when Joel came back in waving a file. "This is nothing. Just one of her client's account info."

"Didn't you look underneath it?" *You really are a supreme moron!* "Uh, maybe there's another file under it."

"This was the only file on her desk, George."

Jeffers pushed past Joel and stormed down the hall. "You want something done right…" *Spender's a genius at predicting market trends, but give him a simple task of finding some coke the size of an eight ball on top of somebody's desk…the man's a retard.*

George stomped around a couple more early arrivals and into Beverly's office. No files, no drugs. He tried the drawers – locked. Either the janitor ripped him out of three hundred dollars, or Joel Spender was a coke-head and pocketed the stash. As anger consumed him, Beverly Wimpole gawked from outside her office.

She was standing between two Minneapolis police officers. *Maybe one of the peons found it and called the cops. Good. This could still work out.*

"That's Mr. Jeffers." She pointed at George. "What are you doing in my office, Mr. Jeffers?" She didn't sound like the shrinking violet of yesterday.

"Are you George Jeffers?" one of the officers asked.

The anger rose again. *Why are they wasting time asking who I am? Idiot, arrest her.* "Yes, but…"

"You're under arrest for the murder of Emily Harper." The officer grabbed hold of his arm. "You have the right to remain silent."

"What the hell are you talking about?" He yanked his arm out of the policeman's grasp.

Three more cops that he hadn't noticed came rushing into the office as the two that were already there threw him hard onto the desk.

"Add resisting arrest," one of the cops snapped.

Between the pummeling and flipping him onto his stomach, they were able to twist George's arms behind his back and cuff him. "Anything you say can and will be used against you in a court of law. You have the right to an attorney."

"But she's the one with the cocaine." George sounded close to panic. He could only see out of one eye now and he tasted blood.

"If you cannot afford an attorney, one will be appointed to represent you."

"Why aren't you arresting her?" The policemen hoisted him to his feet. He tried to twist his body to point at Wimpole, but a police officer stood on each side of him, each one tightly holding an arm.

"Do you understand these rights?"

The vision started to cloud George's good eye. Past the cop standing in front of him spewing gibberish, outside of Beverly's office seven or eight employees had gathered. Each one mirrored the others – eyes and mouths wide open.

"I said do you understand these rights?" Hands like vise grips dug into his arms.

"Yes," George winced.

"Now what's this about cocaine?" the cop asked.

George checked one last time on the desk. Everything that had been on there was now scattered on the floor. He still couldn't find anything resembling an eight ball. Somebody was going to pay. Either the janitor or Spender, George would get his revenge.

"Nothing." For now, all he could do was try to walk out of there with whatever dignity he had left.

--

George sat shackled to a table that was bolted to the floor. His vision had cleared but he knew he'd have one glistening shiner in the morning. On one wall stood a large mirror. He wondered if there might be someone on the other side watching him. There were no clocks, but he guessed that it had been well over an hour, maybe two.

Not more than five seconds after George laid his head in the crook of his elbow, the door opened. He raised his head and squinted. "I know you."

The man held his index finger.

"Who was I supposed to have murdered? They told me her name, but I swear to God I never heard of her." George lifted his hand as far as the chain would let him, the irritation was evident as he jerked it back, and pointed. "I remember you from somewhere."

The man took a seat across the table. He pulled out a mini recorder from his pocket. Glancing at his watch, he pressed the record button. "April twenty-first, eleven forty-two a.m. Detective Gordon Grant interviewing George Albert Jeffers. Before the interview started, Mr. Jeffers mentioned that he knew me. Before we get started I'd like to read you your rights."

"They already read me my rights," George said.

"I just want it on the record, Mr. Jeffers, it'll only take a sec."

"Tell me why you think I murdered someone."

"I'll try to answer your questions after you answer mine. Deal?"

Jeffers yawned through the second reading of the rights.

"Do you understand these rights, Mr. Jeffers?"

George nodded.

"The recorder doesn't pick up a nod, Mr. Jeffers."

"Yes." George sounded bored.

"And you agree to talk to me without a lawyer present?"

"I don't have anything to hide." He again jerked the chains that held his wrists.

"Is that a yes, Mr. Jeffers?"

"Yes."

"To answer your questions, Mr. Jeffers."

"You can call me George."

"To answer your questions, Mr. Jeffers, you and I have met. It was at the office of Stanley Fettig."

"Of course. I guess I didn't recognize you without your Colombo coat."

"That's a good one, Mr. Jeffers."

"Now can we just get this over with so I can go home?"

Grant took out his notepad and pen. "Where were you on the afternoon of April sixteenth?"

"That's an easy one. Day after tax day I was in the office."

"All day?"

"All day."

"Even lunch?"

George thought for a moment. "Probably not. And before you ask, I don't remember where I went for lunch that day. Do you remember where you ate that day?"

Grant ignored the retort. "Do you ever wear a wig?"

"What kind of question is that?" George tried to bring his hand up to his thick salt and pepper mane and growled as he rattled the chain. "Does it look like I need it? Now you on the other hand…"

"How do you know Emily Harper?"

Being glib would not make this go any faster.

"Never heard of her until those cops beat the hell out me. And after I was cuffed I might add. Just so you know, I am going to sue."

"Not my department. You'll have to deal with internal affairs for that. You've never been to 1429 Newberry?"

"I have no idea where that even is."

Grant shifted in his seat. "Here's my problem, Mr. Jeffers." He flipped through the pages of his notebook. "The hair on the wig we found under your bathroom sink…"

"Wait. What wig? I don't know anything about any wig. Ask my wife. And what were you doing in my house?" George began to sweat. It occurred to him that if he didn't answer these questions correctly, he might not be going home tonight, or anytime soon.

"We had a warrant and your wife let us in."

"Why on earth did you think you needed a warrant?

The detective shrugged, probably debating with himself if he should say. George decided he'd demand an answer before he'd say another word. He didn't have to use the threat.

"We got an anonymous tip that we'd find evidence of Ms. Harper's murder under your bathroom sink."

"A judge signed a warrant on that? That's pretty flimsy." George was appalled.

"You a lawyer now, Mr. Jeffers?"

George said nothing.

Grant nodded. "Actually, that's a pretty good question. It was a very specific warrant." He said it like that was all the explanation needed.

"How's my wife taking all this?" It occurred to him that she hadn't come to visit. Maybe she was arranging bail.

Grant sighed. "She's not too happy with you at the moment. Now let's get back to me asking you questions, okay? It'll go much faster that way. You'll talk to your wife soon enough."

"Fine." George motioned for the detective to go on and got annoyed once again at his restricted movement.

"The hair on the wig we found under your bathroom sink matches a couple strands of hair found on the body of

Emily Harper."

Raising his hand to rub his eyes, George cursed as the chain kept his wrist inches from the table. He yanked again, harder, screaming to be set free, and again, thinking he might actually break the links. His curses became incoherent sobs. He only succeeded in hurting his wrists before the tantrum finally subsided.

This time he lowered his head to meet the table. Silently counting to ten, George scrutinized Grant. The man yawned.

"Why won't you believe me?" He stopped in mid breath and his eyes opened wide. "Beverly Wimpole!" His voice became animated. "She was in my bathroom. I bet she planted it there."

"Why was Ms. Wimpole in your bathroom?"

"I was taking her out to lunch and remembered a file I left at home. When we got there she mentioned that she needed to use the facilities." *That bitch! She threw the wig in there and then called the cops on me. Anonymous tip, my ass. Maybe now I'll get her out of the company after all.*

Grant paused as he scanned his notebook. "According to Ms. Wimpole, she ran into the bathroom because she was afraid you were going to rape her."

A swallow got caught in Jeffers' throat. *Does my wife know?*

"Now that might be a motive to frame you for murder, but it doesn't explain how she was able to sneak in a Styrofoam head along with the wig. I've seen her purse. It wouldn't fit."

Defeated, George mumbled, "Maybe it was hiding inside her coat."

"She said you tore off her coat. That's when she ran."

George closed his eyes and tried to sort this all out. Nothing made sense. How could one cocaine buy have gone so haywire? The only thing now certain, he was in a lot more trouble than he previously thought. He let out a long slow breath. "I think I need a lawyer."

Grant checked his watch. "Interview concluded at 11:55 a.m." He switched off the recorder and slid his chair away from the table.

"Can I ask you something off the record?" George asked.

"You can ask." He had the recorder in his pocket, his thumb on Record.

"How much does an eight ball of cocaine cost?"

Grant eyed him quizzically. "You got something else you want to tell me?"

"Humor me."

"Well, I'm not in the drug division, but an eighth of an ounce? Depends on who you get it from, and the quality. I'd guess about a hundred bucks give or take for low end to maybe a couple hundred for the really good stuff. Why?"

George leaned forward, dropping his head on his hands.

Grant walked out of the room leaving George Jeffers alone once more.

Chapter 24

Louise went from watching TV to gazing out the window. The blue sky betrayed no sign of clouds. If she stared hard enough, she could see the little nodes popping out of the branches on boulevard trees. In just days they would turn to buds, and days after that, full-fledged leaves. Soon the street would be under a canopy of green.

She knew she had to call Kate Hanson and accept the job offer, but for the moment she couldn't bring herself to do it. The idea of being a cop again still made her nauseous. "Whaddya think, Peanut? Can I hold off another day?"

Hanson said she needed an answer soon. Louise hoped that maybe, just maybe, she might be able to wait a tad too long and the job would be filled.

The dog lay splayed out on the kitchen floor. When he heard his name he followed Louise with his eye, keeping his blind side pressed against the linoleum. Already he was trying to keep cool and it was only a month into spring.

The Channel Six news jingle quietly emanated from the television set. Just watch the headlines and the temp, and then she and Peanut would venture out for a walk. She needed to work with him for obedience school anyway. In the lower left corner of the screen, the temperature flashed fifty-four degrees. Louise was about to fetch Peanut's leash when she froze, only able to reach the remote control to turn up the sound.

Plastered on the screen was her neighbor's house from across the street. It was old footage. There were no cameras in front of the house now. Louise cranked the volume. Police had arrested a suspect, George Jeffers, in the murder of Emily Harper. It was unknown at this time whether it was related to the arson of the Burlington home across the street. Grant had mentioned his name to her before, but it still didn't ring a bell.

Louise raced to the phone before the news story ended. "They caught the guy who killed our neighbor!" she shouted without even waiting for a hello. She sensed the tension easing away at the other end of the line.

"Are you there?" Louise asked.

After a moment, Karla's relieved voice answered back. "That's fantastic. I think this calls for a celebration dinner."

"I think you're right. I'm cooking. What's your preference, chicken or beef?" Louise pictured Karla at the other end of the phone, twirling her hair with her finger while contemplating. *Please say beef.*

"I think decadence is more in order. Let's go out for pasta. Who makes the best lasagna?"

Louise got giddy inside. She should've known Karla would pick lasagna, even over steak. Plus, now Louise wouldn't have to cook. "You don't have to twist my arm on that, but I thought we were trying to save money." Actually, the idea of mega-carbs sounded ideal. Louise hoped that she hadn't just convinced Karla out of that idea.

"This celebration deserves splurging," Karla said. "Besides, you're calling that woman and accepting the job, right?" There was warning in her voice.

"Yes, Mom. I'll call her this afternoon." *So much for tomorrow.* She scratched Peanut behind the ear in hopes of getting a little sympathy, but like her partner, he gave none.

"Good. I'll be home around five."

"See ya when you get here." Louise had the phone well away from her ear when she heard Karla's voice shouting for her.

"What did I forget?"

"Why don't you ask Andrew if he wants to tag along?"

Louise's heart sank a bit. "You don't want a romantic dinner, just the two of us?"

"It'll be fine. He never comes in afterward. He'll drop us off and leave – might even pick up the check." Her voice transformed to maniacal. "And tell him to bring a date. We'll double."

"You are so evil," Louise chuckled. She was pretty certain her brother hadn't been on a date since that reporter babe took a new job in Dallas.

"See you in a while." Karla hung up.

A giant weight had been lifted off of Louise's

shoulders. She wondered if she'd be able to keep her feet on the ground. She also wondered if she could convince Grant to give her some alone time with this Jeffers guy. She tenderly rubbed her neck thinking there was some serious payback owed.

Peanut still lay stretched out on the floor. He didn't seem nearly as enthused that the police caught the murderer. What would excite him was when Louise would ask if he wanted to go for a walk. Actually, all she really needed to say was the word 'walk.' She loved to watch him jump up and prance to the door like he was some kind of show dog, his little stump tail making his entire butt wiggle. But first, Louise had to bite a bullet in the ass and get it over with. She picked up the phone and called Kate Hanson. After the third ring a recorded voice told her that Detective Hanson was not available and to please leave a message. Louise hung up before the beep.

"Maybe after our…" Before she could say the magic 'w' word, a car parked in her driveway. A Cheshire cat grin spread across her face as the driver's door opened and Gordon Grant stepped out. She and Peanut met him at the door before he had a chance to ring the bell.

"Is it all right for a civilian to hug a detective?" The frown on his face diminished the smile on hers. Peanut resumed his place back on the kitchen floor.

"You might want to take a rain check on that hug." He stepped into the house without an invite and nodded admiringly at the new couch. "Not bad."

Louise closed the door, her elation fading by the second. "Feel free to try it out, and then you can tell me why you're not ecstatic that you yanked another scumbag off the street."

Grant took off his overcoat and folded it over the back of the couch, sat next to it, and then motioned Louise to join him. He picked up the Beretta from the end table and turned it over in his hands, nodding in approval.

"Glad you're prepared."

Now that Grant was seated, Peanut came back and sat impatiently as the detective placed the gun on the cushion next to him. The dog waited to be scratched behind the ears and under and around the strap of the eye patch. Louise grabbed the remote, clicked off the TV and sat at the far end. Satisfied the detective did a decent job, the dog went back to the kitchen and lay down, making sure he could keep track of them both.

"I think we got the wrong guy."

Louise felt it coming, yet she still had a lurch in her stomach. She trusted his instinct too much. "Why?"

Grant didn't hesitate. "If he did it, either the guy is the world's greatest actor, or he's a genius psychopath. After talking to him I didn't get the impression he was very good at it either."

Louise couldn't think of anything to say. She wanted to beg him to reconsider, go over the evidence one more time and change his mind.

"Here's the thing," Grant continued. "A Styrofoam head with the wig on it was found under his sink, right out in the open, not hidden behind anything. It's the perfect surface to pick up fingerprints. The oil from skin sticks to that material like a magnet. Nothing. Why wipe it clean when you're not expecting anybody to find it?"

"Maybe he wore gloves whenever he used it. Maybe he's just really careful." Louise was grasping for anything.

"You should've seen his face when I brought it up. He seemed clueless. I believed him. You would have too."

"Maybe he is a genius psycho."

Grant shook his head. "I really can't believe he's that smart. There's also absolutely nothing to connect him to you or the Burlingtons."

"Well, how else could the wig have gotten there?"

Grant fidgeted like he was afraid of the answer. "I've been thinking about that. If it is the same guy, I'm guessing he had about as much trouble breaking in there as he did here."

Goose flesh broke out over Louise's arms. She didn't want to think about that for the moment. "What about a connection to Walter Farkos?" Her voice shook, betraying her feelings.

Grant's eyebrows arched. "Motive galore there. And no matter what we find out about Harper's murder, he's still a person of interest in that one."

"Can you share info?"

Grant shrugged. "What the hell. You might be able to show me a new perspective. I'm obviously missing something here."

Touched, Louise wisely kept her mouth shut.

"With Farkos out of the way, Jeffers becomes senior partner."

"Sounds like a hell of a motive."

"Here's the snag, and it's a big one. In a nutshell, Farkos snubbed Jeffers in the will, splitting all of his clients with the other two partners and leaving all of his shares of company stock, in other words, control of the company, to his son.

"Sounds like a no-brainer, so far," Louise interrupted.

"Well, just to throw a monkey wrench in it all, Jeffers found out that Farkos had cancer. He knew he was going to die soon anyway, so why kill him?"

"Force him to change the will?"

Grant nodded. "Not bad. He said he knew the son was going to get control of the company." He paused. "I still can't get it to add up."

Louise rubbed her temples. "What about the son, then?"

"From everything I've learned they had no relationship at all. The son just assumed he'd be cut out of the will. Didn't really seem to care. He was shocked that he got anything, let alone control of the company."

"You believe that?"

"Yeah, I do. His sisters confirm it. I was also at the reading of the Farkos' will. The kid looked pretty damned shocked. That leaves the other two partners."

Louise chuckled. "Let me guess; they've got motive, too."

Grant shuffled through the pages of his notepad. "Not that I know of yet, but I've just started doing a prelim. Got a lot more digging to do. Do the names Joel Spender or Leo Carp mean anything to you?"

Louise shook her head. "Never heard of 'em."

"I dunno," Grant said. "This Jeffers guy might've done it. I think he's guilty of something, I just have no idea what. But I don't think it's murder. At least not Harper's."

He put the pad back in his pocket and rubbed his eyes. Louise could see the strain this case had been putting on him.

"Want some coffee? Then maybe we can hash this thing out."

"Sounds good." Grant yawned.

Louise got up and stepped over Peanut on her way to the coffeepot. The dog lifted his head just far enough off the floor to see what she was doing, then plopped back down.

There was coffee left in the pot from the morning. She took it over to the sink, ready to dump it.

"Just reheat it." Grant stood in the doorway. "The stronger the better."

Louise poured a couple of cups, sticking them in the microwave. For ninety seconds she watched the detective squat down and pet Peanut's stomach. Grant's brow furrowed as he found a multitude of scars especially around Peanut's chest. His hand lightly traced over them. Peanut wormed his way from his side onto his back to give greater exposure.

The microwave beeped and the detective grunted as he stood up.

"Poor dog's been through the ringer."

"To hell and back." Louise handed him a cup.

Walking to the living room, Grant stopped, his eyes bore into Louise. "One day when you're finally ready, I want to hear your side of the story behind this dog."

Louise cut him off with a wave of her hand.

Like she knew he would, Grant took the cue and let it go. They both took a seat on the couch. Louise tasted her coffee and grimaced. She observed Grant taking a sip of his and swore that she saw the trace of a smile.

"Okay, what've we got so far?" Louise asked.

"We've got hair from the wig that matches hair found on Harper. We get an anonymous call that we'll find proof that Jeffers killed Emily Harper."

"Male or female?"

"Male. It was made from a cell phone, no ID, probably cloned, traced it to the vicinity of Lake Street and Hennepin Ave."

A sudden chill grabbed Louise and would not let go. "Can I hear that call?"

"I can get a copy. Why?"

"I need to hear Jeffers voice, too."

Grant's eyes narrowed as he set the cup down. He squinted admiringly at Louise. "I think I can get him to say a couple of words." He hoisted himself off the couch. "Let's take a quick trip downtown."

--

Grant parked his car next to City Hall. Queasiness roiled in Louise's stomach as the structure now fondly called The Old Courthouse loomed before her. The granite building took up an entire square block and reminded Louise of a castle. She used to enjoy driving to work during those cold winter mornings when it was still dark and seeing the clock tower, its hands and numbers lit up in red neon. Now, she felt only dread.

Instead of walking in the front entrance where they'd be greeted by a large statue of "The Father of Water," Grant led her to a side entrance that was almost hidden from public view, the door most of the cops used. Louise tried to be incognito, keeping her head down as she followed the detective inside.

"Hey Detective." One of the cops greeted Grant. Per his reputation, Grant ignored him.

The officer did a double take and stared directly at her. She quickly looked down and followed Grant's heels.

"Miller? Is that you?"

No. It's somebody else. She emulated the detective.

"Elevator or stairs?" Grant asked.

"Stairs," Louise answered without hesitation. She would've rather walked to the top of the clock tower than wait for an elevator and stand out like she was on exhibition.

When Grant headed down the stairs instead of up, Louise knew exactly where they were headed.

"Don't we have to go to PSF?" she asked. The Public Safety Facility was where they held a vast majority of the prisoners waiting for their next court appearance.

"He hasn't been charged yet. They're still holding him for probable cause. He's still here."

Instead of entering the tunnel that transformed the Romanesque style of City Hall into the modern blah of the Government Center, the duo made a quick left that brought them to the control room of the detention area. After Grant showed his ID to the deputy behind the Plexiglas, a drawer opened up and Grant took out the form and deposited his gun and car keys. The drawer slid shut.

"We want to see a George Jeffers, being held for PC."

Since she left the force, the only thing PC meant to her now was political correctness. *Arrested for not being politically correct. Maybe he called someone a dyke.*

"Will he need his lawyer?" the deputy asked.

Grant shook his head. "This is just a social visit." He gave the deputy a wink.

The drawer opened up again, sans gun and keys. Grant slid the completed form back in. The drawer disappeared back into the wall.

"Fourth floor, room C," the deputy spoke through an intercom and pointed to the elevators.

They rode up in silence. When the door opened, a guard was waiting for them. He brought them to the interview room, told them it would be just a minute or two, and shut the door behind them leaving the pair alone. On the other side of the white room was another door where Jeffers would be entering.

"I don't think he's going to say a whole lot," Grant said.

"He doesn't have to. I'll never forget that voice as long as I live."

The door opened and a guard escorted a man with a black eye wearing an orange jumpsuit. His shoulder were slumped and his hair disheveled. He walked in like a man who had been utterly defeated. He glanced at Louise. Louise studied him. It was so hard to tell from this angle. Maybe if she laid on her stomach and craned her head back she might recognize him. She tried to picture him in a ninja costume but couldn't.

He shifted his eyes over to the detective. The passive face turned snide. "I'm not saying a word to you without my lawyer here."

The guard hadn't even had a chance to take the cuffs off yet. He looked over to the detective. Grant shrugged, and just like that the interview was over.

Alone once again, Grant regarded Louise. Her heart sank. She felt about ninety percent certain he wasn't the guy who attacked her. Grant took her hand and gave it a fatherly squeeze.

"Too bad you couldn't get him all riled and have him say 'Oh shit.'"

"Maybe we'll have more luck with the phone call," he assured her.

Dejection melded into trepidation as they walked back through the police station. Fortunately, Louise saw no one she knew, and more importantly, no one seemed to recognize her. Grant brought her to an interview room and sat her down.

"I'm going to see if that tape's ready. I'll be right back." He closed the door.

Louise strained to see behind the mirror, wondering if anyone was watching. *You're getting paranoid, Miller. Why the hell would anyone be interested in this?* Still, she thought, why did Grant bring her here instead of his cubicle? She gave him the benefit of a doubt, that he was doing it for her privacy.

A metal ring jutted up from the table where they manacled the perps. Louise wrapped her hand around it. The room reeked of fear and body odor. Maybe there was a touch of stale cigarettes, too. Even though the indoor smoking ban had been in effect for years, the smell would be forever embedded in the walls. She wondered what would happen if she lit one up.

Instead, she reached for her cell phone and debated whether to call Karla and cancel dinner, or Andrew and invite him. If they went ahead with dinner, should she call

Karla and tell her to keep up her vigilance, they got the wrong guy? "Aw, screw it." She pressed number three on her speed dial.

"This is Deputy Miller."

"Vescio's. Tonight. Pick us up at seven. Bring a date." She hung up.

Louise was about to call Karla when Grant walked in holding a mini-cassette. She dropped the phone back into her purse just as it started playing the theme from "Dr. Zhivago." Andrew. She shut off the sound and put the phone away.

Grant shut the door, sat down across the table and rolled his eyes. "Lara's Theme? And to think I respected you."

"Knock it off." She couldn't take her eyes off of the cassette.

"Ready?" he asked, turning serious again.

Louise bit her lower lip and nodded. Grant pressed the button. "9-1-1 operator."

"I was in George Jeffers' house earlier today and I went to use the bathroom. Under the sink I saw a wig and a fake beard and mustache. I pictured what it would look like on him, and it just occurred to me that this was guy on the news who was driving away from that lady's house that got killed."

"What's your name, sir?" Click. "Sir?"

Grant shut off the recorder. "Well?"

Louise had her eyes squeezed shut, concentrating. "Maybe."

Grant rewound the tape and played it again.

"I can't be sure. I swore if I ever heard that voice again, I'd know it."

"Maybe it's not him." Grant slid the recorder into his pocket. "Gave a copy to linguistics. They're going to compare it to the 911 tape made from Harper's house."

Louise replayed the message in her head. "I just don't know. It could be."

Grant stood up and opened the door. "C'mon, I'll give you a ride home. It doesn't sound like you'd be able to swear to it in court, anyway."

"If he's the guy, I'll swear to it."

"I didn't hear that."

Trepidation thickened the air. Louise felt as if she was suffocating while following the detective through the squad room. She got a couple of glimpses from officers she didn't know and her paranoia took over. No way could she ever be a cop again – far too much baggage. She'd have to call Detective Hanson when she got home and decline the offer. Hopefully, Karla would understand. *Oh my God! What if Grant's taking me to her now? I don't want to tell her to her face.*

Louise wasn't even aware that she successfully passed through the gauntlet until Grant opened the door and a cool spring breeze slapped at her face.

"You okay? You're looking a little pale."

"Actually, I'm not feeling all that great."

On the way home Louise listened to dispatch talk to other officers over the radio. Grant pulled the car into Miller's driveway. She opened the door and stepped halfway out.

"So, have you decided to rejoin the fold?" he asked.

She saw it coming but still wasn't prepared. "Yeah." *Where the hell did that come from?* She wanted to get inside before she spit out another lie. She had her key in the lock and almost had the door open.

"Hang on a sec." Grant got out of his car and walked toward her. His manner frightened her. "He's been here before. How about I check it out first?"

"Holy shit!" The thought hadn't occurred to her. She'd used up all her paranoia at the police station.

Grant had his hand near his holster as Louise swung open the door. Peanut danced in a circle before nuzzling into her leg.

"I think I'll be fine."

Grant agreed and headed back to his car.

Chapter 25

The first time he stepped out of the elevator as a kid, Walter had been in awe. In huge gold letters, Farkos Jeffers Spender & Carp shone above the ebony wood doors. His name came first. Well, it had been his dad's name, but Walter Sr. did say that one day it would all be his. Walter Jr. was seven at the time. He had never dreamed that his dad would keep his word.

Fifteen years later, he was still impressed. The letters weren't solid gold like he believed at one time, but it was still one hell of an entrance.

Walking past the double doors, Walter was greeted by a smiling receptionist, maybe twenty-five, sitting behind a large oak desk that curved around almost giving the woman her own office, or at least a high-class cubicle. She could've just as easily come from a model shoot. Blonde hair, professionally curled, rested on her blue chiffon shoulders. Her makeup was not overbearing, but enough to highlight her cheekbones and green eyes. The top two buttons of the blouse were undone, not quite exposing cleavage. Sitting with her back straight, the woman's legs were planted under the desk.

He became self-conscious, wearing blue jeans and a Minnesota Twins T-shirt under a tattered leather jacket. When he dressed that morning, he thought it would make a nice rebellious statement. Now it felt stupid.

"I've got an appointment with Leo Carp."

Her eyes grew as her smile widened. She pushed back her chair and stood up, extending her hand. "It's such a pleasure to meet you, Mr. Farkos." She had a firm handshake, full of confidence.

"My father was Mr. Farkos. I'm Walter. And you are?"

The woman returned a coy smile. "Megan. Megan Walston."

She's good. She didn't seem the type to be embarrassed or caught off guard easily.

"Maybe I should just call you boss," she said with a flirtatious voice.

A slight smear of lipstick on her otherwise bright white teeth turned him on. He could easily see her converting him into her lap dog if he wasn't careful. He should probably exert some authority. The thought made him wonder if his dad had ever had sex with this Megan. He shuddered and tried to bury the image.

"I think that would be a bit presumptuous. I believe Leo is expecting me." Damn, he did sound like a boss.

"Of course." Megan sat and lifted the receiver. She pressed a couple of buttons. "Mr. Carp, Mr., er, Walter Farkos is here to see you." She winked at him, a well practiced wink. "I'll send him right back."

It was as she hung up the phone that Walter noticed the large cluster of diamonds banded around her 'Back Off, I'm Married' finger. *Probably for the best.*

"Through the door, all the way down the hall and turn left. Third door in."

A keypad barred the entrance. Before Walter could ask for the combination, before he could utter a word, the door buzzed and clicked.

"Go right on in," Megan said. The lipstick seemed to be growing on her teeth.

The devil played inside Wlater. "Just in case you're not here sometime that I need to get back there, what's the combination?"

"There's always somebody at the front desk. Company policy."

Her professional smile was beginning to annoy him. "You know who I am, right?"

"Of course." Her demeanor faltered, just a little.

"What's the combination?"

Her smile faded. "Mr. Jeffers made it clear that only employees have access. Current employees," she mumbled.

"Look at me, Megan." She did which fed into his growing power. An evil leer spread across his face. "In a matter of days I'm going to be George Jeffers' boss. Who would you rather deal with?" *I'm having way too good a time at this.*

The smile slowly returned to Megan's face. "One-seven-nine-two."

She had launched a torpedo straight into his chest. His legs became wobbly and he reached out to the doorknob for balance. The door swung open and Walter fell to his knees, but bounced back to his feet as if it were a dance step.

Megan jumped up from her chair. "Are you all right?"

That look of surprise was the first real emotion Walter had seen from her.

"I didn't think the old man even remembered," Walter said.

"Excuse me?" Megan strode out from behind her desk.

Walter held up one hand to stop her, with the other hand he kept the door pried open. "Nothing. I'm fine. It's just that January seventh, nineteen ninety-two, is my birthday." He let the door swing shut behind him. He'd had enough of Megan for a while.

No one else had seen his Fred Astaire imitation. Voices floated over the cubicle walls. Some were telling people to sell, others saying now was the time to jump back in these stocks were ready. Across the aisle from the cubicles were the offices to the elite – the execs who probably did the least amount of work, but made the vast majority of the money.

Walter was halfway down the hall when Leo Carp appeared around the corner. Leo seemed genuinely happy to see him as he picked up his pace, an arm already extended.

"It's been way too long." Leo grabbed Walter's hand and gave it a firm shake.

"We just saw each other at Dad's funeral."

Leo put his arm across Walter's shoulder and led him back into the office. "I mean the last time we had a chance to talk."

"When was that, Leo?" Walter couldn't think of a time they ever talked before.

"You're probably too young to remember."

Walter let it slide. If there ever had been a time, it certainly couldn't have been of anything consequential. It probably went something like, 'You're getting to be quite a big man.' 'Yes sir.'

For a partner, Leo had a rather modest office. Next to the door a floral patterned couch rested against the wall. Behind it hung an early Picasso print of a girl balancing on a rock while a man sat and watched. In front of the couch sat a glass coffee table, financial magazines neatly placed on top. Across the room were the generic round table and fancy black leather business chairs. On the opposite wall hung a painting of a clown holding a copy of the Wall Street Journal, a tear dripping down the clown's cheek. Walter liked the painting, but questioned if it might be sending the wrong kind of message. *Goddammit! There I go thinking like a boss again.* Behind Leo's desk, windows lent a partial view of the city past the Mississippi river. Most of the scene, however, was blocked by another skyscraper across the street.

Leo sat at the table and motioned for Walter to join him. Walter took a chair opposite and as if on cue, a man and a woman walked into the office. The man he knew from before, but the woman he only recognized from the funeral. He couldn't remember either of their names, if he ever knew them.

"You remember Joel Spender," Leo said.

Walter shook his hand without getting up.

"And this is our newest partner, Beverly Wimpole."

Walter stood and bowed his head when she didn't offer her hand. She did give him a nice smile, though.

When all four were seated, Leo spoke, directly to Walter. "You heard about George Jeffers, didn't you?"

Walter shook his head.

Leo did not seem fazed. "Mr. Jeffers was arrested this morning for murder." His voice came out very smug.

Excitement wrapped itself around Walter as his heart beat faster.

"My father?"

"Do you think George murdered your father?" Joel's eyes widened.

Walter was amused with Joel's reaction. "It had crossed my mind."

"I just can't believe he'd ever do that." Joel rushed to Jeffers' defense.

Leo shook his head. "No, some woman, totally

unrelated.”

“Was probably having an affair with her,” Beverly mumbled.

The room became silent as Walter, Joel, and Leo all shifted their eyes toward Beverly. She blushed at the attention.

“Beverly, do you know something we don’t?” Leo asked.

She shook her head without saying a word.

“Speaking of affairs, is there maybe something I ought to know?” Joel asked, leering at Leo.

Leo gave back a crooked stare. “What the hell are you talking about?”

Walter shifted uneasily in his chair. This was sounding more like eighth grade. Maybe he should sell. He wouldn’t admit it to himself, but he gained a new respect toward his old man. If this is what he’d had to work with, it was amazing the company had flourished.

“Maybe I should go.” Walter slid his chair back.

The tension broke when Leo raised his hands. “I’m so sorry.” He closed his eyes and inhaled deeply. “We’re so sorry. I’m not sure what’s going on here, but it’s certainly not how I wanted to introduce you to the company. You don’t need to get involved with our petty grievances.”

Joel and Beverly nodded in agreement.

“All right.” Leo let out an exasperated breath. “Let’s get down to business here. Barring any court challenges, Mr. Farkos here now owns the majority of the company.”

“I haven’t signed anything yet,” Walter interrupted.

Leo waved a dismissive hand. “I guess the first question we all have, is what are your intentions?”

Walter gave Beverly a mischievous grin. “I promise to have her home by midnight.”

Joel’s laughter sounded typical suck-up. Beverly had a habit of blushing and turning away.

“Can we be serious for a minute?” Leo was not amused. “I have to be at a seminar in forty-five minutes. Would you agree, Mr. Farkos, that we do have a right to know?”

What a fucktard. “Fine, Leo.” Walter matched the

man's intensity. He began to feel like a boss again. "The first thing I'm going to try and do is get rid of George Jeffers."

He studied their reaction. Joel choked on his breath like he swallowed that kiss-ass grin. Leo folded his arms across his chest, smug. Walter knew he had an ally there. Beverly he couldn't read. She wouldn't look him in the eye. Her face could've read surprise, or relief.

"Hopefully this murder charge, whatever it is, will make it a no-brainer. I don't know if you all knew this, but my father never trusted the man."

Again, it was Joel Spender with the shocked expression.

Can you really be that naïve? "Anything past that I really haven't decided."

Walter strolled to the window and marveled at the scenery across the river. "I've got an idea." He noticed his reflection in the glass and saw what a man he'd become in just twenty-two years. "Why don't you each write up a proposal and tell me which direction you want to see this company take." He spun around to the trio. "I'd prefer you not talk about it with each other. I'd like to get a feel for each of you." He waited, giving them each a chance for any sort of dissent but got none. "Good. You've got," he looked at his watch, "let's say three days." He winked at Beverly.

Before they had a chance to respond, Walter walked briskly out the door. Closing it behind him, Walter heard Joel. "What seminar? I didn't hear about any seminar."

Walter took his time making his way back to the lobby. *This just might be a lot more fun than I anticipated.*

--

Storm clouds slowly rolled in from the east as Walter turned into his late father's driveway, now Elissa's. He hoped he could get his twin sister to the airport and himself back home before the clouds broke. As he stepped from the car, the front door to the house opened and Jessica strutted out, her bag strapped over her shoulder. Walter headed toward her. Jessica stopped as he passed and kept walking.

"I wouldn't go in there if I were you."

Walter stopped. "Just wanted to say hi to Lissa."

Jessica grabbed his shoulder. "Drew is ready to kick

your ass."

Walter furled his brow, then got angry. "He's a wuss. What's the bug up his butt about?"

Jessica punched him in the arm.

"Oww!"

"I'm ready to kick your ass too."

Walter seemed genuinely hurt. "What did I do?"

"Jesus Christ, Walter, I almost had to wipe the drool from your mouth as you watched Elissa walk up the stairs. I thought you were going to stick your hand down your pants."

The memory filled his head and embarrassment blanketed his face. He wished he could freeze time and disappear. Instead, he focused his attention up at the clouds as they got darker and nearer. Ozone permeated the air. He could smell it. A storm of either rain or snow was getting ready for an attack.

"I was pretty drunk. I don't remember." Walter couldn't look his twin in the face.

Jessica punched him in the arm again. He scowled and took a step back but didn't say a word.

"Don't bullshit a bullshitter. She's your half-sister for god's sake. Your married half-sister. What the hell were you thinking?"

"I don't even remember it." He stuck with his story.

"Drew told Elissa, now she's pissed as hell at you too."

Walter had to bite his lip to keep from swearing out loud. "I'll just go in and apologize. Tell 'em the champagne must've affected me and I don't remember a thing."

"Tell them later. Just get me to the airport. I got to be there in half-an-hour."

"But it's the truth! I really don't remember."

"Your face says you do."

The disgust in Jessica's eyes made him give up for now. Maybe if it wasn't raining or snowing after dropping her off, he'd swing back. Or maybe not. A phone call might work better. Then he wouldn't have to worry about punching out Drew.

Walter reached for Jess' bag. The strap slid down her

arm and she let him take it. That was a good sign. He threw her bag in the back seat and then opened the front passenger door. She slid in without acknowledgment. A drop of water splashed on Walter's head as he got into the car.

By the time Walter rolled down the driveway, rain was pelting the car. As he entered the ramp to the freeway, large clumps of snow entered the mix. He switched on the radio. "Cars" by Gary Numan filled the Buick with synthesizer music. He upped the volume. Jessica turned it down.

"I like this song. Haven't heard it in years."

"That clapping sound gives me a headache," Jessica said.

Walter merged into traffic. Overly cautious cars were traveling between twenty and thirty miles per hour. The fearless were weaving in and out between sixty and seventy.

"They're all fucking idiots," Walter said. "Half of 'em drive like they've never seen snow before, and the other half think it's a damn racetrack. Morons!"

He got stuck behind a Honda traveling thirty-five while an SUV sped past on the left.

"Fucking snow in April, I can't believe it. This is supposed to be spring, isn't it? April showers bring May flowers?"

"Only in Minnesota, huh?"

Jessica gazed out the side window. Snow was already sticking to the branches and power lines. "It is beautiful, but I'm glad I'm getting the hell out of here."

Wall of Voodoo started singing "Mexican Radio." Jessica cranked the volume. Walter hit a patch of ice and almost fishtailed into the ditch before righting the car back into his lane. A Ford behind him laid on the horn. Walter flipped him the middle finger and slowed to twenty-five.

"Be careful!" Jessica had her hands clenched.

Walter ignored her. By the end of the song they were only a couple of miles from the airport. Rain had pretty much turned to snow, the flakes wet and heavy. The DJ announced the temperature was a balmy forty-one degrees with lows dipping down to the upper thirties. At least the rain wouldn't form an ice sheet on the roads. The song ended and commercials came out of the radio. Walter shut it off. The silence felt good. Jess seemed to enjoy the solitude also.

Turning into the long stretch of road that led past the car rentals to the parking lot and departure gates, Walter asked, "Do you want me to go in with you?"

Jessica shook her head. "That would be pointless. With security you can't even get past the main area without a ticket. Just drop me off."

"Hell, didn't anybody tell you? We're rich. I can buy a ticket just to see you off, then throw it away."

"Money already poisoning your brain, baby brother?"

The remark hurt until he saw her smile.

Cars were double parked along the curb. People scurried to get their bags out of trunks, while others waited impatiently to get their cars free so they could get the hell out. Walter stopped at Jessica's airline sign, becoming the first triple parked car. The car behind him stomped on the breaks. There was a quick screech of rubber burning into tar.

Walter got out of the car and smirked at the guy behind him. The man threw up his arms in a what-the-hell-is-this gesture. He got back an insincere shrug as Walter opened the trunk.

"What are you doing?" Jessica asked. She already had her bag.

Walter handed her a small box. "A going away gift."

Jessica's eyes widened. "Thank you. Can I open it here?"

"You're going to have to move your car now, sir." The red cap's voice was polite but stern.

Jess ran over and gave her brother a quick peck on the cheek. "You go. I'll open it inside. Whatever it is, it better fit in my bag because I'm not checking luggage."

Walter gave his sister a hug. "Hope you like it. And don't worry. It was on sale. Money hasn't rotted my brain – yet."

Under the watchful eye of the red cap, Walter closed the trunk, got into his car, and drove back into the falling snow. In the rearview mirror he saw his sister opening the box as she walked through the sliding glass doors. He couldn't see her reaction.

Ideas were popping into his head faster than the miles per hour of the Buick. George Jeffers was in jail. If Walter was going to do anything about getting rid of him, now was the time. Actually, he hadn't been impressed with any of the partners. He wondered if he could get rid of all of them? A sudden surge of fear and powe overtook him. Walter junior was becoming Walter senior. He pushed that thought aside.

First, he had to smooth things over with Elissa. That wouldn't be easy, especially with Drew as her little fuck monkey. Now that they were all rich, he felt confident that Lissa's marriage with Drew wouldn't last. It was just a feeling, but he learned to trust it. Still, he decided to give them a year. If they hadn't split by then, he'd help them along their way.

There were just so many, many things to think about.

Chapter 26

Louise sat at her kitchen table wearing sweats and T-shirt studying the Walter Farkos murder file. Detective Grant had bent the rules and emailed her a copy, asking her to take a gander. How could she refuse? He actually used the word gander. Peanut lay on the floor, his chin resting on her foot.

A blow to the upper right side of Farkos' head had been the cause of death, but he had also been tortured. Superficial cuts had sliced his belly and throat. A tiny nick of a paper-cut had been found on the pinky of his right hand. The report read they were smooth cuts, no serrated edges. It could have been an incredibly sharp knife, but more likely a scalpel or razorblade. *Or a box cutter.* Louise would have to remember to tell that to Grant. The police had the murder weapon, one of Walter's paperweights. Walter's face showed other bruising, 'but at the time of this report, it has not been determined if they were caused by said paperweight or maybe a fist.'

Piecing it together, Louise imagined herself tied to the chair, a killer standing over her. Walter had been able to free his left arm. Was he defending himself against the knife when the killer picked up the paperweight? The angle of the wound showed the two were face-to-face. She pictured Walter grabbing the man's wrist, using all of his strength to fend off the attack. That meant that the attacker would be right-handed. But if there hadn't been a fight and the killer just picked up the weigh – that would most likely make him left-handed.

The headache started at the base of her skull and slowly climbed to her forehead. Louise popped a couple of aspirin and bent down, scratching Peanut between the ears. He rubbed his face against her shin. The eye patch made a quiet popping sound as it was pushed inward. The dog didn't seem to mind.

"What do you think? Why didn't he use the knife to kill him?"

Peanut looked at her with love, exhaled a bubble of snot, and nestled his chin harder onto her foot.

"You're so romantic."

With effort, Louise slid her foot from underneath the dog. His chin softly smacked the floor. She made her way to the other side of the kitchen and poured herself another cup of coffee.

"I think there was a struggle. There had to have been."

Unimpressed, Peanut got up and stretched, then plodded his way to the back door. Louise set down the cup and followed. "Snow? What the fuck, Peanut! Not only had it snowed, but it had snowed enough to stick to the grass. She had been so buried in that report she never noticed the weather.

"What the hell?" Louise scratched the dog while opening the door. "You have something to do with this?"

She hooked the cable to his collar and watched as he ambled down the back steps, then rolled onto his back, wiggling himself a massage on the wet grass.

Life's simple pleasures.

She sat back at the table, hoping something from the report would leap out.

With the dog outside enjoying the cold, Louise jumped at the sound of the front door opening. Her first reaction was *where's the gun?* All of her confidence had followed Peanut out the back door. In her head were Gordon Grant's words. *"I'm guessing he had about as much trouble breaking in there as he did here."*

"Hello?"

The tension eased. Louise closed her eyes and took a deep breath. "In here."

Karla walked into the kitchen, leaned down and gave Louise a quick peck on the lips.

"I'm starving. Had lasagna on my mind all afternoon."

Louise rubbed her eyes with thumb and forefinger. "Uh, about that." Just coming in from outdoors, Karla's hand felt cool on her shoulder. Still, Louise pressed her cheek into it. "Grant stopped over this afternoon. Told me they got the wrong guy." She didn't go into any other detail.

A small gasp escaped past Karla's lips as she wrapped her arms around Louise. Louise sank into the embrace.

"No lasagna?" Karla half pouted, half cooed.

Louise muffled a giggle in Karla's shoulder.

"Andrew's not picking us up?"

"Oh shit!"

Louise broke from the hug and dashed into the living room, grabbing the cell phone from her purse. She had been so nervous at the old courthouse, she'd forgotten about Andrew. While she punched in the code, Karla stood in the kitchen doorway holding up an open bottle of merlot. Louise nodded and then listened to Andrew's message.

"He'll be here at seven, unless you want me to phone him back and cancel," she called. Karla had disappeared from the doorway.

No sound emanated from the kitchen and a shudder spread through Louise starting at her spine and shooting down her limbs.

"Karla?" Her voice cracked.

No answer.

"I'm guessing he had about as much trouble breaking in there as he did here."

"Karla!" Louise's voice held an urgency as she searched for her gun. *It was on the damn table. What did I do with it?*

"Uh huh."

A wave of relief washed over Louise. *Get hold of yourself, woman!*

Two glasses of wine sat on the table. Karla studied the report, lost for the moment in Walter Farkos' world.

"The killer knew where to find the safe," she said without taking her eyes off the report. "Only one painting was taken down. Either he knew, or he was a very good guesser."

Recovered enough to breathe, Louise took a seat across from her partner. "Or maybe Walter told him." She picked up a glass and gulped the wine. She was beginning to feel a little better.

Karla glanced up. "That doesn't make any sense. Why would he tell him where to find the safe, and then get himself killed by not telling him the combination?"

Louise examined her empty glass. *Why the hell didn't I think of that? Shit, now even Karla is a better detective than me.* "You gonna drink that?" She pointed to the full glass of wine.

A thud at the back door startled both women. Two massive paws were pressed against the glass.

"I'll get him." Louise pushed back her chair and made a detour to the counter, grabbing the merlot on the way. Behind Karla's back she took a swig from the bottle.

With one hand, Louise expertly unhooked the dog. Peanut galloped over and squeezed his head between Karla's elbow and rib cage. With the dog in a headlock, Karla gave him a noogie, ignoring the cold and wet fur pressed into her clothes. He snorted his approval. Louise snuck up from behind and scratched his rear. His little nub of a tail, stood straight up, gyrating.

Long shadows grew across the table and an empty bottle of merlot as late afternoon stretched into evening. Louise absently flipped on the kitchen light. She had studied every detail of the report, and now Karla had done the same. They agreed it had to have been an inside job. It was no great revelation; the police were going on that theory too.

"If it's not Jeffers, I want to know about the other two partners," Karla said.

"I'll talk to Grant in the morning. He said he had follow-up to do with them."

Peanut sprang from the floor and trotted to the front door. A moment later the bell rang. Both women looked up at the kitchen clock in unison. Two minutes to seven.

"Oh my god!" Karla shot from the table. "I've got to change." She raced from the room.

"You? You look great." A couple splotches of red stained Louise's shirt. She hadn't remembered spilling any wine. The coffee stains on her sweats were old.

The bell rang again. Peanut used his clawless paws to dig at the door.

"Shit." *Andrew is going to be so pissed I'm not ready.* The thought made Louise smirk.

An incredibly hot, and vaguely familiar-looking Asian woman stood in the doorway. Apple Bottoms jeans were molded to her long, shapely legs and tucked inside black leather boots. She stood an inch smaller than Louise, but where Louise was long in the torso, this woman was all legs. A black leather coat hung unbuttoned down to mid-calf. Her cherry lips matched the red cotton sweater. "Well, are you going to invite us in?"

Louise hadn't even noticed her brother standing next to the woman. "Um, yeah." Louise held the door open.

Halfway through the entrance, the woman gasped. She stood frozen, her eyes staring at the rottweiler. Andrew gallantly stepped in front of her and scratched the dog's forehead.

"See. He's so tame, he wouldn't hurt anybody." Andrew shot Louise a warning glare.

The girl timidly held out an arm. Peanut sniffed and then licked the back of her hand. The magical barrier had been broken. She followed Andrew into the house.

A shit-eating grin spread across Louise's face as she pointed at the visitor. "You're the waitress."

"Ahn Kim you remember my sister, Louise?"

Louise couldn't wipe off the grin as the two shook hands. "Kim the waitress?"

"Don't," he warned, and then leaned over to his date. "'Kim the Waitress' is a rock and roll song."

"By Material Issue, I know. Believe me, I'm very familiar with it." Ahn rolled her eyes. Her voice held no trace of an accent.

Peanut wedged himself in between Andrew and Ahn, almost knocking the woman into the wall. She grabbed Andrew's arm for support.

"I think he likes you," Louise said.

"So, sis," Andrew interrupted. "You work all day at getting this dolled up?"

"I was working."

The bedroom door opened and Karla emerged wearing brown tweed slacks and a white silk blouse. Around her neck she wore a thin gold braid chain with a tiny lighthouse pendent. Where the light should be was a small diamond. Louise bought it for her on their six-month anniversary.

Karla's jaw dropped as she went over to give Andrew a hug. "She's gorgeous," Karla whispered.

"This is my sister's partner, Karla Spires."

"Ahn Kim." She held out her hand.

Karla released Andrew. "Uh-uh. Not good enough." She gave the woman a hug.

Louise playful slapped Karla on the butt. "While you're stealing Andrew's date, I'm going to change."

"Take your time." Karla winked at Ahn.

Ahn's face blushed almost as red as her lipstick.

--

A half-block away, a car sat idling, the heater blowing full blast. He thought he had every contingency covered, but had omitted the possibility of a goddamn sheriff bringing a date over for dinner. A dog and two dykes he could handle. Throw in a lawman and that lowered the percentage of success considerably.

The temperature dropped as the sun disappeared from the horizon. Still, his rage kept him warmer than the car heater. He'd already stayed parked longer than anticipated. Seven o'clock he had planned to go to the door, a pizza box in one hand, a gun in the other. Even though they hadn't ordered anything, they'd still open the door. No smartass neighbor peeking out their window would give it a second thought.

Now, it wasn't safe to stay any longer. On his way over one police cruiser made a pass down the block. He didn't know when they'd be coming by again, but figured it might be soon. Who knew how long that stupid brother would be staying?

Just as he was ready to turn the headlights on and drop the car out of park, Miller's front door opened. The four of them were laughing as they piled into the brother's car.

This could work out after all. He might not be able to get Miller tonight, but he could certainly get rid of the dog. He figured he had at least an hour minimum to play with the beast before they came home. They would open the door and start a game called 'Find the Doggy.' They'd find a piece in every room of the house.

Sometimes things just work out for the best. Killing the dog will cause a lot of pain and grief for the bitch. And isn't that what life is all about?

Chapter 27

The snow eased to light flurries as the setting sunlight wedged its way through cracks in the clouds. Snow crystals in front of the windshield reminded the detective of tiny flash bulbs popping before his eyes. Grant flipped down the visor. It didn't help.

The ice was long gone off of Lake Minnetonka, but with the snow still dusting down, the scene could pass for a Christmas postcard. Grant wasn't in the mood to appreciate it. An aerial view of Lake Minnetonka made him think of a Rorschach inkblot. Driving around the winding roads, he felt lost in a maze. The voice on his GPS told him to turn right in half-a-mile. He envied, admired, and disliked Leo Carp for being able to afford to live in this area.

Around one of many sharp turns, Grant's car hit a slick of black ice and fishtailed. A Beemer coming the opposite way blew its horn and narrowly missed Grant's rear taillight. Instinctively, the detective flipped the guy off.

Grant turned right and was immediately disgusted at the row of McMansions lining the bay. He reminisced back to childhood when his dad used to take him fishing here. They'd rent a small boat, try to find the quietest spot on the lake and spend an entire day catching sunfish, carp, and an occasional bass. Bonding the way a father and son should. As a small boy he marveled at the fancy houses. Now, the few old ones that remained were like shacks in between castles.

"Turn right, here."

Grant obeyed the small box and turned into a circular driveway leading to a three-car garage. He stepped out of his car, flipped up his collar, and wondered what had happened to that eighty-degree day from less than a week ago. A sign hung from a gas lamppost in their front yard. A fish, most likely a carp, was sculpted above the Carp name. Grant pictured Leo's face on the body of a carp. The thought made him chuckle as he pressed the doorbell. He hoped his smile wouldn't frighten the man into silence.

"Who's there?" The female voice came through an intercom.

212

"Detective Gordon Grant. Minneapolis PD." He took out his badge and looked around to see if a camera might be pointed at him. If it was, it lay well hidden.

"What can I do for you, Detective Grant?"

He leaned down to put his mouth closer to the speaker. "I have an appointment to speak with Leo Carp."

"He's not here. Tonight's his bowling night."

Bowling? The son of a bitch was supposed to meet me here. The anger of a wasted trip trailed behind the surprise of Leo Carp bowling. Other than watching the professionals, he'd never seen, or even heard of a rich man go bowling.

"Can you tell me what bowling alley he went to, ma'am?"

"I think it's called Lucky's, or something like that. If you turn left out of the driveway, it's a couple miles down the road, across the street from the Holiday Station. But I'm not sure if that's the name of it. It's right on this road, though."

Anger slowly simmered beneath Grant's skin. "Does Joel Spender usually bowl with him?" It took effort to sound polite.

"I have no idea. I don't think so."

Grant swore under his breath. "As long as I'm here, could I ask you a few questions?"

"About what?" For the first time her voice sounded uncertain.

"Your husband's relationship with George Jeffers." *For starters.*

"I really don't know anything about that."

He wanted to tear the intercom out of the wall. "Can we talk face-to-face, ma'am?" Irritation crept into his voice.

"I really don't have the time, detective."

He mouthed the words along with her. That seemed to be the standard answer.

"I promise, it won't take long," came the standard reply.

After a pause an exasperated voice came back. "Just a minute."

Grant looked through a small window in the door as

he waited. The door was built from solid oak and it wouldn't have surprised him if the window were made of unbreakable glass. Even if someone did break it, a muscular arm wouldn't fit, and even if it did, the window was high enough they wouldn't be able to reach in and unlock the door. This had been built with security in mind.

Through the window a handsome woman walked down the stairs. Wavy dark-brown hair hung past her shoulders. As she approached he instinctively held up his badge and I.D. A moment later the deadbolt slid and the door opened. She motioned for him to enter.

"Thank you. Mrs. Carp?"

She nodded. "Call me Charlotte."

The woman had an olive complexion, most likely Middle Eastern descent, a bump on the bridge of her nose, and very thin lips. But her large brown eyes seemed to put everything in proportion. A pretty woman, but a normal pretty, she only came up to his chin. Gray roots peeked up from the scalp. She probably had an appointment at the salon in another day or two. Grant chided himself for being an ass.

"Thank you, but professionally I'd better stick with Mrs., or Ms. Carp."

She nodded. "Sorry it took me so long to answer the door. I tried calling Leo on his cell, but it must be turned off."

"I appreciate your taking the time to talk to me."

"I really don't think I can tell you anything, detective." She closed the front door, but didn't invite him any further inside the house.

"Did your husband ever do anything social with George Jeffers?" He wanted to keep her focused on Jeffers. As soon as she found out he was more interested in her husband as a suspect, Grant knew he'd be walking out the door, probably with a push from behind.

"Not for years." She leaned in like they were conspirators. "Leo said he's anti-Semitic."

Grant pulled out his pen and notepad. "Did he ever say why he thought that?"

She shook her head. "Just the typical ignorance and stereotyping. He never got into specifics."

"How did he get along with Walter Farkos?"

"My husband or Jeffers?"

The woman was sharp, but she just opened up an opportunity he thought he'd have to skirt around.

"I meant Jeffers, but as long as you brought it up, let's start with your husband." Before she could get suspicious he added, "And any motive he could come up with as to why Jeffers might want Farkos dead."

She looked from the foyer into the living room, and then at her watch. "I have to leave in ten minutes to pick up my daughter from gymnastics. But take off your shoes and come in. You've got five minutes."

He slipped off his shoes grateful he'd put on the pair of socks without holes that morning. He followed her into the living room. This area of the house was strictly for entertaining. There was no evidence to show that the fireplace had ever been used. Above it hung an enlarged photograph of a traditional rabbi standing behind a young girl who was reading from the torah.

"Your daughter?" Grant asked.

Charlotte Carp's eyes sparkled with pride. "Ruth's bat mitzvah. That was taken three years ago."

For the first time, Gordon Grant thought of Leo Carp as a husband and father rather than a suspect. He hoped Carp had nothing to do with either murder.

"Please sit down," she said.

Mrs. Carp sat at the end of the sofa. Grant took a seat in the middle, careful not to invade her space.

"I'd offer you something to drink, but there's really no time."

"That's quite all right. Now about Walter Farkos, did your husband ever mention a reason why anyone, not just George Jeffers, would want him dead?"

She concentrated on the question, something Grant learned to appreciate from witnesses, not so much with perps. When perps started actually thinking, they were usually smart enough to demand a lawyer. He waited patiently.

"You really need to talk to Leo about this," she finally answered. "He said Jeffers was a kiss-up to Walter

Farkos and everybody laughed behind his back about it, including Walter. Maybe Jeffers found out and snapped. To be quite honest, Leo rarely brought baggage home from work. He's a strict believer in separating work life and family life."

"What about your husband's relationship with Walter Farkos?" The question he really wanted to ask her.

She caught on way too quick. Her eyes went from friend to predator. Her personality changed instantly. "They were very good friends." Her voice could freeze water. "It's time for you to leave, Detective Grant."

Mrs. Carp followed him back to the foyer, her eyes burned a hole into his back. She had the door wide open before he had his shoes retied.

"One last question."

She glared, standing rigid.

"Has your husband ever mentioned a Louise Miller?"

He could add hatred to predatory.

"Do I need to call my attorney?" she spit through clenched teeth.

"No, ma'am. Thank you for your time."

Even though the snow had stopped, the temperature was cold outside. But not as frigid as it felt inside. Grant circled around the driveway and turned left. Two-and-a-half miles down the road he saw the Holiday Station. Across the street, Lucky Strike Lanes was closed for remodeling.

Leo Carp became a suspect again.

Chapter 28

Their car slowed at the corner then turned right. After it was out of sight he slowly counted to sixty and started his car – his new temporary car. To avoid suspicion he drove around the neighborhood until he figured the car would be erased from any neighbor's memory. That's why he liked to steal Toyotas – they blended in, especially the Camry. People didn't give them a second glance. He would be taking a chance, but it would be worth the risk.

He turned back onto Miller's block and into her driveway. Again, just in case of neighbors, he carried the empty pizza box. In his other hand, he held his lock-picking tool. A Colt XSE nestled in his pocket. He hoped the first shot wouldn't kill the dog. The ugly beast should be alive for as long as possible while being eviscerated. Miller would get home, see the mess, and do a room-to-room search. The only thing she'd find would be doggy bits scattered throughout the house.

A pang of fear stabbed at his chest. Why didn't he have a back-up plan? This one was too risky. He should've parked the car a block or so away and snuck in the back. But now his car was in the driveway. What if he backed out and someone was watching? That would be something to stick in a person's mind. He hadn't planned on no one being home. He should have thought of that possibility.

Think!

Things were not going well. For the first time, he felt stupid. After this, no more ad-libs. From now on everything would be thought out, including a fallback plan.

He closed his eyes until the clouds in his mind dissipated. A pizza deliveryman would not be inside a house for any extended period of time. The car might be noticed. *Okay. This can still work.* He'd go to the front door and ring the bell. When nobody answered, he'd make a show of double-checking the numbers above the door, slap himself upside the head like he got the wrong address, then drive off. He'd park on the next street over and sneak in the back door. Not perfect, but it would do.

Beads of sweat formed on his brow as he stepped

from the car. The temperature made them feel like ice. A nervous energy bounced around him as he walked up to the door. Ideally no one would be at their windows, but another part of him wanted to put on a show even if the audience was invisible.

As his finger reached for the bell a thud crashed from the inside of the door. He jumped, the box fumbled from his hand and he did a quick juggling act to catch it. Another loud crash slammed against the door. After a momentary panic his breathing returned to semi-normal. *Last time I was the one inside with you outside wanting in.*

Just to irritate the mutt, he rang the doorbell several times.

The hell with it. I'm here. Let's get this done. He inserted the pick into the lock. A bright light slid across the house and stopped, focusing on him like a star attraction. A pair of headlights froze in the driveway, blocking his car from escape.

Bringing his arm up to shield his face, he dropped the pick, covering it with his foot. The driver's door swung open and through the glare and burning in his eyes, he made out the shape of the lawman.

"Can I help you with something?"

Nerves jumbled close to panic. The Colt pressed against his leg. *Don't lose it! You can get through this.*

"You live here? I got your pizza."

From inside the door another crash made his heart lurch. He had to lower his arm, using both hands to keep the box from dropping. The backdoor to the car opened. The bitch stepped out.

"If I hadn't forgot my purse, you'd be standing there all night."

Don't panic! Now he needed to deliver one hell of a performance.

He glanced up at the numbers above her door. "One pepperoni, mushroom, and black olive for 1427 Milestone Road." He lowered his hand closer to the gun.

The bitch laughed. "This is Newberry. You're a block off."

"You're kidding." He squinted down the block like

he might actually be able to see the street sign. "This isn't Milestone?"

"Newberry," she called back.

This time he was able to ignore the thud against the door. "Man, do I feel like an idiot."

"Easy mistake," the lawman chuckled as he slid back inside.

A set of keys flew out the back door of the car. The dyke snatched them out of the air just like a guy.

"Thanks, sweetie. I'll be right back," she said into the car.

He could feel and hear his heart start to gallop then turn into a drum roll as she walked up the path. A smile crossed her lips as she approached. He hid his face from her and had a flashing thought of pulling out the gun, shooting that smug lesbian face.

He started to breathe again as the car backed out of the driveway, freeing his own. He skidded his foot along the cement as he walked toward her, hoping to push the lock pick into the grass. He didn't dare risk to see if he was successful.

"Hey, that actually sounds pretty good. Let me get my purse and I'll buy it from you."

Think! "That really wouldn't be fair to the people that ordered it, would it?"

They brushed past each other, rubbing elbows. He fought every urge to make a full-out run to his car.

"Spoil sport."

Another thud vibrated the front door.

"I'm coming, Peanut, settle down."

The key slid into the lock and, as nonchalantly as he could, he stepped up his pace. The cool temperature couldn't stop the sweat that rolled down into his shirt. He opened the car door at the same moment she opened the front door. The dog tried to bolt, but she caught him by the collar and they both fell.

Backing out of the driveway, he tried to laugh but his nerves were prickling every pore in his body. Dropping the gear in drive, he managed to give the lawman a half-assed salute while passing him by.

Louise wrestled with Peanut as he struggled beneath her weight trying to get to his feet. He finally squeezed out from under and dashed down the path. Andrew leapt from the car and skillfully grabbed the dog's collar, hoisting him up so the dog was standing on his hind legs like they were dancing in the middle of the street.

"What's wrong with you?" he scolded. The dog settled down. "You okay, sis?"

Karla sprang from the car and ran to Louise. Helping her up, a piece of metal by the step, not much larger than a toothpick, caught her attention.

"What's this?" Karla asked, handing it to Louise.

"Oh shit!" Louise's eyes grew and she boosted herself up using Karla as leverage.

"Meet me on Milestone," she yelled to her brother. Louise tore off around the house.

Andrew shouted to Karla. "Take care of the dog, we'll be back in a minute."

Louise kicked and tripped over the drainpipe jutting out from the gutter. She almost caught her balance, and would have had the grass not been wet. Falling to her knees, she cursed. Another pair of slacks ruined. Just one more thing added onto the payback list when the bastard was caught.

Though no fence separated Miller's back yard from the neighbor behind, a row of lilac bushes did an equally good job. In the summer, the leaves and sweet smell would be intoxicating. Now in the darkness of early spring, they were just invisible sticks scratching her flesh as she ran past.

Running between the houses, Louise dashed all the way to the sidewalk before stopping. Tires squealed as Andrew rounded the corner. Louise stood bent over, panting, her hands on knees. Andrew slowed to a stop, his window down. There were two Camry's parked on the block, neither one the same color as the pizza guy's.

"I let the goddamn son of a bitch walk right by me!" She scanned the addresses across the street and pounded the roof of his car with her fist. "There is no 1427 on this block."

Louise glared at her brother. "I knew something was

off. Pizza smell should've been oozing out of that box. I never smelled a thing. And the way he carried it? I bet you a night with your date there was nothing in that box but air." She looked past her brother at Ahn. The girl's face looked ashen, but exhilarated at the same time. Louise softened.

"First dates are always the best, huh?" she said, her breath wheezing.

Andrew evil-eyed his sister. "Don't go there."

"Give me your cell." All serious again, Louise cut him off with her demand.

Andrew handed her his phone. "Cripes! I had him blocked in and let him go!"

"Okay, we're both morons. Let it go. Do you have Grant's number?"

Andrew thought for a moment. "Yeah, he called me a couple days ago."

"Do I want to know why?" Without waiting for an answer, Louise scrolled through his received calls until she found the detective and pressed send.

"Yeah, it's me. I saw the motherfucker up close. I actually touched him!"

--

Traffic was light as he made his way to the Mall of America. Finding a parking place in the most crowded section of the lot, he wiped the car of prints and rolled up the pizza box, tossing it in the trash. Not too busy a night, he easily made his way down to the light rail with little attention and boarded a train for downtown.

The gentle hum of the wheels on tracks calmed him. Still, his hands jittered. *That was beyond stupid!* He checked his watch and was surprised at how the evening had sped by. Quite a walk from the train, he'd parked his car in the Target store ramp. But that was okay. *Places to go, people to see.*

He closed his eyes, concentrated on his breathing, and thought about the mistakes he'd made. He had been very lucky. As much as he hated that bitch with every molecule in his body, he had to admit to himself that she wasn't stupid. If she hadn't yet, Miller would eventually make the connection.

Usually it's three strikes and you're out, but he'd been granted a reprieve. Miller had seen him with no disguise. He could no longer afford to play games with her. Next time they met would be their last. His face would be the last thing she would ever see.

Chapter 29

With a little bit of charm and the threat of rank, Detective Grant cajoled the sketch artist away from his family to meet with Louise Miller in her home. Grant wanted to be there, but not only wasn't it necessary, he also didn't want to spread around his bad luck. He got nothing but hate from Mrs. Carp. Leo Carp had blown off the interview to allegedly go bowling. Joel Spender couldn't be found, either.

Worse news came just before Miller had called – they were releasing George Jeffers first thing in the morning. Grant knew Jeffers wasn't the one after Miller, but he still had a lot of questions to ask about the Farkos murder. And then there was the whole issue that Miller let a possible murderer walk right on by. Curiosity would gnaw at his gut until he heard the details of that story.

Hoping the day wouldn't be a total waste, he wished his one last interview would pan out. He'd stop off at Miller's afterward. Hell, the way his day had been going, he very well might get stood up again. *If I didn't have bad luck, I'd have no luck at all*; the lyrics from an Albert King tune lingered on his mind. Just maybe with a little good luck, by the time he finished, the sketch artist would be done and the perp's face would be plastered on the police computer. With a little more luck, he'd recognize the son of a bitch.

Grant hated the 494 strip into Bloomington. The traffic was always rush hour heavy. With the frame of mind he was in, when Carp was found, he'd be hauled in for questioning, none of this conveniently in your home bullshit. The more he thought about Carp, Grant wondered if the man might be having an affair. He wondered the same thing about Spender. That got him to thinking that they might be having an affair with each other. He'd seen crazier things in his lifetime.

A sudden chill iced itself around his body. Lovers nothing. What if they were working in tandem? He started forming scenarios in his mind and they all added up. The two could easily frame Jeffers for the murder, or murders. One could be in the ponytail, the other in the ninja costume. One would divert attention away from the other. Genius. But as much as he added it all up, he still couldn't figure as to how all of that tied in with Louise Miller. The conclusion? It didn't matter. He would fill in the holes later.

Grant called in an all-points-bulletin for Leo Carp and Joel Spender. He didn't want them arrested, just located. Probable cause didn't cover hunches and he didn't feel he could legally detain either one. But a new urgency to know where they were overwhelmed him. He picked up his phone to warn Miller of his new suspicions and punched in her number, clearing it before pressing Send. She was already on alert, no point in panicking her. He tried to picture her in a panic, but got no clear vision. Besides, what were the chances? It was just a hunch. Still, if he didn't call, and something were to happen, he doubted he'd be able to live with the consequences of his inaction. This time he completed the connection and got her recorded voice telling him to leave a message.

--

A little out of breath, Leo Carp walked into a small Thai restaurant located on LaSalle Avenue, just a block off and past the end of Nicollet Mall in downtown. Quiet, with low lighting, it provided the perfect atmosphere for privacy. Beverly Wimpole sat alone at the table with an empty glass. "You're late," she said as he walked up.

Before taking off his coat, Leo signaled the waitress and ordered a drink. " Is Joel here yet?"

Beverly asked for another cosmo "Not yet. So what's this all about?"

Leo sat. "We'll wait for Joel. I don't want to explain things twice." Leo couldn't ignore her stare. "Let's just say it's important enough that I blew off a meeting with that detective."

The two waited in silence. The seconds stretched to minutes.

Agitated, Leo took a sip of his vodka and tonic and looked at his watch for the third time in five minutes. Beverly hadn't yet touched her second cosmopolitan, the cranberry color fading to pink as the ice melted.

"Please tell me what's going on." A rare sternness resonated in Beverly's voice.

Leo jerked his head toward the door. "About time."

Joel waved and ambled over. "Sorry, couldn't find a place to park."

Leo couldn't get too upset with that excuse. The restaurant had no parking lot and with all the apartments in the area, street parking was hard to come by.

Joel draped his coat over the back of the chair and sat with his partners. In an instant, a waitress appeared, placing a small napkin in front of him.

"What can I get you?"

"Hmmm, I think I'm in the mood for a tequila sunrise."

The waitress winked and walked off.

"You've got to be kidding. I used to drink those in high school," Leo said.

"What was so damn important that it dragged you away from your bowling night?" Joel asked.

"The lanes are closed, but even if they weren't, this is too important to wait."

"It's about time." Beverly sipped her drink.

Joel noticed the drinks already on the table. "Let me guess. Vodka tonic?"

Leo nodded.

"Well aren't we the international trio; Leo from Russia with his vodka, me, from Mexico with my tequila, and you, Bev, from the Caribbean with triple sec."

"I'm Russian, too," Beverly said. "There's also vodka in cosmopolitans."

"If you don't mind," Leo interrupted, like a parent admonishing his two children. "We've got serious problems here."

The waitress returned and set Joel's drink on the napkin. "Anything else? Any food tonight?"

Leo shook his head. "We're fine, thanks." The dismissal was curt.

When the waitress was out of hearing range Leo leaned in like a conspirator. George and Beverly did the same.

"I called and asked about our partner." Leo spoke barely above a whisper. "They're letting him out tomorrow." He waited for the reaction to sink in.

Beverly appeared to be alarmed than Leo would have expected. Joel seemed clueless.

"It means that it's going to be much harder to force him out if he's walking around free as a bird."

Beverly lifted the straw out of her drink and took a gulp.

"Maybe we shouldn't try forcing him out in the first place." Joel stirred his drink with a straw.

"Your allegiance to him amazes me, Joel. The only thing George Jeffers cares about is George Jeffers. He used you like he used all of us, to get ahead."

Joel waved a finger between Leo and Beverly. "Speaking of allegiances, what about you two? What's going on there?"

"Excuse me?" Beverly stared, wide-eyed.

"What the hell are you talking about?" Leo demanded.

Joel drank from his glass. "There's a rumor around the office that you two are, well, kind of an item."

"That's ridiculous!" Beverly shouted. "He's married, for god sakes!"

The bartender, two waitresses, and the only other occupied table became interested at the outburst.

Leo reined in his ire and spoke as calmly as he could. "It's bullshit! There's absolutely nothing going on between me and Ms. Wimpole. Just who is spreading this vicious piece of fiction?"

Joel looked from Leo to Beverly. Her stare was equally harsh. He gazed down back into his drink. "George mentioned that he saw some papers on Beverly's desk."

"He's feeding you a bunch of crap," Leo snapped. "Let me tell you something about your friend."

"He tried to rape me."

Leo stopped in mid-sentence. Beverly's eyes were brimming with tears and she looked straight at Joel. Leo tried to speak, but the words caught in his throat.

"What the hell. When?" Joel asked the question that

Leo couldn't.

Beverly dabbed at her eyes with a napkin and took a sip of her drink. The two men waited patiently. "That day he took me to lunch. He said he asked you two, but you didn't want to go."

Leo and Joel couldn't speak. Leo gave a slight shake of his head and Joel shrugged. Finally, "What are you talking about?" Leo asked. "When?"

"It was right after the will reading. He said you didn't think it was proper."

"That never happened," Joel told her. "Asking us to lunch, I mean."

"I figured as much later." Beverly sniffed and blew her nose into the napkin, then downed the rest of her drink. Picking at her napkin, Beverly's voice shook. "He said he had to pick up some files from his house. We got inside and he was all over me."

The waitress came over and picked up the empty glass. "Can I get you another one?"

Beverly nodded. With the waitress gone, Joel placed his hand on Beverly's wrist. "He didn't succeed, did he?"

She shook her head. "I locked myself in the bathroom. He finally came to his senses. Said it would be beneficial for both of us to forget 'the incident' ever happened."

"That son of a bitch." Joel whispered.

Beverly took a deep breath. "I was hoping I'd never have to lay eyes on that man again."

The waitress placed a fresh napkin on the table, a new cosmopolitan on top and made a quick exit.

Showing concern on the outside, Leo couldn't help but smile on the inside. With all three of them united, and the new Farkos on their side, George Jeffers would be out.

"What about testifying against him?" Leo asked.

"What do you mean?" Alarm shook Beverly's voice.

"If they don't throw him in prison for murder, maybe you can put him away for assault and attempted rape."

She shook her head emphatically. "No. No. I couldn't do that."

"Why not?" Leo asked. "You could make sure you'd

never have to see him again."

"I think she's gone through enough already." Joel squeezed Beverly's arm.

Surprised, Leo had never seen Joel's eyes hold such sympathy. Beverly gazed at Joel like a damsel who had just found her white knight.

The sympathy vanished as Joel spoke. "You can see how painful it is for her to tell us. Can you imagine what a lawyer would put her through?"

Leo held up his hands in surrender. "You're right. I'm sorry. It would never hold up anyway. I guess I just want to see Jeffers suffer." His voice became tender as he took Beverly's other hand. "We'll make sure you never have to cross paths with him again."

"How do we do that?" Beverly asked.

Leo liked the way she used the word we.

"Leo and I will talk to him. I'm guessing that most of his clients watch the news. And most of them are going to be calling us in the morning wanting a new investor. With few clients bringing in little money, I think we'll be able to buy him out cheap, and without a lot of trouble."

For the first time in years, Leo admired his friend. This was the Joel Spender he knew before George Jeffers had made him into a sniveling toady.

With the rape attempt on Wimpole, Jeffers had unwittingly released the hold on his only ally. In an instant, Joel reverted back to his old, confident, take-no-prisoners self. In the big picture, Leo thought the attack had probably been the best thing that could've happened to everyone seated at the table.

"What if he won't sell?" Beverly asked.

Joel got a gleam in his eye. "Then we get nasty."

"I think after we talk to him, he'll be ready to resign." Leo raised his glass. "To Spender, Carp and Wimpole."

The three clinked glasses and the atmosphere around the table became noticeably lighter. A woman at the other table, earlier so engrossed in their conversation, glanced over a couple of times but quickly lost interest.

With two cocktails inside her, Beverly became

chatty. She shared bits and pieces of her life, the majority of the conversation directed at Joel. Leo wondered if the two might be sharing a house tonight, and if so, whose.

Beverly looked at her watch. "It's getting late."

Joel downed the rest of his tequila. "Are you okay to drive?"

"I'm fine."

"Well at least let me walk you to your car."

Beverly slid back her chair and stood up. Joel got up and helped her with her coat.

"It's so nice to know chivalry still exists," she said.

"One little seed I want to plant before we part." Leo held up his hand and motioned them to sit. "It will only take a minute."

Uncertain, Beverly and Joel sat.

"About our new boss," Leo said. "I've been trying to figure him out and I don't have a clue."

"Who," Joel asked. "Walter Jr.? He seems nice enough. Smart as a tack."

Beverly snickered. "Sharp as a tack, silly."

"I'm sure we can mold him. He'll be fine," Joel added, and stood back up. Beverly followed his lead.

"I hope you're right. All I'm saying is we need to keep a very close eye on him is all."

Joel waved goodbye. "Say hi to Charlotte and give her a kiss for me."

Joel put an arm around Beverly and they walked together out the door.

Chapter 30

Grant turned into the parking lot of the Hotel Sofitel. Considering she would be left with practically nothing, Muriel Farkos seemed to be doing pretty well for herself staying at a place like this – at least for now.

The Hotel Sofitel. Now he remembered why it kept gnawing at him. During Wimpole's interview she mentioned that's where Jeffers was going to take her for lunch. It made him wonder if Jeffers and Muriel Farkos might have rendezvoused here before. That might make for an interesting discussion. He also wondered if anybody in the family would have anything left after the attorneys got their cut. This was brewing to be one hell of a fight over one hell of an estate.

With only four customers in the bar, Muriel Farkos was easy to spot. Alone at a table, she watched a news report from a silent TV. Wearing a black dress with a slit up the side, Muriel sat with her legs crossed, exposing a lot of thigh. She had gotten a perm since he last saw her and wore the make-up a little heavy. But beneath the call girl exterior he could still see the grieving widow, although no doubt grieving more for herself than her husband.

The bartender walked over and placed a tall glass in front of her, taking away an empty one. Grant recognized the Long Island iced tea. *Shit!* Even if she only had one previously, this would be a difficult interview. He hated interviewing drunks. They seemed to talk a lot without ever really saying much. And the few times they did say something relevant, it took too much brain power to sort it through all the crap. *If I didn't have bad luck I'd have no luck at all.* The song still echoed in his mind. *Well, at least she's here.*

Muriel questioned the bartender. He pointed to a gentleman sitting at the far end of the bar. The man winked and raised his glass to her. She signaled permission for him to join her.

Before the man made it halfway across the room, Grant took a seat across from Muriel. Her eyes were red and glazed.

"I know you," she said.

"Detective Grant. I spoke to you on the phone earlier, said I had some questions? You told me to meet you here."

"But we've met before," she insisted.

"At your husband's lawyer's office. I need to ask you a few questions about Walter."

The man stood over Grant and cleared his throat. Tall, lean, young, and drunk, he bobbed on the balls of his feet ready and wanting to kick some ass.

"I believe she's my woman."

"Got a receipt?"

The man jabbed his fingers in Grant's shoulder. "You think you're funny?"

Grant kept his eyes on Muriel. "I thought that was a pretty good one, yeah."

"Why don't we take it outside and you can laugh about it all the way to the hospital." He winked at Muriel. "Just to let you know, I have a black belt in Tae Kwon Do. I'll give you one last chance to walk away."

"Very impressive. But I'm still betting I'd win." Grant shifted his attention to the young man. He opened his coat and showed his badge, making sure the guy saw the butt of his .45 resting in the shoulder holster.

The man's face instantly sobered. Grant wasn't sure if the guy even saw the badge.

"Now how about I give *you* one last chance to walk away?" Grant said.

The man stepped back, bumping into another table. Almost tripping over a chair, he fled the bar.

Grant smirked. "Amazing what the sight of a gun and badge does to a person." He couldn't read her face. She reminded him a little bit of Mona Lisa. "Sorry about that."

"He was too young for me anyway." She gave a half-shrug and held up her glass. "Got a free drink out of it."

"Do you know why anyone wanted your husband dead?"

"All business. I respect that." She took a large gulp and let the alcohol slide down her throat. "These taste just like iced tea."

Muriel handed the glass over to him. Grant shook his head. "Please. If you could just answer my questions."

"You guys already asked me this." She took back her glass and had another sip.

"I know," he said sympathetically. "But that was before I was assigned. Please humor me." He'd pretty much memorized her statement and wanted to see if she had anything new or different to add.

"Well, I'm sure he was sleeping with a half-dozen sluts. Maybe a jealous husband found out?"

In her original statement she could think of no one.

"Where were you the night he was killed?"

Muriel peered into his eyes daring him to challenge. "I was in the Hamptons with my girlfriends."

That was the same answer she used in her original statement, but with a little investigation, her girlfriends turned out to be one Dr. Milton Hammond. Grant thought about pressing, but decided he'd rather have her talking friendly for now. They could always revisit her answer later.

"What about your husband's work associates?"

Muriel shook her head. "He never talked to me about work. He knew it bored me to tears."

"What about his co-workers – he ever talk about them?"

Muriel shook her head. "We saw his partners occasionally, but not for a long time."

"You don't know if any of the partners might want him out of the way? Maybe Jeffers?"

A nostalgic look shone on Muriel's face. "Poor George."

The fuse of Grant's temper was burning down. He resisted the urge to ask if she'd ever met him here before. "Even if he killed your husband?"

Reminiscence transformed into anger. "Especially if he killed my husband." Her voice sounded terrifyingly sober.

"Is there something you want to tell me about you and George Jeffers?'"

Her features softened as she smiled and reached across the table, taking Grant's hand. "Let's talk about something else. I don't know anything about you, detective."

Blood rushed to Grant's face. Muriel Farkos did something that no one had been able to do for more years than Gordon Grant could remember – she embarrassed him. He jerked his hand out of her grasp and as a diversion grabbed his notepad. The temperature suddenly felt twenty degrees warmer. The bartender turned his attention to the TV. A glance around the bar, he noticed everyone else had gone.

Sweat formed on his brow, and Grant cleared his throat. "What about your kids?" *Dammit!* She had thrown him off his game plan. He hadn't finished talking about the business partners yet. He needed to get back to Carp and Spender. One or both could be headed to Miller's while he was wasting precious minutes. But at the same time, she seemed more relaxed. He'd spend a couple minutes on the kids, then weave the conversation back to the partners. Hopefully, once she gushed about her offspring, she'd still be talkative regarding Carp and Spender.

"I'm very proud of them." Delight shone on Muriel's face.

"What about Elissa? She's not yours, is she?"

Muriel put a finger over the opening of the straw. She removed it from her glass and stuck the other end in her mouth, sucking the liquid.

"Do you know of any reason she'd want to harm Walter?"

Muriel chuckled and put the straw back in her drink. "That little tree hugging bitch? Ha, if she had killed him, she would've used his body as mulch. Good for the environment."

Grant tried to picture the image, and then thought it best not to. "What about the twins? What about Walter Jr.?"

Muriel shook her head. "He's a good boy. Besides, I don't think he cared about his father enough to kill him. They hardly knew each other, let alone ever saw each other. Walter Jr. wanted to live life on his own terms. Made it clear he never wanted his daddy's money. I think that's why my husband got so fed up with him. His only son was the one person in the world he couldn't buy."

"What about Jessica?"

"She was in school out east."

"Could she have hired someone?"

A mischievous smirk spread across Muriel's face. "Let me ask you something, Mr. policeman detective. If someone were paying for your education at Yale Law School, plus sending you a monthly check for room and board and other incidentals, would you want to kill him?"

Grant smiled and shook his head. "No, ma'am, I guess I wouldn't."

"No, you wouldn't." Muriel craned her neck around toward the bartender. "Jerry, my friend here doesn't have anything to drink."

"What can I get you, sir?"

Grant became uncomfortable once again. "I'm fine, thanks."

"He's on duty. Bring him a Shirley Temple."

Grant sighed. "A club soda with a twist of lime."

Muriel again placed her hand on his arm. This time Grant gently lifted it off and placed it on the table. The expression on her face didn't change.

He tried to focus back onto the interview. "Did you and your husband ever do anything socially with the Carps and/or with Joel Spender?"

"It's a shame though," she said.

The bartender placed the club soda on the table. Grant reached for his wallet.

"Put it on my tab," Muriel said.

"I can't allow that, Mrs. Farkos." Before Grant could explain about proper police etiquette, the bartender told them it was on the house. That, he'd accept.

"What's a shame?" Grant watched Jerry amble back behind the bar and play with the remote until the TV stopped on a rerun of Cheers.

"About Walter and his father."

Damn! Grant had hoped to get her back to talking about the partners again. He feared the alcohol might become the dominant factor in her conversation and needed her to concentrate on his questions.

"What about Walter and his father?" He tried to formulate a way to weave the interview to where he wanted it to go.

“One of the last conversations I ever had with Walter, I told him he needed to be a father to Walter Jr., that his son deserved that. It was one of our more genital conversations.”

“You mean genteel?”

“What did I say?”

Grant shook his head. “Doesn’t matter. So he needed to be more of a father.”

Embarrassment washed over Muriel’s face. “Oh my God. Did I say what I think I said?” Talk about your Freudian slip.” She laughed and took another long pull from her straw.

“Please. What were you saying about your husband needing to be more of a father?” Grant rubbed his eyes. He figured he’d tapped Mrs. Farkos of all the useful information he’d get. He didn’t like the way she was making eyes at him, either.

“Oh, hardly worth mentioning.” Muriel broke her gaze and stared into her glass, her faux pas already forgotten. “Walter did make an effort. And even more amazing, Walter Jr. seemed to crave the attention. I thought they were actually going to become friends. They were getting along great. Then poof, it was over.” Her demeanor changed from seductress to hurt mother. “Walter buried himself in his work again, totally ignoring his son.”

“Why do you think that was?” Grant was just being polite. In a moment he’d thank her for her time and head out.

“My husband was never the same after that DWI.” Muriel glared. “Do cops usually point their guns at a guy’s head just for driving drunk? That really scarred my husband. He never got over it. Good God, out of nowhere, he’d start ranting about police brutality. If I tried to say anything –” She lowered her voice trying to sound like Walter. “When a gun is pointed at your head, then I’ll listen.”

Grant tried to keep in check, but his heart pounded. With every ounce of concentration, he kept his voice calm and steady. “How did your son react to that?”

Muriel gave a slight shrug. “He was very upset and let down at first. You would be too if your father became a part of your life for the first time, and then suddenly stopped.

But you know kids. He got over it. Things just went back to the way they always were between them."

"Is that right?" Grant pushed back his chair and stood up from the table. "Thank you for your time, Mrs. Farkos." He quickly exited the bar.

"We haven't even started talking about you yet."

Grant had a new theory, one that didn't involve either Carp or Spender. He opened his cell and called Louise's number. Again, he got a recorded voice. Before he left a message about another hunch, he wanted to check something out first.

Inside the car, Grant logged onto the computer. He punched in the codes and cursed at how long it took to develop an image. Finally, his bad luck had found a sliver of good. The sketch artist had completed his job.

Chapter 31

The vibration next to Walter's crotch aroused him. He let it buzz a couple of times before he reached in his pocket for his cell phone. Looking at the caller ID, Walter grimaced. With no desire to talk to his mother, he motioned the waitress to bring him another Scotch on the rocks. There was also a message from his sister. He punched in the code.

Hey baby brother, I just wanted to say thanks for the sweater. That was so sweet. How did you know I love cashmere? And I must say, I look pretty in pink – get it? But what's up with the sleeves? Were you having a tug-of-war? Let me guess. It was the last one and you and some woman were fighting over it. Well, I'm glad you won because I love it. Thanks again. Call me.

Just as he was about to put the phone back in his pocket, it vibrated again. This time he had a new voice mail from Muriel. Walter debated whether he should bother wasting his time. The waitress came over and set his drink on the table. With a fresh scotch in front of him, he decided to risk it.

Hi Walter, honey. She sounded drunk. *I just had the most interesting conversation with that Detective Grant.* Walter held the phone closer to his ear. He wanted to yell at the entire bar to shut the hell up. This was important. Instead, he put his hand over his free ear. *He seemed most interested in your relationship with your father. He wanted to know all about you. I told him there was no way in the world you could possibly have anything to do with...*

Walter absently folded the phone, set it on the table, and stared straight ahead looking at nothing. That son of a bitch figured it out. If the detective knew, Miller knew. Or she would shortly. "Oh shit!" If he was ever getting another shot at her, it had to be tonight. It had to be now. Then he had to get the hell out of Minneapolis. He closed his eyes hoping a plan would formulate in his head. For incentive, he shot back the whisky. While sucking on an ice cube it came to him.

Halfway into calling Miller's number, he stopped. If she didn't know who he was yet, why push it? He signaled the waitress.

"Get you another one, hon?"

Walter gave a contrite smile. "Actually, I was wondering if you would do me a big favor?" He twirled his phone on the table. "My date never showed up and my battery is dead. I was wondering if you'd be so kind as to let me borrow your phone just so I can call and make sure she's all right?"

The girl fidgeted. Walter plucked a fifty-dollar bill out of his pocket and laid it on the table.

"I promise it will only take a second. You can even stand here while I make it."

A grin creased her face. "It's in my purse. Don't go anywhere."

Walter leaned back and closed his eyes. In his head he recited Louise Miller's phone number, a number he'd etched into his memory.

"Ahem."

He snapped back to attention. Another cell phone sat next to his in place of the money.

"I'm just going to deliver these drinks. I'll be right back." The girl left with a full tray and a fifty-dollar bill.

Walter leered as she wiggled her ass, walking off to deliver drinks. She glanced back at him with a wink and a smile. Walter returned a half-wave. While she tended to her customers he snatched the cell and punched in Miller's number. After four rings the answering machine kicked in.

He spoke soft and menacingly. "I think it's finally time we meet face-to-face. No more pretenses. Be at the casino at midnight. And come alone – or else." He turned off the phone, sat back and laughed. Miller would have a field day with that. By the time the cops found and interviewed the waitress, Miller would be dead, and he'd be on his way to a country that didn't have reciprocity with the United States. He had enough money saved to leave his life and Minnesota behind. More than enough coming that he'd never have to work again. He trusted his sister to take care of arrangements in his absence.

"Is your friend okay?" The waitress bent over and reached across the table, taking back her phone. She also gave Walter a view of ample cleavage.

"She's just fine," he said, taking advantage of her generosity.

"Get you another one while you're waiting?"

Walter removed a twenty from a wad of bills out of his wallet and slapped it on the table. "Places to go, people to see, things to do." He shoved his phone back into his pocket and grabbed his coat.

"Hey, if you want, I get off work at one-thirty. Maybe we can get coffee or something? My name's Brenda."

Walter walked out of the bar.

--

Louise checked the caller ID on her answering machine and shrugged. "Do you know a Brenda Wilkens?"

Karla shook her head. Louise ignored the ringing phone and returned her attention to Andrew's date. "Tell us more about growing up in China."

Ahn Kim squirmed uncomfortably at being the center of attention, but Louise didn't care. Andrew sat protectively close to Ahn ready to deflect questions if they got too personal. He gave Louise an evil eye, the second one of the night, warning her to stay away from the sex life.

Before Ahn could open her mouth the answering machine beeped and they heard *his* voice on the speaker: "I think it's finally time we meet face-to-face. No more pretenses. Be at the casino at midnight. And come alone – or else."

No one spoke. Louise couldn't take her eyes off the phone until Andrew placed a hand on her shoulder. That broke her trance. She hadn't even realized he'd gotten up. With no warning, a laugh that she couldn't contain tumbled from her throat. Three sets of eyes stared at her like she'd gone crazy.

"Or else what? He's going to kill me?" None of them cracked a smile. "Work with me, people. He's going to try to kill me anyway. What the hell difference is it going to make if I come alone?"

"It's not funny," Karla said.

Andrew agreed. "Not funny, sis. Was that the pizza guy?"

"I'd swear to it."

"Call Grant?"

The phone rang. Louise glanced at the ID and picked up. "Speak of the devil. I was just going to call you." Her eyes hardened. "No shit! That son of a bitch."

The three stood, frozen like statues.

"He just called – told me to meet him at the casino at midnight. And to come alone, or else. How damn dramatic is that?"

With a couple of mm-hmms and a few head nods, Louise hung up.

"Well?" There was an edge in Andrew's voice.

"Walter Farkos' kid. Some crazy-ass bullshit about me busting his old man."

"Did they pick him up?"

Louise shook her head. "APB. I'm going to the casino to meet him."

"Let's go." Andrew grabbed his jacket.

"Alone." Louise walked over behind Karla and massaged her shoulders, then spoke at her brother. "I'll be fine. Grant doesn't want you to go. Walter Farkos knows you. Grant's going to send half the goddamn force to cover the area. Along with the casino's security, Jr. won't get within one hundred yards of me."

Andrew punched his fist in his hand. "I still want to go. Maybe follow you in from a safe distance.

The smacking sound brought Peanut out of the kitchen. Karla made a kissing sound and the dog trotted over. He assumed the position and Karla scratched his haunches.

Louise locked her eyes on her brother. "I want you here, protecting the home front. Just in case."

She waited for her partner to protest that she didn't need a babysitter, but Karla didn't say a word. Ahn Kim fidgeted on the couch. Louise noticed her distress.

"There's time. If you want, Andrew can take you home."

Ahn shook her head. "No way. I haven't had this much excitement in, well…ever."

Louise winked at her brother. "I like her." She glanced at her watch, then at the three faces. Peanut's face was buried in Karla's side. "In that case, how about a game of Pictionary before I go?" She hoped they hadn't noticed the quiver in her voice.

Chapter 32

Walter let the cool night air wash over him as he strolled down a mostly deserted Nicollet Mall. The cops were probably trying to locate him by now, and no doubt keeping an eye out for his car. One last stolen vehicle and he'd call it a career. He strolled into the parking lot, nonchalantly took the elevator to the sixth floor, and went to his car. In the glove compartment he took out an extra clip for his gun and thought about the pain it would inflict. Best to be prepared. He patted the hood of the car like an obedient pet and went in search of something easy to steal.

--

Grant got off the phone with the casino security. They were going to coordinate with the Hiawatha Police Department. He also called a dozen Minneapolis cops, ones he hoped didn't have a grudge against Miller, and filled them in. They all agreed that tonight was a perfect night to get out and play some cards. As much as he wanted to go, Grant wouldn't risk showing up at the casino. Walter, Jr. knew his face. Instead, he headed off to Miller's place. Maybe he'd catch her before she left and he could go over last minute instructions – not like she'd ever listen.

--

Louise went over to the hall closet and standing on the tips of her toes, reached behind the towels for her Beretta. "Shit." *That's right.* She'd had it out and now couldn't find it. Last she'd seen the gun, it was sitting on the table next to the couch. *What the hell did I do with it?*

Casually walking back into the living room, Louise stood over her partner.

"Really, I'll be fine." She leaned down and pressed her lips against Karla's mouth, harder than a normal good-bye kiss. She pulled back a couple of inches and mouthed the words, "I'll be fine." Karla brushed Louise's cheek with her finger.

Louise went to the side of the chair and bent down, playfully tugging Peanut's ears while giving him a kiss on top of his head. "You take good care of everybody."

Andrew followed her into the kitchen. Opening the door to the garage, she stopped and gave Andrew an uncharacteristic hug and then the two shared an unspoken message with their eyes. She smiled evilly and called over to Ahn. "If you two hit it off, we'll do lunch and I'll tell you all the embarrassing things about my brother."

Andrew punched her in the arm, a little harder than she deemed necessary. Nerves. She didn't retaliate.

--

Walter stood huddled across the street, hidden in the shadows next to the Harper house. At eleven-thirty, Miller's garage door inched up. A moment later the brother appeared. Finally he was leaving. *Stupid shits!*

The brother's car rolled out of the driveway, Miller followed suit in her Saturn. Of course she wouldn't go to the casino alone. Deputy brother would follow. Perfect. That left the dog and the dyke lover alone.

Walter's jaw dropped. He couldn't believe the sudden gift of good fortune the gods smiled down upon him. *How could the bitch be so stupid as to forget to close the garage door?* In a flash, the gods' generosity turned. The brother parked at the curb and got out of his car. He walked back into the garage and as he entered the house the garage door closed.

"What the fuck?"

Stomping back to his new found car, Walter fumed. The gay bitch didn't trust him. He regrettably admitted she was smart, but he didn't expect *her* to have a Plan B. Although unexpected, not unplanned for – Walter had his own Plan B. Unfortunately, it involved patience, something Walter felt a shortage of at the moment.

He got into his car and parked a few doors from Miller's house, hidden as best he could in the shadows between trees and streetlights. No way would he be freezing his ass standing between houses. He settled in for the long wait. When the bitch got home, the brother would leave. Then Walter would break in and kill them. Regrettably, he wouldn't have the pleasure of seeing the dyke's face as she discovered her dog and lover's body. But now time was as much an enemy as Miller.

Another idea, a Plan C, popped into Walter's head as he fruitlessly tried to see through the blinds covering Miller's front window. How fun it would be for her to come home and find her lover and her brother both naked in bed – dead, of course. The risk factor shot way up, but so did the entertainment factor.

While contemplating the pros and cons of Plan C, headlights pointed at him. Walter ducked beneath the windshield as the car approached. The headlights passed as the car turned into Miller's driveway. Walter sat up.

"She leaves and they're having a goddamn party?"

The police detective got out of the car and walked to the front door.

"Shit!" As much fun as it would be for her to find that threesome naked in her bed, the risk now far outweighed the entertainment. Walter settled back into Plan B.

Not more than two minutes passed when the front door opened. The brother and some Asian chick walked out.

"Jesus Christ," he whispered. He'd forgotten all about her. That could've been a very costly mistake. Maybe the gods were smiling down upon him. He went back to thinking about Plan C. The plan remained the same; just one of the characters would be different.

The two lawmen chatted while the girl waited patiently. Even from a distance Walter could see her shivering. "You keep her waiting much longer, you ain't going to be getting any tonight, cowboy."

The brother pointed to the detective's car, then the two shook hands. He put his arm around the woman's shoulders as they walked to his car. She leaned into him. He opened the passenger door. Before he could close it her arms reached out and lured him down. A couple seconds later he came back up wearing the stupidest face Walter had ever seen.

"I guess you are going to get lucky tonight." Walter thought about his original Plan C, seeing the brother's naked dead body in Miller's bed. "You're lucky in more ways than you'll ever know, cowboy."

As Mr. Lucky drove away, Walter's heart lurched. Nothing he'd done could deserve this good fortune. The detective was pulling his car out of the driveway too. Plan A took form once again.

The euphoria only lasted a moment as the detective's car took the place of the brother's. "Duh!" They were just keeping the driveway open so Miller could drive back into the garage. *Back to Plan B.*

--

As Louise neared the giant parking lot her nerves ignited. Unless the psycho had a death wish, he'd probably make a play between the car and the front door. She could only hope that the Hiawatha cops and casino security knew their jobs. If not, she swore she'd come back as a ghost and haunt Sergeant Crabtree.

The lot was well lit as Louise cruised down the aisles, scrutinizing for any movement inside of cars. In the third row she found a spot and parked. She used her cell and called Grant.

"I'm here. Nothing yet." She disconnected.

Keeping low she got out of the car. The door to the casino stood about fifty yards away. With a fast gait, Louise zigged and zagged toward the entrance. She might look spastic, but she was damned if she'd give the kid an easy shot.

Out of breath and with only a few odd stares, she made it to the front door. Inside, warmth wrapped up her like a blanket. The tables were busy but not crowded. If she had the urge, she wouldn't have to wait for a chair. Then the thought slapped her. When they caught the asshole, who could blame her for playing a few hands? *Just an hour or so to unwind*. She realized how stupid that sounded – even to her. Maybe that meant she was making progress.

Louise scanned the room for anyone resembling the pizza delivery guy, and also searching for blond beards and ponytails. A number of players scattered about seemed to be more interested in their surroundings than in the cards. A couple of them gave her a quick glance before turning back to their hands. She recognized one of the off duty cops.

After her second pass around the tables, Louise wandered toward the bar. Bargirls in fishnet stockings and black dresses hemmed at mid-thigh made for a pleasant distraction. Taking in the sights, Louise heard one of the girls complain to the bartender. "Lana better get here soon. I should've gotten off at midnight and it's almost twelve-thirty."

Stunned at the passage of time, Louise confirmed it on her own watch. Panic stabbed at her as she snatched the phone from her purse. Convinced this had been a ruse, she called Karla. Relief when her partner answered. Karla sounded equally relieved. After convincing each other that everything was fine, Karla said, "Grant wants to talk to you."

"Anything?" he asked.

"I'm beginning to think he's just jerking us around. Maybe this was a diversion so less people would be searching for him while he ran."

After the obligatory lecture of how many resources and how much taxpayer money was wasted on her tonight, Grant told her to come home.

"Are you serious? You're putting all this on me?"

For the first time in her life, she heard Gordon Grant laugh. He hung up on her – another first.

Almost one o'clock. It wouldn't be long now. Adrenalin coursed through Walter's body. As if on cue, headlights turned down Newberry. Walter ducked below the steering wheel as garage door went up and the Saturn pulled in. When the door was safely down, he exited the car and hid behind a boulevard tree, pulling his gun.

The front door opened and the cop said his good-byes. Walter's ears filled with white noise as the detective reached his car and unlocked the front door. Like an eagle swooping silently toward its prey, Walter charged.

The man never even turned around before the butt of Walter's Colt smashed into his skull. The cop went down with hardly a grunt. Walter fell on top of him striking repeatedly until blood splashed into his eyes.

Stripping the detective of his coat, Walter threw him in the front seat and quietly closed the door. He snuck around to the back of Miller's house, scratched on the door and ran around to the side peeking around the corner. A moment later the door opened.

"Take it easy, fella. What's wrong with you? You were just out a little while ago." Miller's lover hooked the dog to the cable and shut the door.

Putting on the detective's coat and turning up the collar, Walter jogged to the front door. He knocked then turned his back. Miller opened the door. "What did you forget?"

The door flew open and Louise was flung against the wall, banging her head and cracking a hole in the sheetrock. Her legs gave out and she went down. A hand grabbed her arm and yanked her to her feet, flinging her into the living room. Louise tripped over the corner of the coffee table and onto the floor. In an instant the man was on top of her, his knees pinning her shoulders. The muzzle of the gun pressed against her forehead.

Speckled red, Walter Farkos Jr. sat on top of her. The coat was soaked in blood. Louise let out a whimper as it dawned upon her whose it was. Insanity flashed in the young man's eyes as they darted around the room.

"Get out here this second or I shoot the bitch NOW! You got 'til the count of two. One!"

"Wait!" Karla appeared in the kitchen doorway, a hand behind her back.

"Get over here, dyke. What are you hiding?"

"Nothing." Her voice cracked, but Karla held her hands in the air like a gun was pointed at her.

"Sit down over there." He cocked his head toward the couch.

Karla obeyed, sitting at the far end.

Even with his weight on her chest, Louise could breathe again when he lifted the muzzle off her forehead. The back of his hand crashed across her face, blinding her for a moment. She heard Karla yelp, then a crash at the back door. Her vision came back to see Peanut standing on hind legs, his body pressed against the window trying to paw and bite his way in.

Farkos aimed the gun toward the dog but Louise squirmed, freeing her arm and grabbing his before he shot. It earned her a fist to the jaw.

"Don't move!"

Louise couldn't if she wanted to. Through blurred vision she saw the gun pointed at Karla.

"Why?" Louise tasted blood.

Air rushed into her lungs as the weight lifted off of her chest. Walter grabbed a handful of her hair and twisted. Together they got to their feet. He threw her to the couch.

Lighting coursed through her knee as it connected the corner of the coffee table. She tripped and fell back into the sofa. A new pain stabbed at her tailbone. Her .45 had somehow slid under the cushion behind her. With all the blood on her face she easily hid the smile.

"You have the gall to ask me why?" The gun shook in Walter's hand as he became more riled.

He picked an ashtray off the table and hurled it. Louise ducked and felt the breeze as it sailed past her face.

"Because I finally had a father until you came along and pointed a gun at his head." He stormed over and jammed his gun in Louise's cheek. "How does it feel?" He pressed and twisted hard enough to break the skin. A new trickle of blood flowed down onto her neck.

"Or this?" He slapped Louise with the side of the gun. With one knee on the couch, he stood between Louise and Karla. He pointed the gun at Karla's temple. "How do you like it when it's pointed at someone you love? Does it feel good?" His voice verged on hysterics.

Even though she saw double, Louise noticed a flash of steel protruding from Karla's sleeve. She shook her head hoping Karla would get the signal not to try anything stupid. That was her job as she tried to inch the Beretta into her hand.

"What does this have to do with me pointing a gun at your father?" The words bubbled out of her mouth along with the blood.

Walter glared, his eyes growing wilder. "He said he was going to leave me the company. He was becoming a real father! Then after you came along he went back to threatening me out of the will, telling me I was worthless. I had to get the newest copy of the will before he handed it over to his lawyer." Tears flowed down his face. "It was just a bluff. He was always going to leave me the company. He just wanted me to shape up." Walter released a grieving wail that echoed in Louise's head. "He never knew it was me. The bastard didn't even recognize his own son!" He sniffed back his snot. "I didn't mean to kill him."

Half the blade was out of Karla's sleeve when Walter saw the glint of metal.

"NO!" Louise shouted as she brought her gun up from behind the cushion.

Gaping at Louise, and in a panic, Walter pulled the trigger as he drew the gun away from Karla's head, switching his aim to Louise. The bullet grazed Karla's cheek.

Although the bones had healed enough to take the cast off, Louise had trouble getting her finger around the trigger. A throbbing head and double vision made it worse. As she struggled, Walter had the gun pointed at her face. Through Louise's eyes it seemed as if his gun just disappeared. Now you see it, now you don't. But she heard it bounce off the table and onto the floor. Blood shot from his wrist as Karla dug the knife into his flesh. He screamed while Louise concentrated on getting her finger around the trigger. When she tried to aim, Walter and Karla struggled for control of the knife. Louise didn't dare shoot.

Walter wrestled the knife away and grabbed Karla's hair, holding the blade at her throat, using her body as a shield. Blood streaked down from her cheek. He dragged her through the kitchen toward the back door.

"Drop the gun or I'll kill her."

"Drop the knife or I'll kill you."

Louise and Karla locked eyes. Louise gave a barely perceptible nod and Karla pushed Walter's arm and dropped. Louise squeezed the trigger.

The window to Walter's right shattered. Louise tried to adjust her aim and saw Peanut still on his hind legs. Walter flung open the back door sending the rottweiler tumbling down the three stairs to the lawn. In one easy leap he cleared the dog. Louise tried to clear Karla just as Karla sat up. She tripped over her partner, landing on her stomach.

The rottweiler scrambled to his feet and gave chase.

"Peanut, come!" The dog not only blocked her shot, but he'd snap his neck when the cable ran out.

The dog gained ground but Walter made it past the cable's reach. From her stomach, Louise got ready to scream again, but the screws connecting the cable to the house shot out from the wall. The dog leapt past where Walter thought he was safe. The scream reminded Louise of the time she saw an owl stick its talons in a rabbit and carry it off. She had never known rabbits could shriek until that moment.

Louise raised herself to her feet and stood in the doorway. Through the blackness, she made out flailing as the dog reverted to its primal self. Even though the dog couldn't bark, the sounds coming from his throat made her shiver.

Karla raced past her, frantic. "He's going to kill him!" She yanked the cable trying to pull the rottweiler.

Louise jerked the cable out of Karla's hands and let it drop to the ground. "Get back in the house. I'll handle this." Her voice sounded all cop, totally taking control of the situation.

Lights from neighboring houses came on as Walter's screams faded to moans, then to silence. Louise limped across the yard. Peanut ceased his attack as Louise approached. Walter's eyes were wide open and staring at the starless sky as he gasped for air. Blood poured from his mouth and a gash in his neck. A death rattle gurgled in his chest.

Louise patted Peanut on the head.

Chapter 33

Karla sat in the atrium of the Hennepin County Government Center. She shared the same section as the people waiting for their numbers to be called to get or renew licenses. Since the last time she'd been there, the County shelled out some taxpayer money for a few TV monitors.

The most popular one showed an episode of SpongeBob SquarePants. Karla had to laugh. There were far too many adults watching that screen to compensate for the number of children around them. She had the CNN section mostly to herself.

Minneapolis had made it big on the national news scene. Detective Gordon Grant solved the case of a double murder and arson. Though his heroics were almost fatal, he also prevented the murder of two others. While Detective Grant risked his own life, the intended victim's dog attacked and killed the suspect.

When interviewed by police, Karla claimed to have been in the house the entire time. She had no desire to hear Louise's skewed story, tying Grant in the street out front with Peanut on the other side of the house. But however she did it, Grant became a hero. Karla had no argument with that. She did, however, have issues with her partner. The callousness she showed Walter, even though he deserved it, scared the hell out of her.

How warped am I? Karla would've had no problem stabbing him to death, even less of a problem had Louise shot him. But letting the dog kill him? Why was that so different? Then she remembered Louise's face as she watched – total indifference. They hadn't seen each other since. She asked Louise to stay with Andrew. Karla needed to sort things out. Louise reluctantly agreed. Now they were going to meet and Karla wanted her back but still had no idea what to say. Hell, she didn't even know if Louise would still want to come home. Maybe she'd gotten fed up herself.

CNN ran a related story in business news: The company of Farkos Jeffers Spender and Carp has brought a lawsuit against former partner George Jeffers. Since the murder of Walter Farkos by his son, and his son's death,

George Jeffers quit the company and started his own, taking many of company's clients with him.

--

A warm sixty-degree breeze greeted Louise and Kate Hanson as they walked out of the Hennepin County Medical Center. The sun actually felt good on Louise's skin. Neither one had said a word since leaving the detective's room.

"My car is right over here. Need a ride?"

Louise shook her head. "Karla's waiting for me at the Government Center. We've got a meeting with the DA."

"I can give you a ride there."

"The walk will do me good."

Hanson nodded. "See you on Monday?"

Louise pointed to her own head and grinned. "When the doc gives me the okay. Concussions can take a while." She planned to milk it for as long as she could.

Detective Hanson returned a malicious smile. "I'll be talking to your doctor."

The four-block walk did feel good. When Louise got to the entrance of the GC, she lit a cigarette and mingled with the other smokers. The employees congregated in one area, defendants and clients were pretty much scattered around. One guy was going ashtray to ashtray picking out the semi-smoked butts and placing them in a small baggie. Louise admired him. He didn't ask for handouts, just went about minding his own business. She strolled over and gave him two from her pack. He smile like he won the lottery, and without a word stuck them in his shirt pocket like he didn't want to contaminate them with the used ones.

Louise found Karla staring up at the TV screen. The scratch that traveled along her cheek looked sexy. Louise hoped she'd opt to keep the scar over plastic surgery.

Standing behind, Louise put her hands on Karla's shoulders. She leaned over Karla and took a chance. Her heart fluttered as Karla tilted her head back, tugged at the lapels of Louise's blouse, and kissed her with hope and longing. She didn't give a damn who might be watching. As they parted, Karla took her hand and spun her around in a

253

pirouette until Louise was in front of her.

"Come home?" Karla's blue eyes sparkled.

Louise couldn't speak. Her bottom lip trembled as she nodded. She squeezed Karla's hands in hers.

"How is he?"

Louise cleared her throat, grateful for the change in subject even though it pained her even more. "Out of IC. He's got brain damage. They have no idea how much, and won't know for a while. His cop days are over."

Karla closed her eyes and took a deep breath. Louise took her hand and kissed her partner's knuckles. "He'll be okay."

When Karla got her voice back, she told Louise about the story on CNN.

After clearing the metal detectors, the two women rode the elevator up to the twenty-second floor of the Courts Tower. They checked in with reception and before they had a chance to sit down, a man appeared in the doorway. "I'm assistant County Attorney Gary Marx." He shook their hands. "Thank you for coming. If you'd follow me, please."

Unlike the glorified offices on TV, Marx's room was not a whole lot bigger than a cubicle, but at least he had walls. Shelves behind his desk were packed tight with law books. Stacks of files littered his desk. More files were piled on the two chairs in front. Marx took the files from the chairs and placed them on the floor. "Please sit."

The women did as asked and the attorney took a seat on the corner of his desk.

"I'm sure you've seen on the news that a number of people are calling for tighter laws on dangerous dogs. They want to make an example of yours."

"He was defending his home and family." Karla's voice raised an octave higher than normal."

"And that's a drop in the bucket compared to the protests that will happen if you try to prosecute a hero dog." Louise glared at the attorney ready for a fight.

Marx smiled. "That's exactly what I told my boss, who in turn convinced the mayor. It wasn't a hard sell."

"You shit." Louise gave him an I-want-to-punch-you-in-the-face-then-buy-you-a-beer smirk. "We had to come down here for that? You could've called. When can we pick him up? I think Peanut's been locked up long enough."

"As soon as you're done here I'll call and let them know you're on your way." The lawyer turned serious and opened the top file from one of the stacks. "We know the history of the dog." He handed her a document from the file. "We can't force you, but here's some information on a trainer who's really good. The Humane Society uses him when they get fighting dogs, especially pit bulls and rotts. He's kept a lot of dogs from being put down." He handed her the remainder of the file. "There's vouchers in there. When you get a bill, just send it with one of those and we'll take care of it."

Louise's grin turned into I just want to buy you a beer smile. They all shook hands, but Marx closed the door before Louise and Karla could leave.

"What I'm about to say doesn't leave this office. And if word ever gets out I'll deny it."

Louise really liked where this was going. She squeezed Karla's hand.

"That dog saved the taxpayers of Hennepin County a lot of money and our office a lot of man hours that we don't have. On behalf of the county attorney's office, I just want to say thank you."

Louise glowed as they left his office. She caressed the wound on Karla's cheek. "You sure you're ready for me to come home?"

Karla kept her gaze on the elevator doors. Her smile answered the question.

www.ingramcontent.com/pod-product-compliance
Lightning Source LLC
Chambersburg PA
CBHW072259130726
47910CB00012B/2172